THREE THIEVES
BOOK FIVE

Pirates of the Silver Coast

Kids Can Press acknowledges the financial support of the Government of Ontario, through the Ontario Media Development Corporation's Ontario Book Initiative; the Ontario Arts Council; the Canada Council for the Arts; and the Government of Canada, through the CBF, for our publishing activity.

Published in Canada by
Kids Can Press Ltd.
25 Dockside Drive
Toronto, ON M5A 0B5

Published in the U.S. by
Kids Can Press Ltd.
2250 Military Road
Tonawanda, NY 14150

www.kidscanpress.com

Edited by Yasemin Uçar
Designed by Scott Chantler and Marie Bartholomew
Pages lettered with Blambot comic fonts

The hardcover edition of this book is smyth sewn casebound.
The paperback edition of this book is limp sewn with a drawn-on cover.
Manufactured in Buji, Shenzhen, China, in 6/2014 by WKT Company.

CM 14 0 9 8 7 6 5 4 3 2 1
CM PA 14 0 9 8 7 6 5 4 3 2 1

Library and Archives Canada Cataloguing in Publication

Chantler, Scott, author, illustrator
    Pirates of the Silver Coast / Scott Chantler.

(Three thieves book 5)
ISBN 978-1-894786-53-9 (bound)   ISBN 978-1-894786-54-6 (pbk.)

    1. Graphic novels. I. Title. II. Series: Chantler, Scott. Three thieves ; bk. 5.

PN6733.C53P57 2014   j741.5'971   C2013-908318-9

Kids Can Press is a *Corus*™ Entertainment company

ACT ONE

Fortune

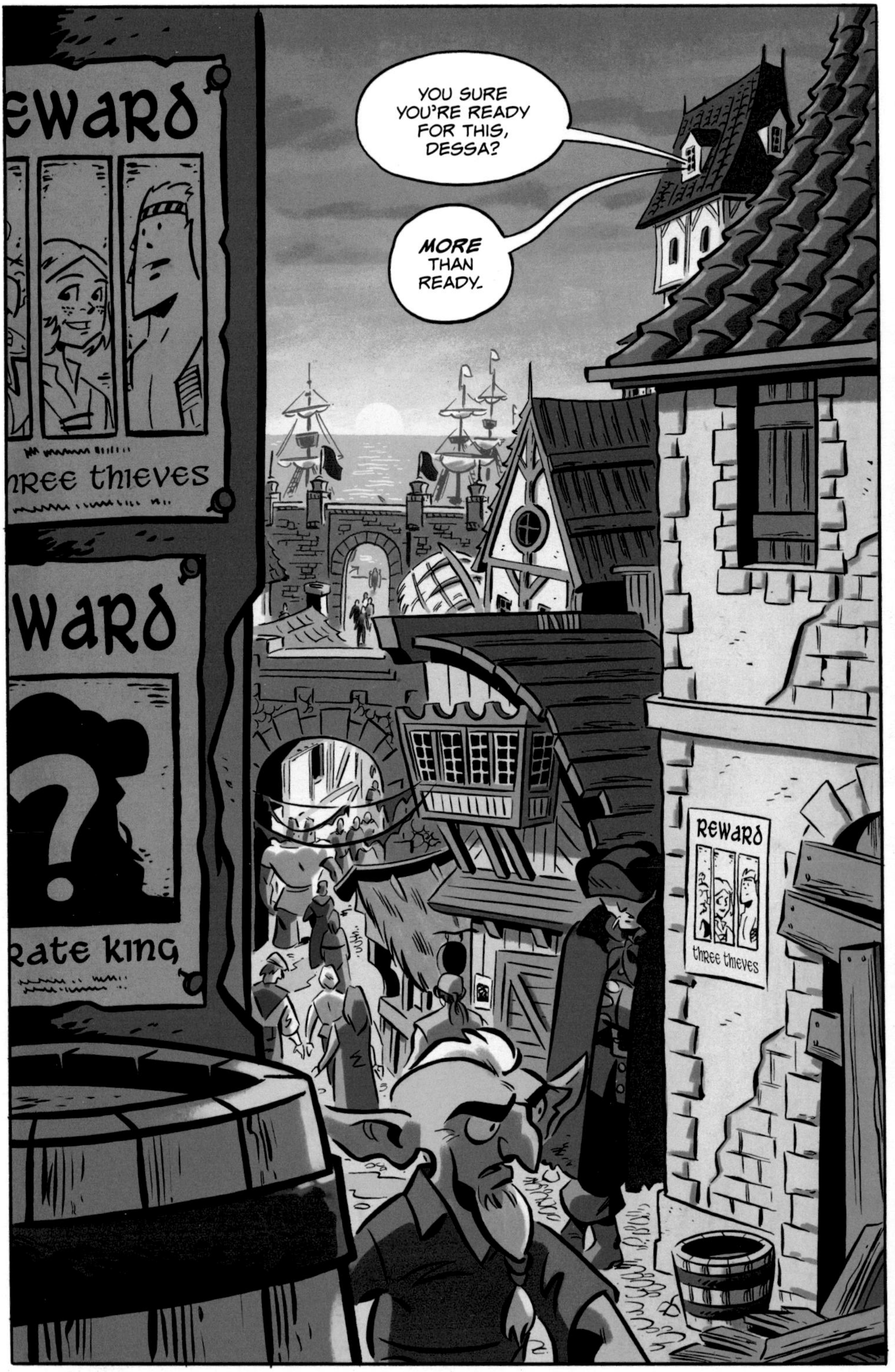
YOU SURE YOU'RE READY FOR THIS, DESSA?
MORE THAN READY.
EWARD
HREE THIEVES
WARD
RATE KING
REWARD
THREE THIEVES

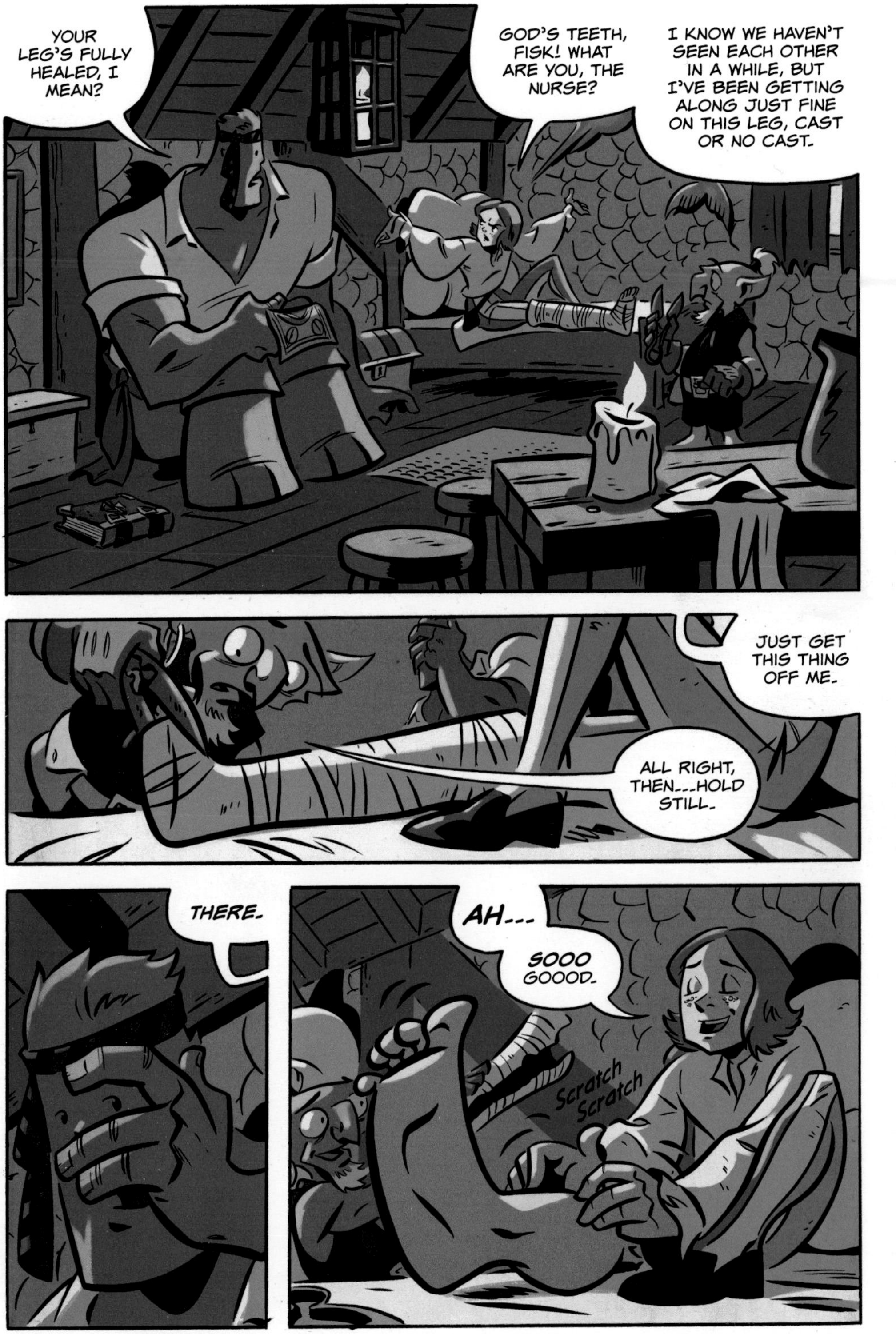
YOUR LEG'S FULLY HEALED, I MEAN?
GOD'S TEETH, FISK! WHAT ARE YOU, THE NURSE?
I KNOW WE HAVEN'T SEEN EACH OTHER IN A WHILE, BUT I'VE BEEN GETTING ALONG JUST FINE ON THIS LEG, CAST OR NO CAST.
JUST GET THIS THING OFF ME.
ALL RIGHT, THEN...HOLD STILL.
THERE.
AH...
SOOO GOOOD.
Scratch Scratch

I HOPE YOU TWO HAVE ENOUGH MONEY TO KEEP RENTING THIS ROOM, BECAUSE I PLAN TO DO NOTHING BUT SCRATCH THIS LEG FOR THE NEXT SEVERAL DAYS!

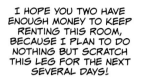

Scratch Scratch Scratch

WE'RE BROKE, AREN'T WE?

I'VE BEEN PICKING POCKETS IN THE MARKET DISTRICT...

...BUT MOSTLY WE'VE BEEN LYING LOW, TRYING TO KEEP OUT OF SIGHT WHILE WE WAITED FOR YOU.

<SIGH>

PENNILESS. LIKE OUR CIRCUS DAYS ALL OVER AGAIN.

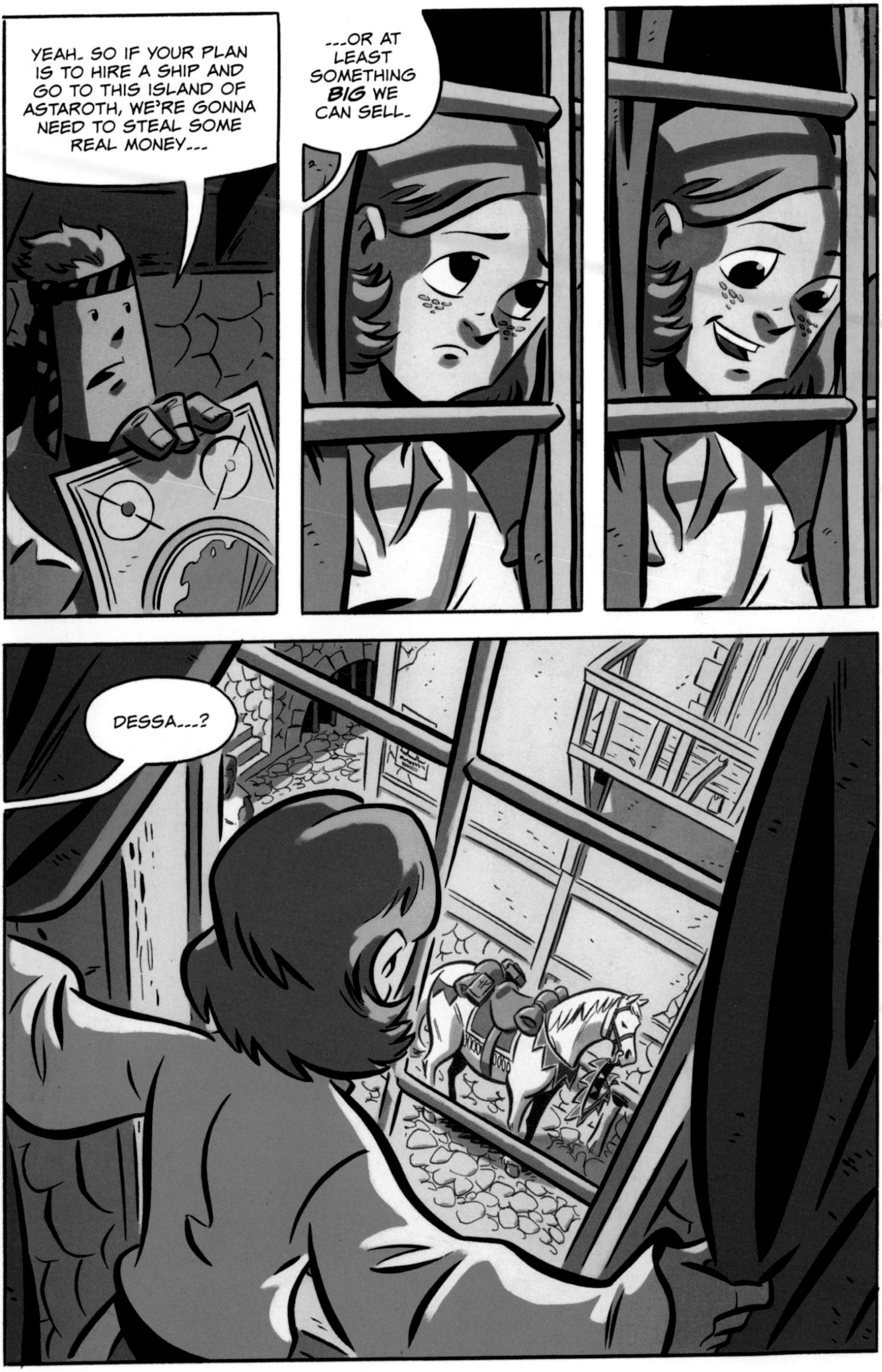
YEAH. SO IF YOUR PLAN IS TO HIRE A SHIP AND GO TO THIS ISLAND OF ASTAROTH, WE'RE GONNA NEED TO STEAL SOME REAL MONEY...
...OR AT LEAST SOMETHING BIG WE CAN SELL.
DESSA...?

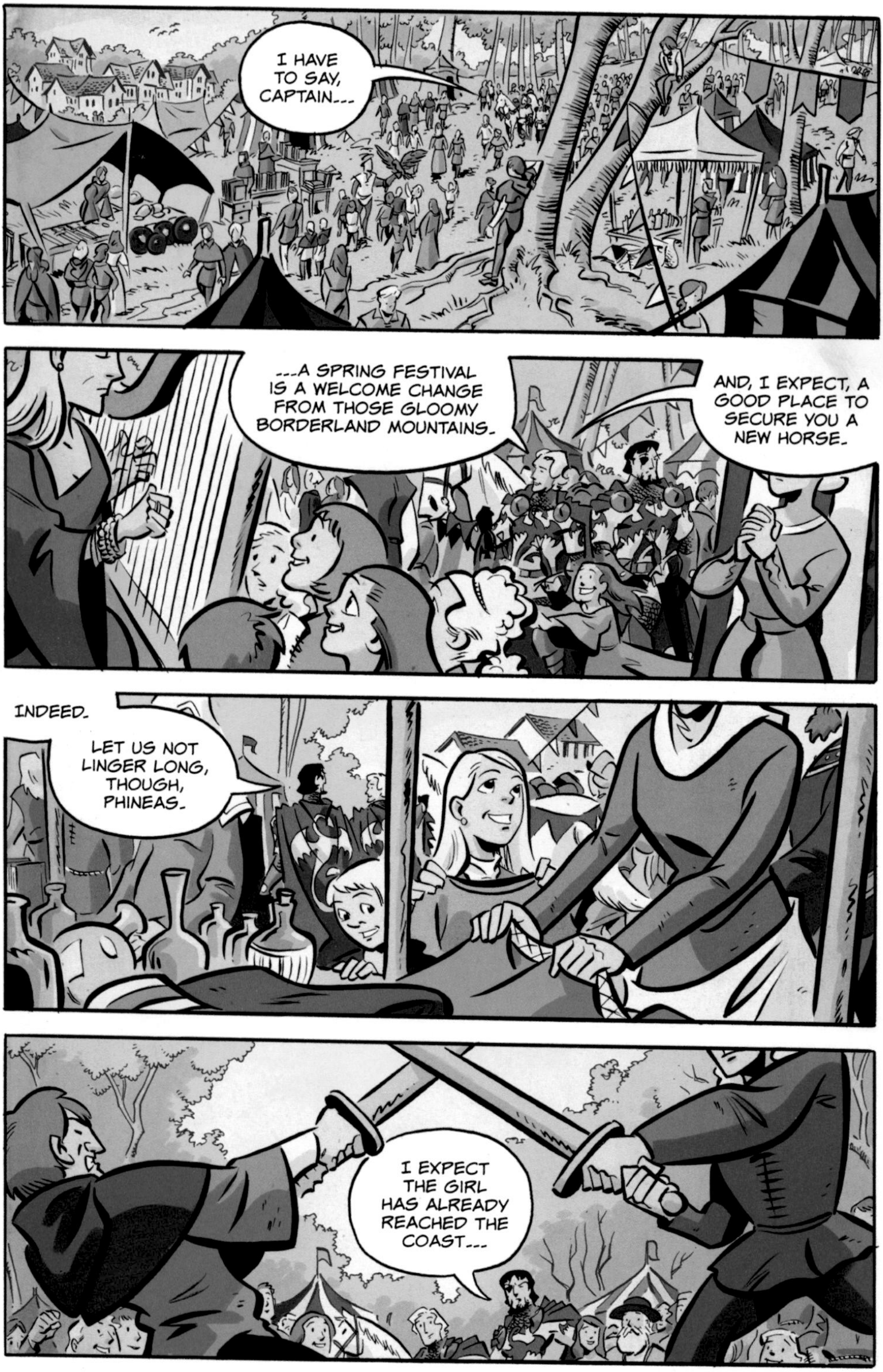
I HAVE TO SAY, CAPTAIN...
...A SPRING FESTIVAL IS A WELCOME CHANGE FROM THOSE GLOOMY BORDERLAND MOUNTAINS.
AND, I EXPECT, A GOOD PLACE TO SECURE YOU A NEW HORSE.
INDEED.
LET US NOT LINGER LONG, THOUGH, PHINEAS.
I EXPECT THE GIRL HAS ALREADY REACHED THE COAST...

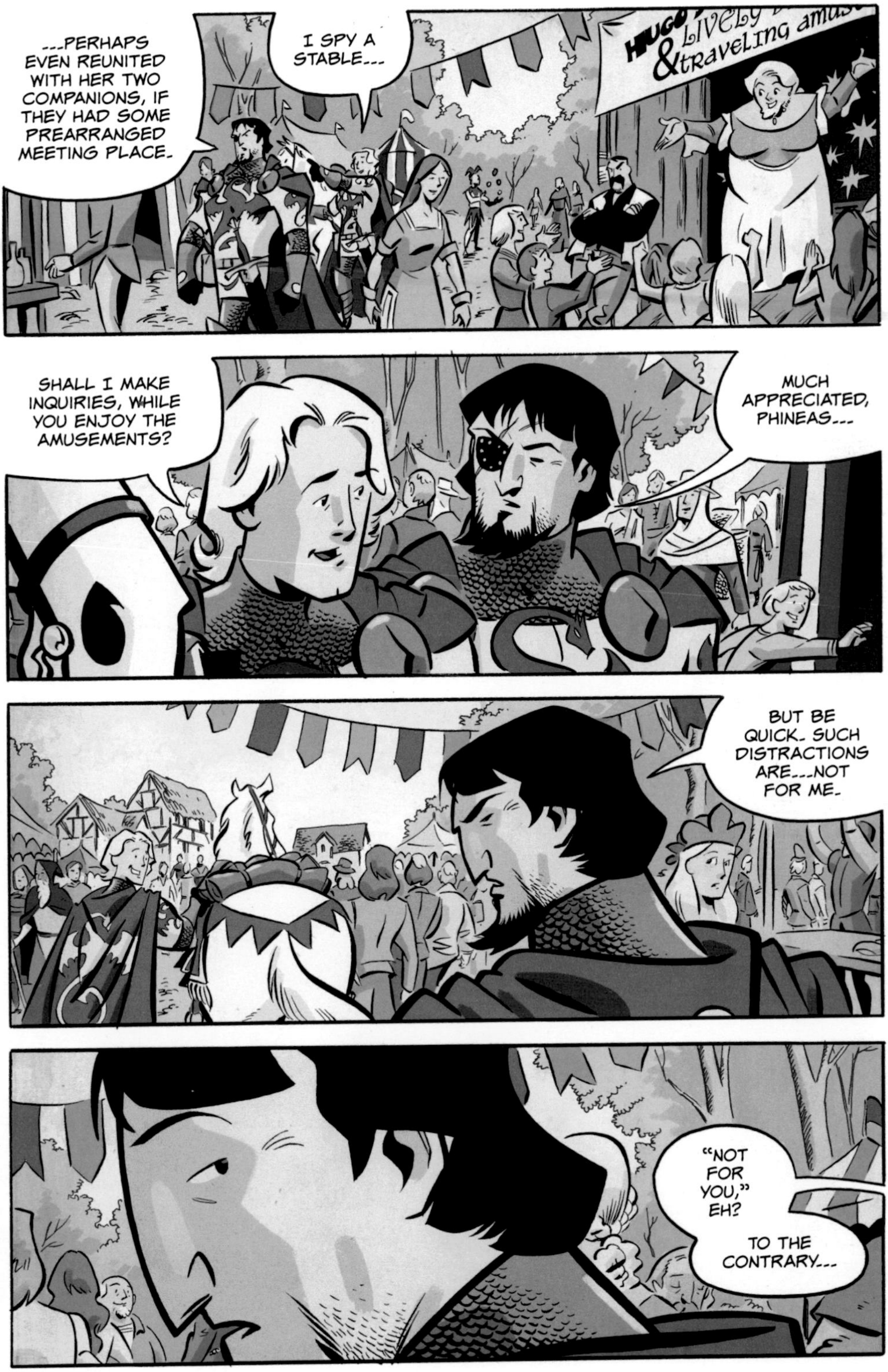
...PERHAPS EVEN REUNITED WITH HER TWO COMPANIONS, IF THEY HAD SOME PREARRANGED MEETING PLACE.
I SPY A STABLE...
LIVELY
&traveling
SHALL I MAKE INQUIRIES, WHILE YOU ENJOY THE AMUSEMENTS?
MUCH APPRECIATED, PHINEAS...
BUT BE QUICK. SUCH DISTRACTIONS ARE...NOT FOR ME.
"NOT FOR YOU," EH?
TO THE CONTRARY...

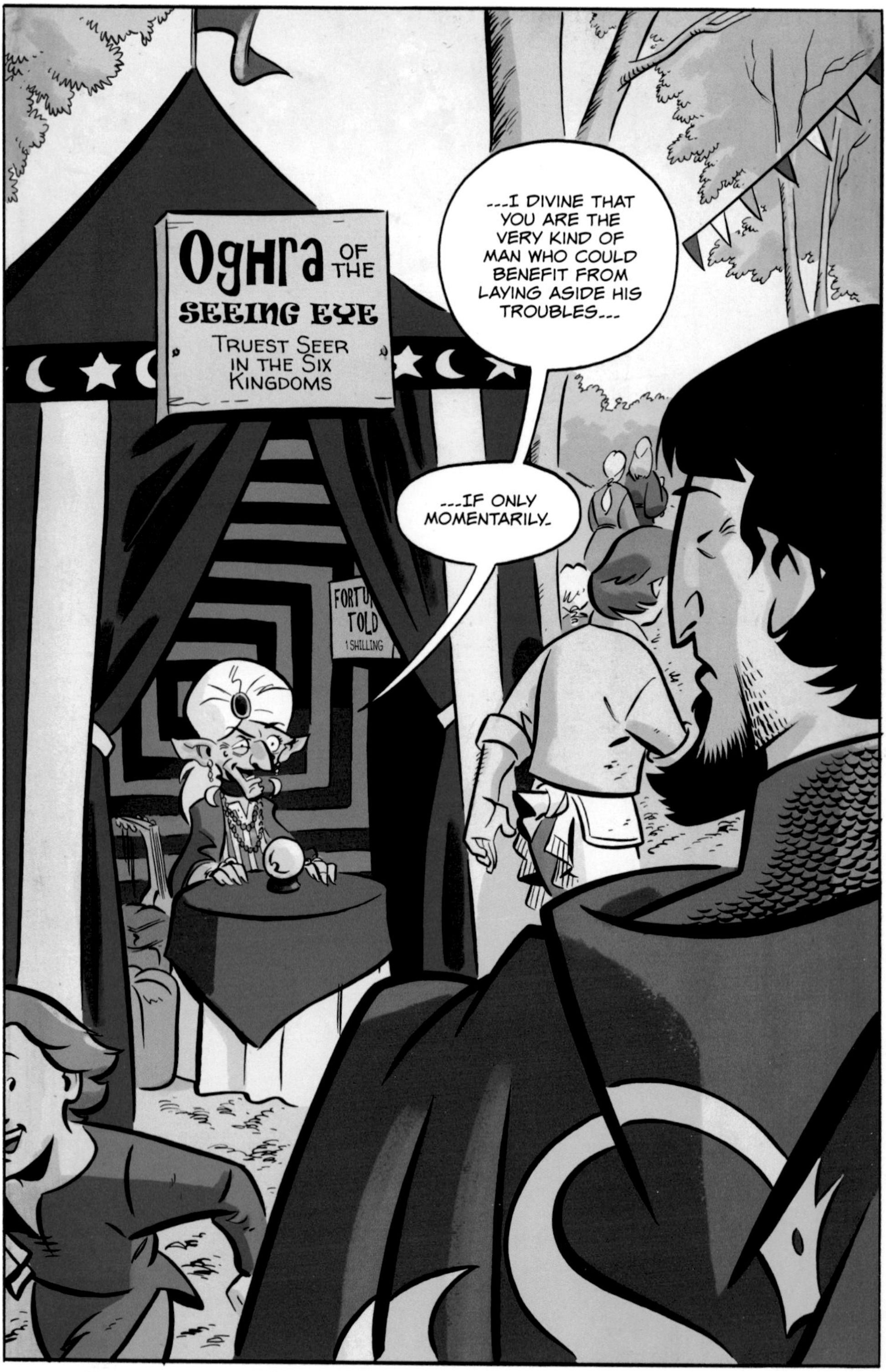
Oghra of the
Seeing Eye
Truest Seer
in the Six
Kingdoms
---I DIVINE THAT YOU ARE THE VERY KIND OF MAN WHO COULD BENEFIT FROM LAYING ASIDE HIS TROUBLES---
---IF ONLY MOMENTARILY.
Fortu[ne]
Told
1 Shilling

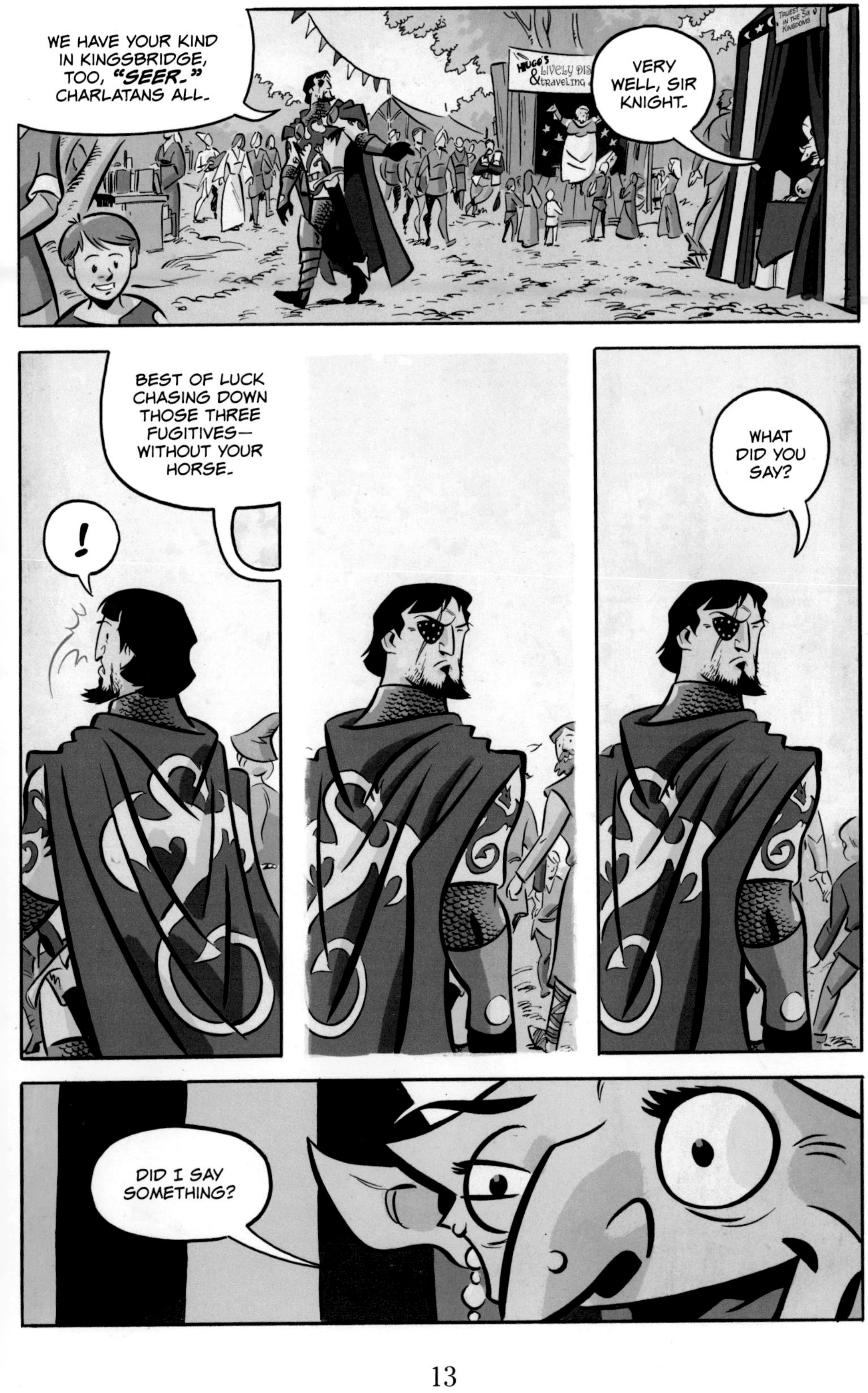
WE HAVE YOUR KIND IN KINGSBRIDGE, TOO, "SEER." CHARLATANS ALL.
VERY WELL, SIR KNIGHT.
BEST OF LUCK CHASING DOWN THOSE THREE FUGITIVES— WITHOUT YOUR HORSE.
!
WHAT DID YOU SAY?
DID I SAY SOMETHING?

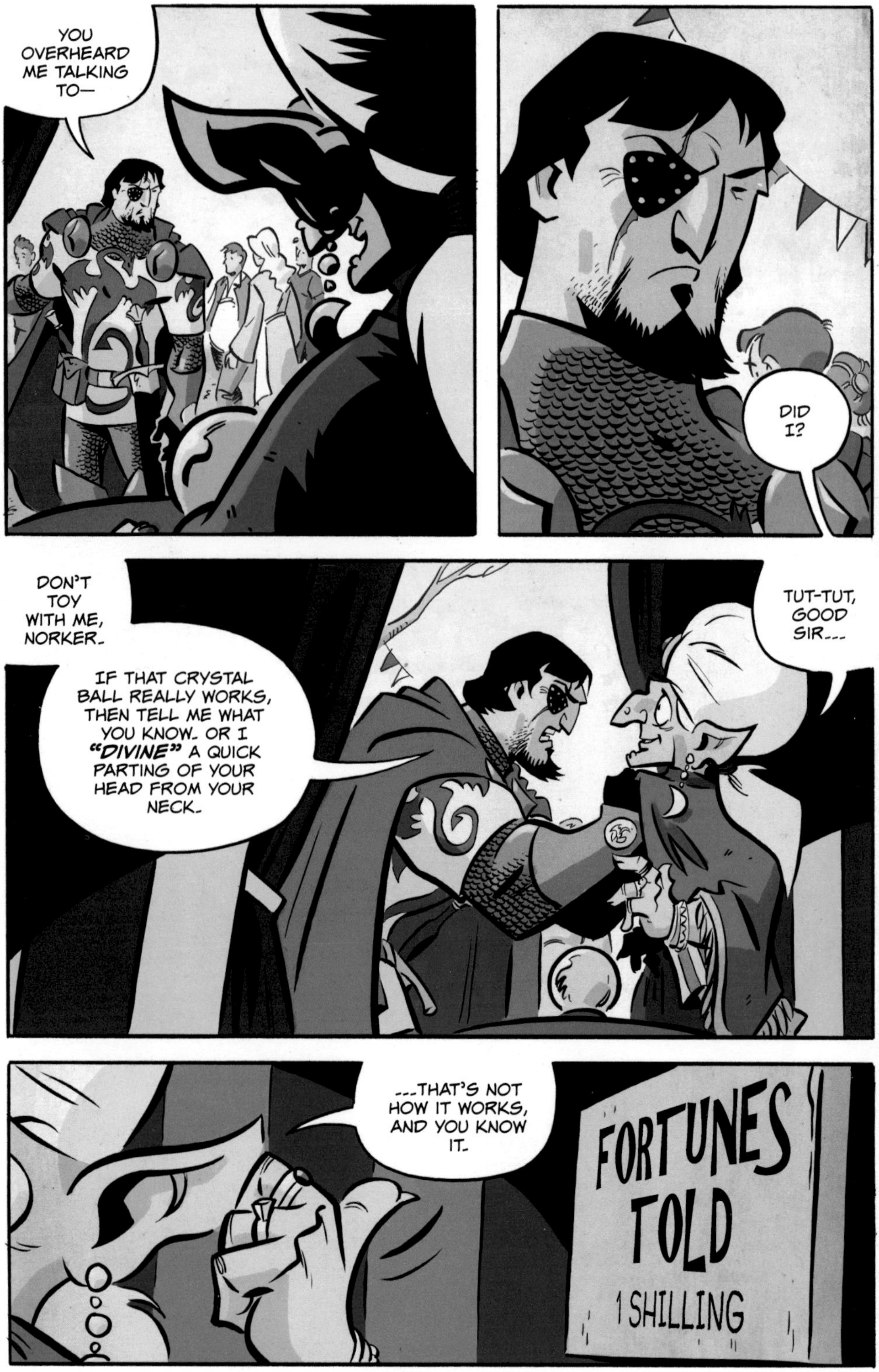

YOU OVERHEARD ME TALKING TO—
DID I?
DON'T TOY WITH ME, NORKER.
IF THAT CRYSTAL BALL REALLY WORKS, THEN TELL ME WHAT YOU KNOW. OR I "DIVINE" A QUICK PARTING OF YOUR HEAD FROM YOUR NECK.
TUT-TUT, GOOD SIR...
...THAT'S NOT HOW IT WORKS, AND YOU KNOW IT.
FORTUNES TOLD
1 SHILLING

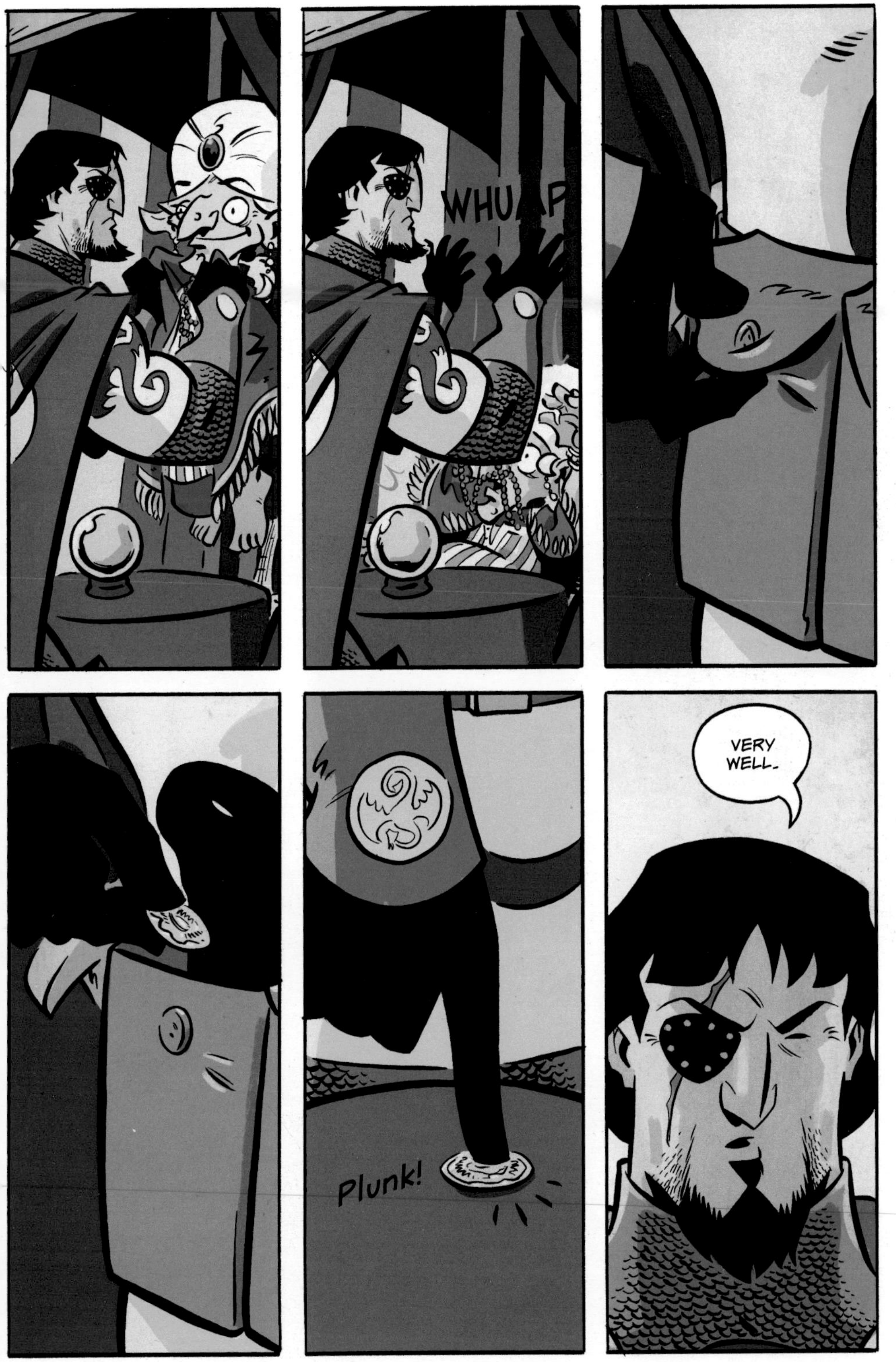
WHUAP
Plunk!
VERY WELL.

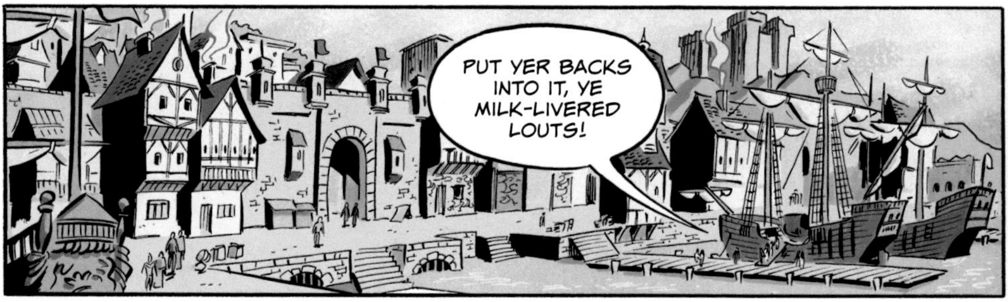
PUT YER BACKS INTO IT, YE MILK-LIVERED LOUTS!

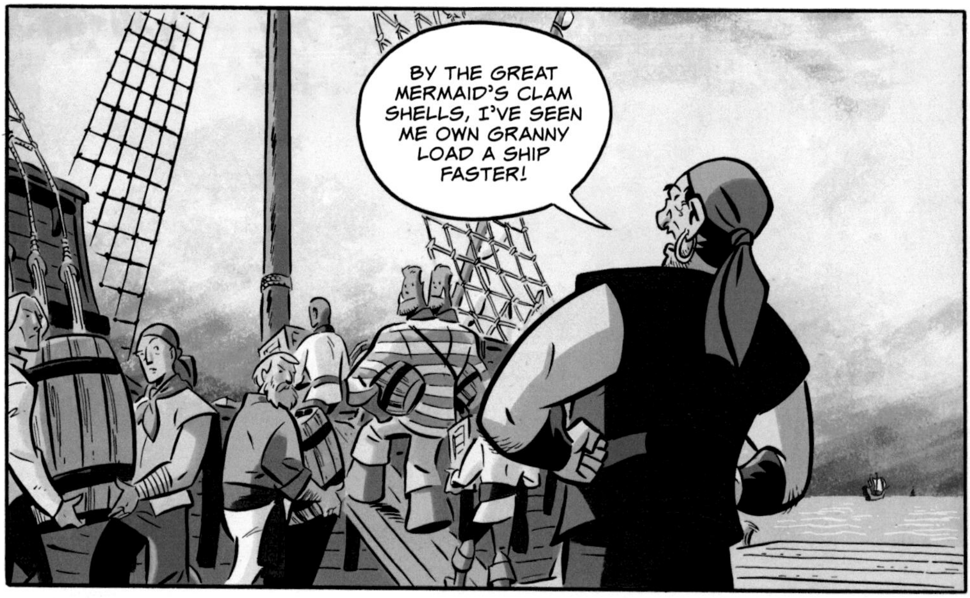
BY THE GREAT MERMAID'S CLAM SHELLS, I'VE SEEN ME OWN GRANNY LOAD A SHIP FASTER!

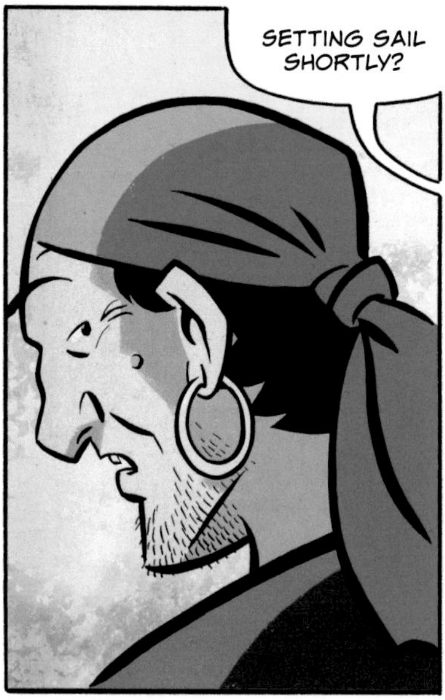
SETTING SAIL SHORTLY?

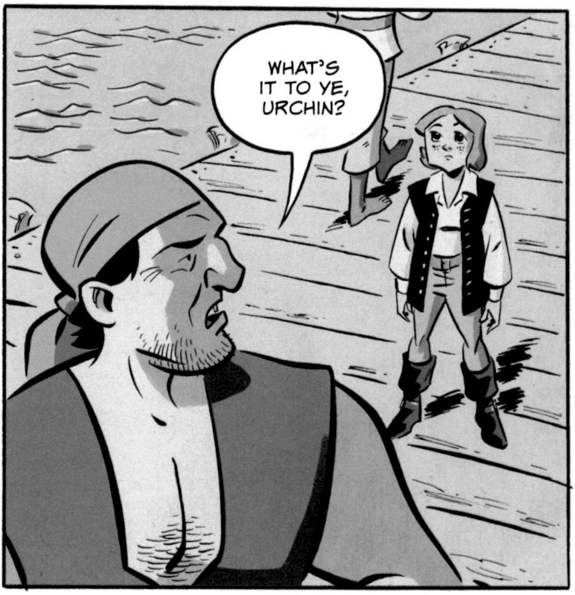
WHAT'S IT TO YE, URCHIN?

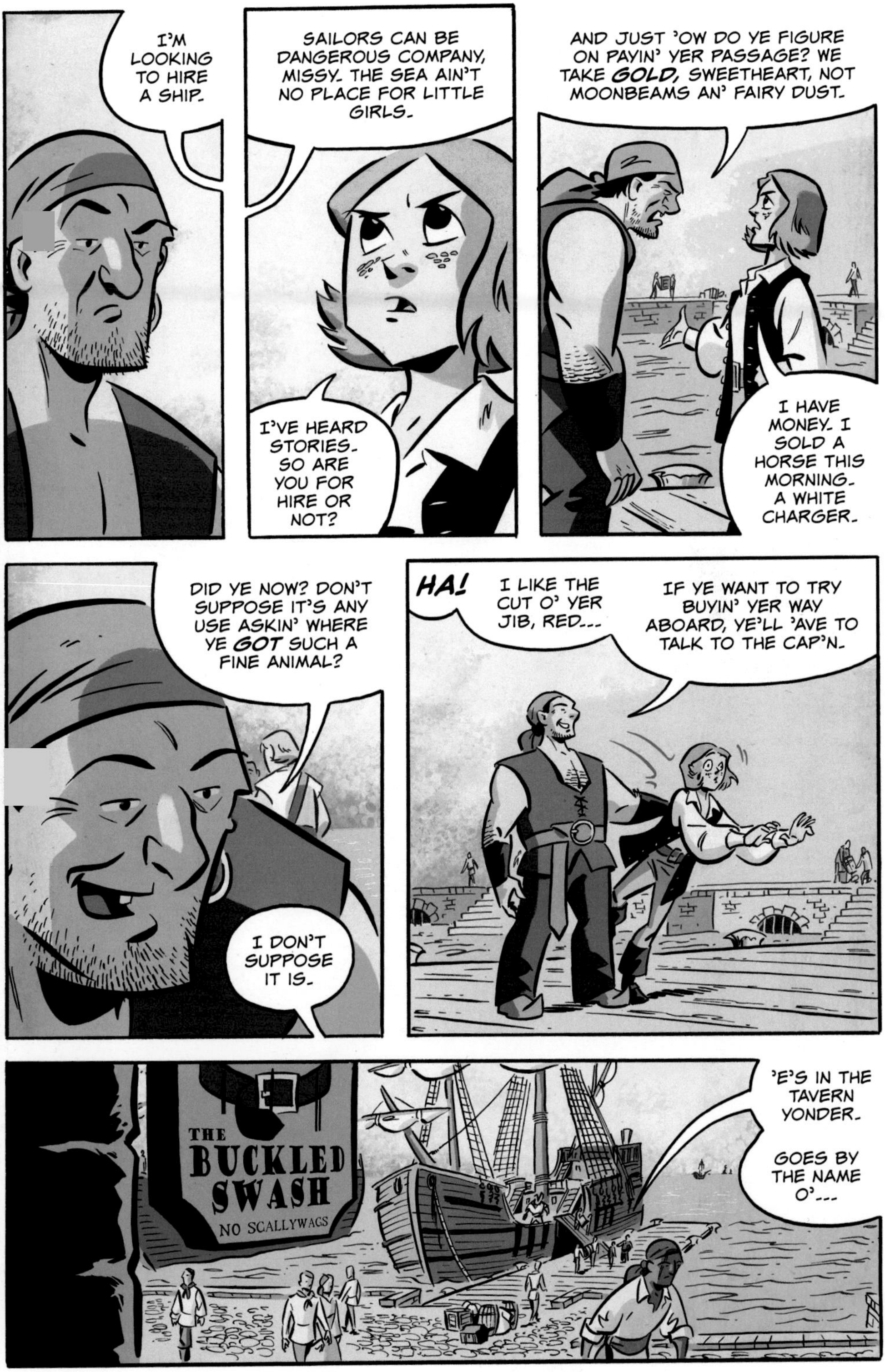
I'M LOOKING TO HIRE A SHIP.
SAILORS CAN BE DANGEROUS COMPANY, MISSY. THE SEA AIN'T NO PLACE FOR LITTLE GIRLS.
I'VE HEARD STORIES. SO ARE YOU FOR HIRE OR NOT?
AND JUST 'OW DO YE FIGURE ON PAYIN' YER PASSAGE? WE TAKE GOLD, SWEETHEART, NOT MOONBEAMS AN' FAIRY DUST.
I HAVE MONEY. I SOLD A HORSE THIS MORNING. A WHITE CHARGER.
DID YE NOW? DON'T SUPPOSE IT'S ANY USE ASKIN' WHERE YE GOT SUCH A FINE ANIMAL?
I DON'T SUPPOSE IT IS.
HA!
I LIKE THE CUT O' YER JIB, RED...
IF YE WANT TO TRY BUYIN' YER WAY ABOARD, YE'LL 'AVE TO TALK TO THE CAP'N.
THE BUCKLED SWASH
NO SCALLYWAGS
'E'S IN THE TAVERN YONDER.
GOES BY THE NAME O'...

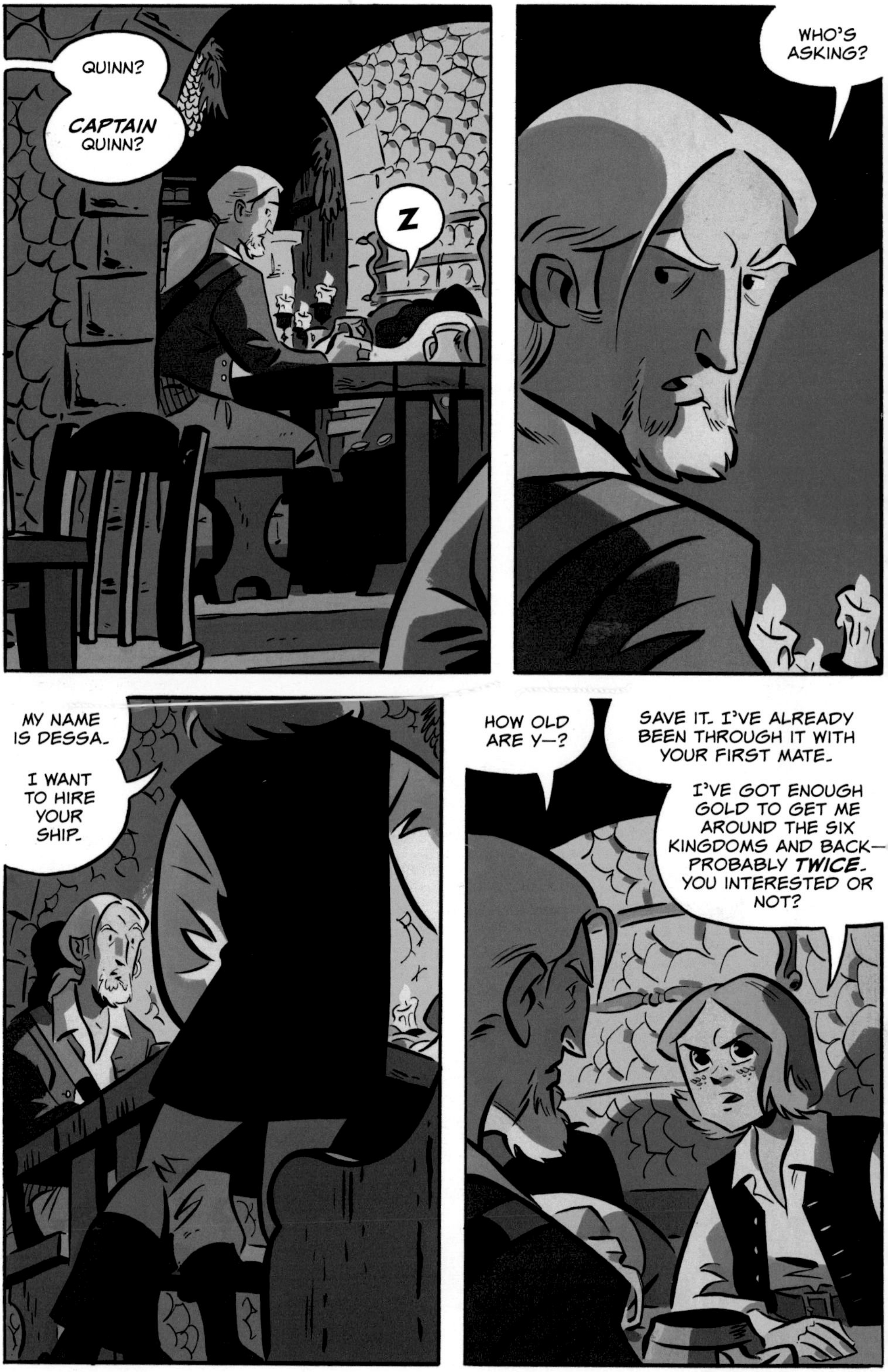
QUINN?
CAPTAIN QUINN?
Z
WHO'S ASKING?
MY NAME IS DESSA.
I WANT TO HIRE YOUR SHIP.
HOW OLD ARE Y—?
SAVE IT. I'VE ALREADY BEEN THROUGH IT WITH YOUR FIRST MATE.
I'VE GOT ENOUGH GOLD TO GET ME AROUND THE SIX KINGDOMS AND BACK— PROBABLY *TWICE*. YOU INTERESTED OR NOT?

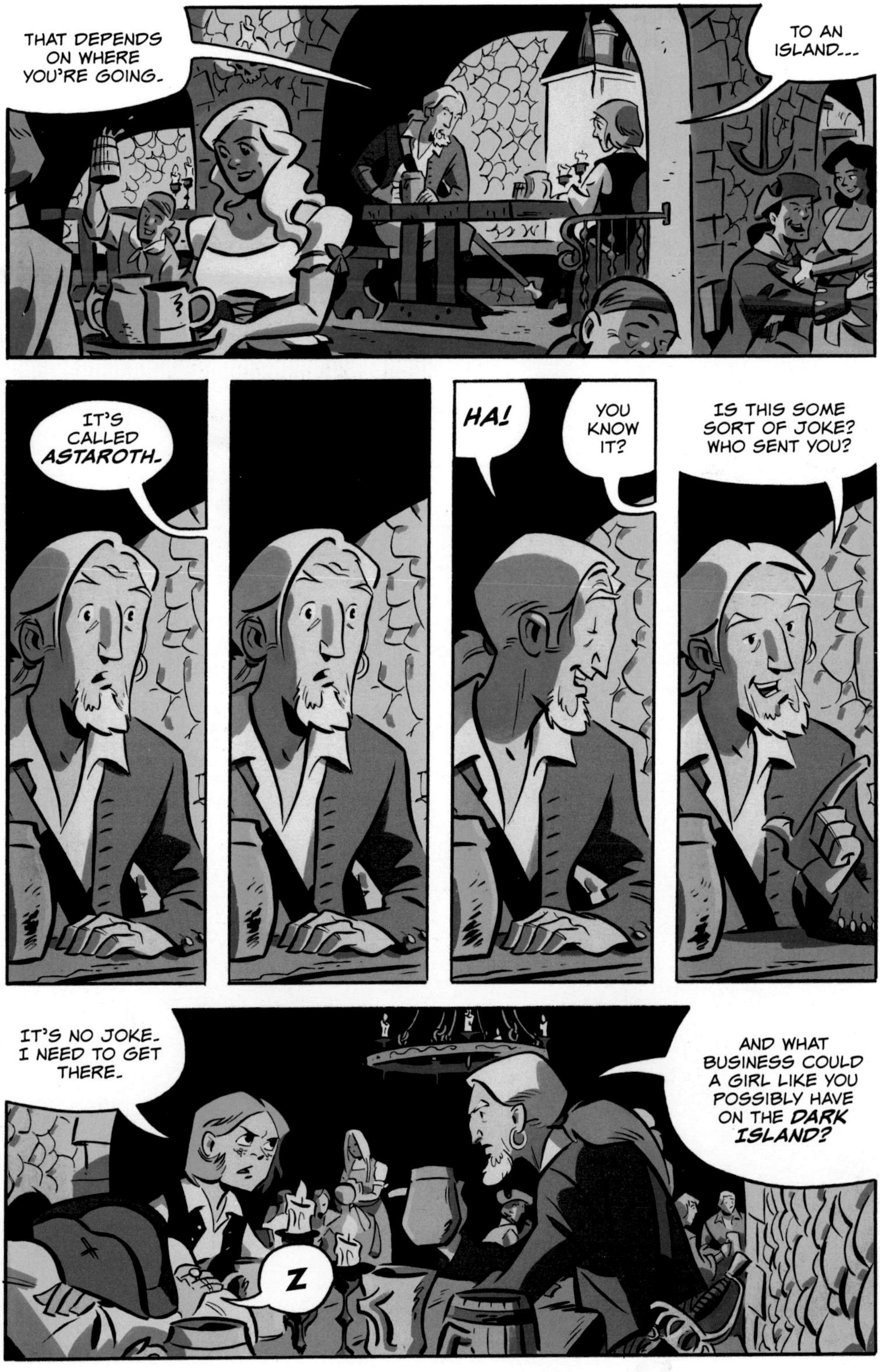
THAT DEPENDS ON WHERE YOU'RE GOING.
TO AN ISLAND...
IT'S CALLED ASTAROTH.
HA!
YOU KNOW IT?
IS THIS SOME SORT OF JOKE? WHO SENT YOU?
IT'S NO JOKE. I NEED TO GET THERE.
AND WHAT BUSINESS COULD A GIRL LIKE YOU POSSIBLY HAVE ON THE DARK ISLAND?
Z

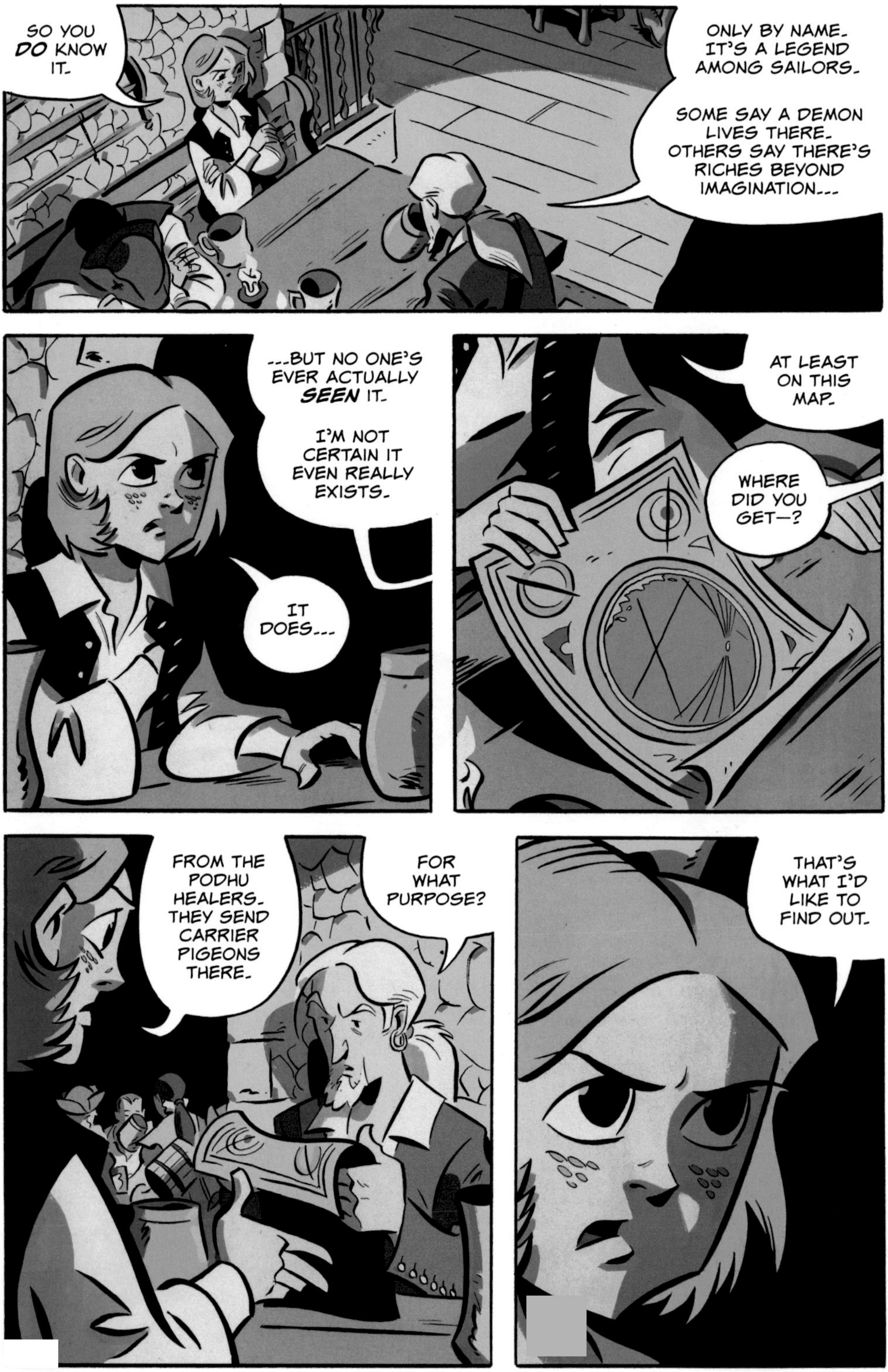
SO YOU DO KNOW IT.
ONLY BY NAME. IT'S A LEGEND AMONG SAILORS.
SOME SAY A DEMON LIVES THERE. OTHERS SAY THERE'S RICHES BEYOND IMAGINATION...
...BUT NO ONE'S EVER ACTUALLY SEEN IT.
I'M NOT CERTAIN IT EVEN REALLY EXISTS.
IT DOES...
AT LEAST ON THIS MAP.
WHERE DID YOU GET—?
FROM THE PODHU HEALERS. THEY SEND CARRIER PIGEONS THERE.
FOR WHAT PURPOSE?
THAT'S WHAT I'D LIKE TO FIND OUT.

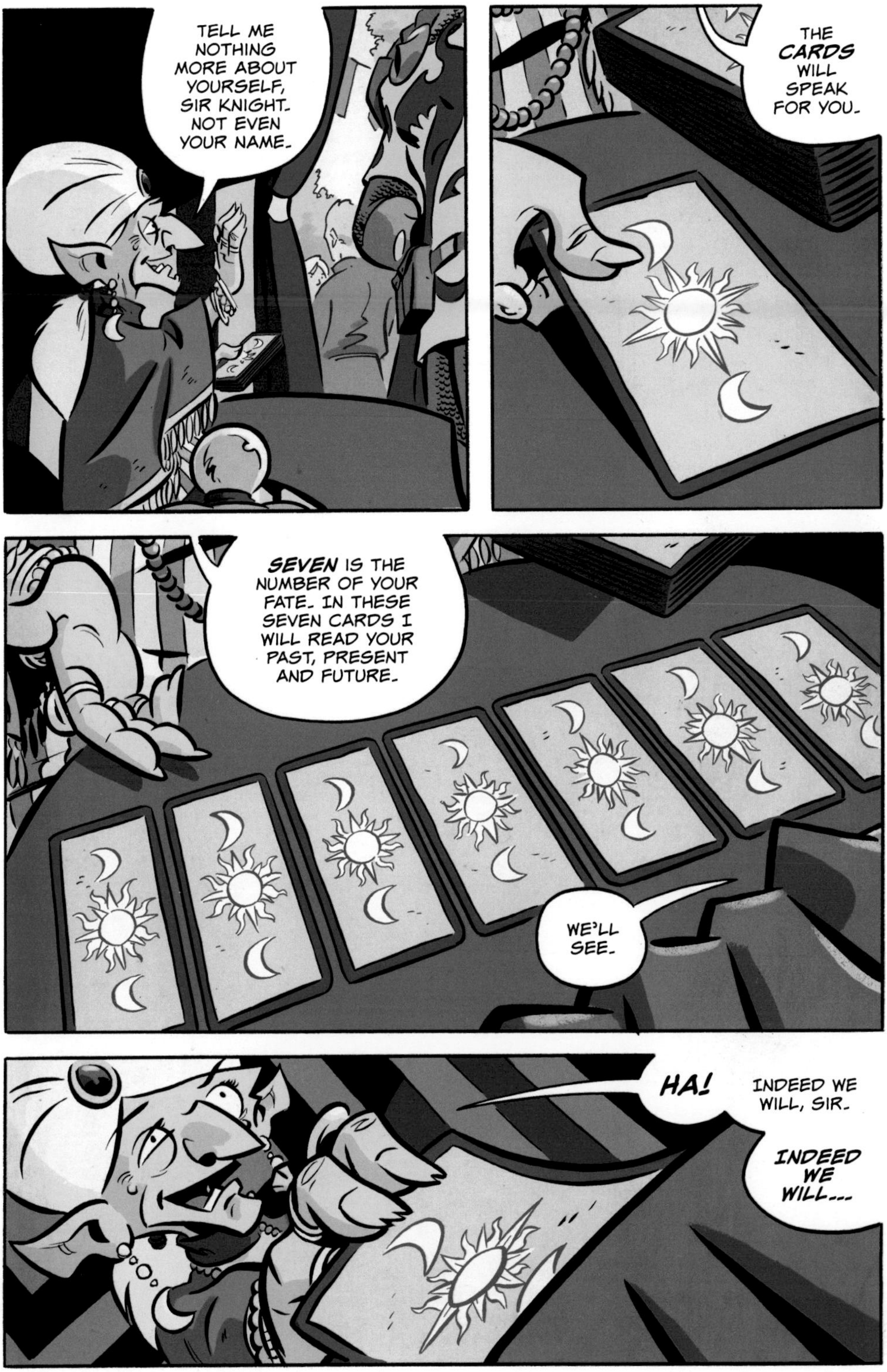
TELL ME NOTHING MORE ABOUT YOURSELF, SIR KNIGHT. NOT EVEN YOUR NAME.
THE CARDS WILL SPEAK FOR YOU.
SEVEN IS THE NUMBER OF YOUR FATE. IN THESE SEVEN CARDS I WILL READ YOUR PAST, PRESENT AND FUTURE.
WE'LL SEE.
HA!
INDEED WE WILL, SIR.
INDEED WE WILL...

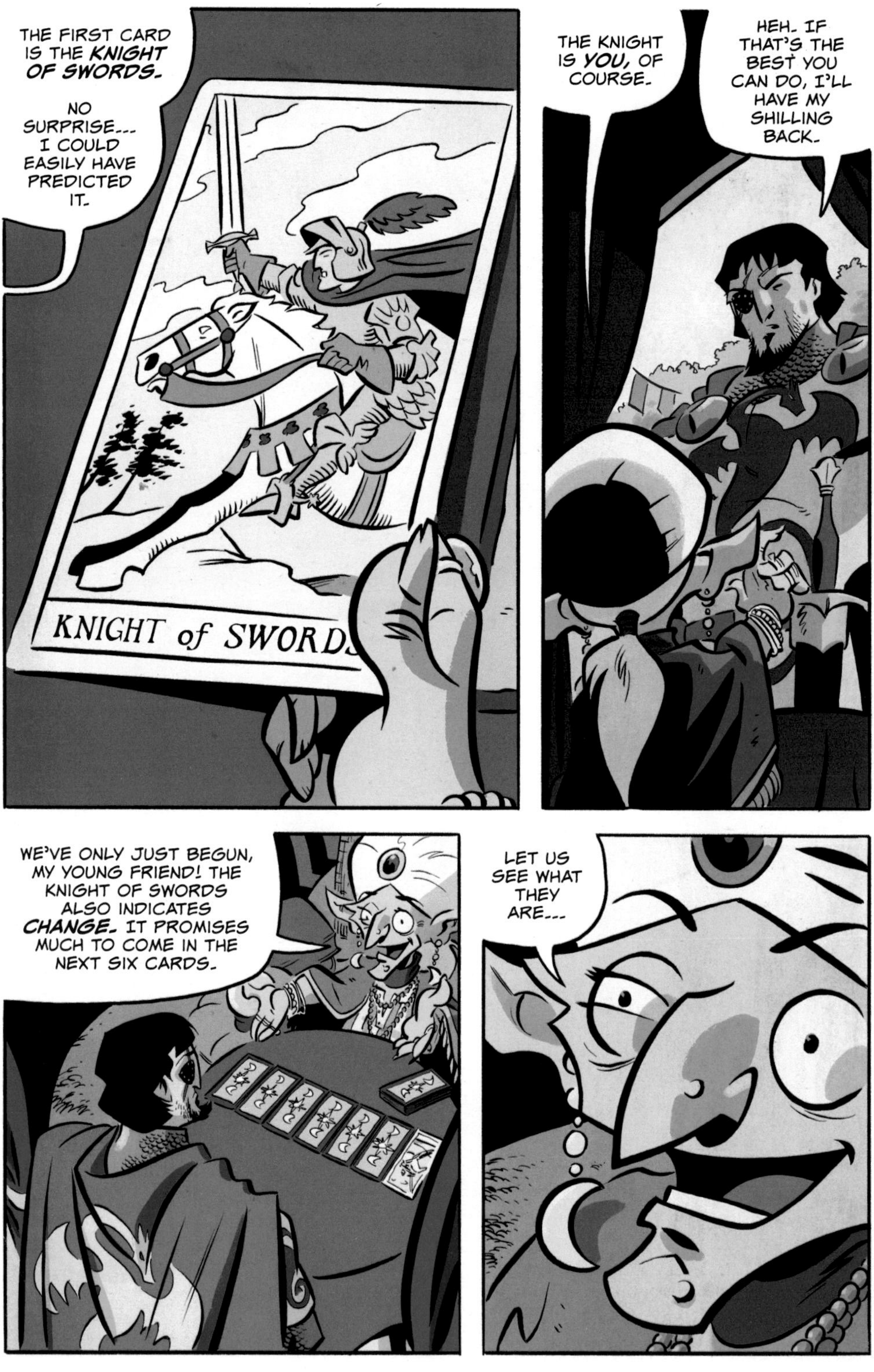
THE FIRST CARD IS THE KNIGHT OF SWORDS.
NO SURPRISE... I COULD EASILY HAVE PREDICTED IT.
KNIGHT of SWORDS
THE KNIGHT IS YOU, OF COURSE.
HEH. IF THAT'S THE BEST YOU CAN DO, I'LL HAVE MY SHILLING BACK.
WE'VE ONLY JUST BEGUN, MY YOUNG FRIEND! THE KNIGHT OF SWORDS ALSO INDICATES CHANGE. IT PROMISES MUCH TO COME IN THE NEXT SIX CARDS.
LET US SEE WHAT THEY ARE...

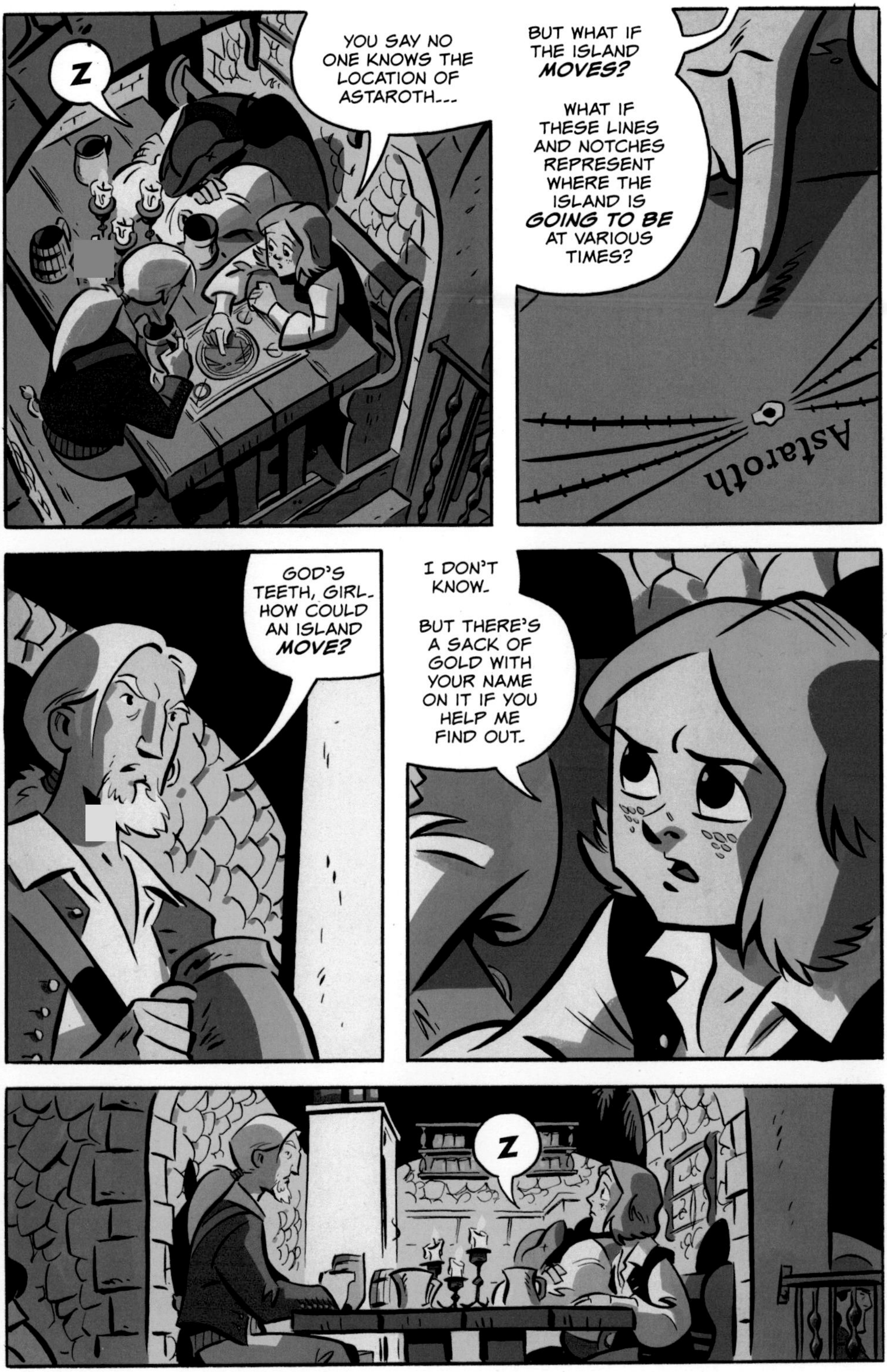
Z
YOU SAY NO ONE KNOWS THE LOCATION OF ASTAROTH...
BUT WHAT IF THE ISLAND MOVES?
WHAT IF THESE LINES AND NOTCHES REPRESENT WHERE THE ISLAND IS GOING TO BE AT VARIOUS TIMES?
Astaroth
GOD'S TEETH, GIRL. HOW COULD AN ISLAND MOVE?
I DON'T KNOW.
BUT THERE'S A SACK OF GOLD WITH YOUR NAME ON IT IF YOU HELP ME FIND OUT.
Z

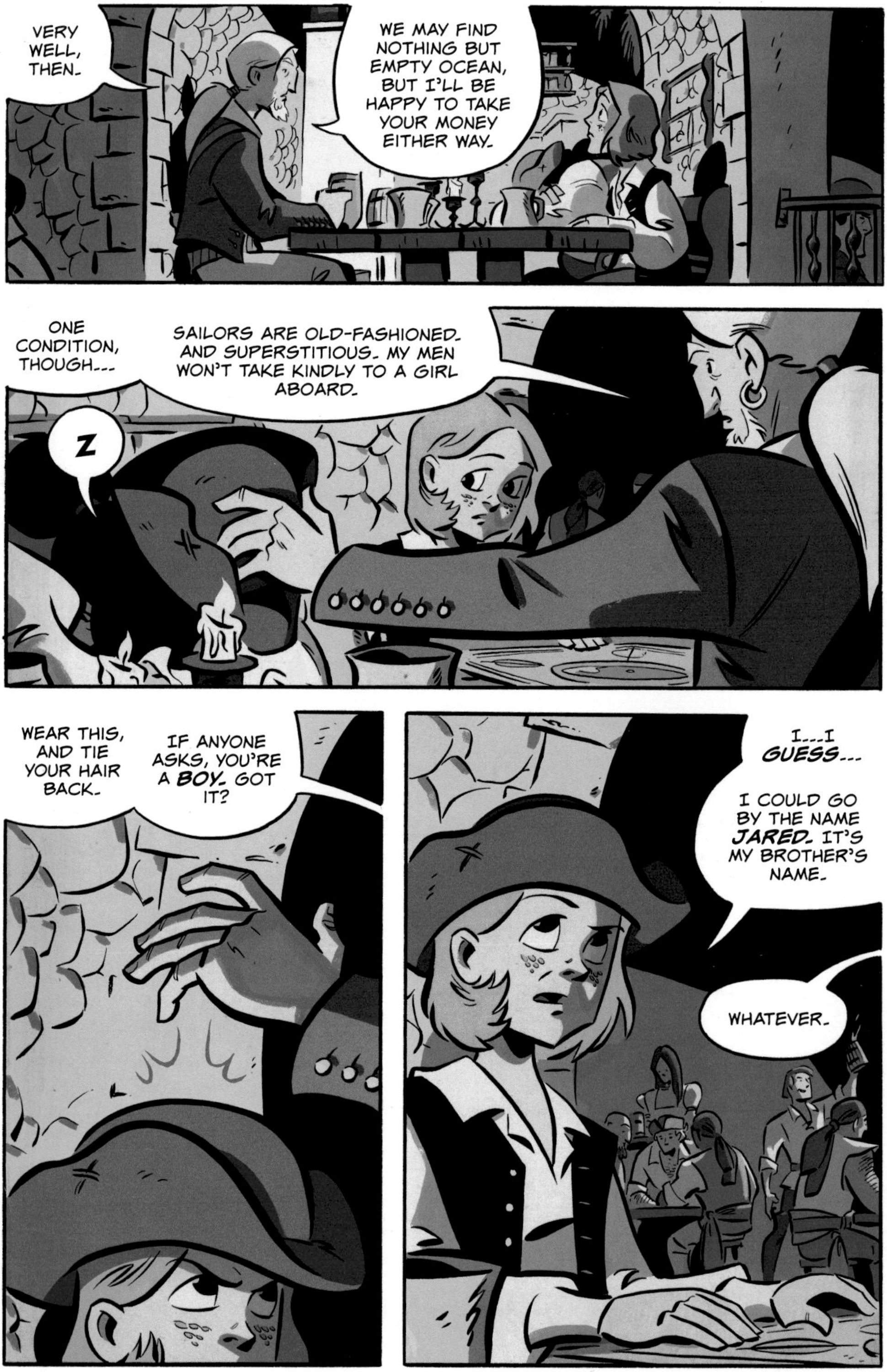
VERY WELL, THEN.
WE MAY FIND NOTHING BUT EMPTY OCEAN, BUT I'LL BE HAPPY TO TAKE YOUR MONEY EITHER WAY.
ONE CONDITION, THOUGH...
SAILORS ARE OLD-FASHIONED. AND SUPERSTITIOUS. MY MEN WON'T TAKE KINDLY TO A GIRL ABOARD.
Z
WEAR THIS, AND TIE YOUR HAIR BACK.
IF ANYONE ASKS, YOU'RE A **BOY**. GOT IT?
I...I ***GUESS***...
I COULD GO BY THE NAME ***JARED***. IT'S MY BROTHER'S NAME.
WHATEVER.

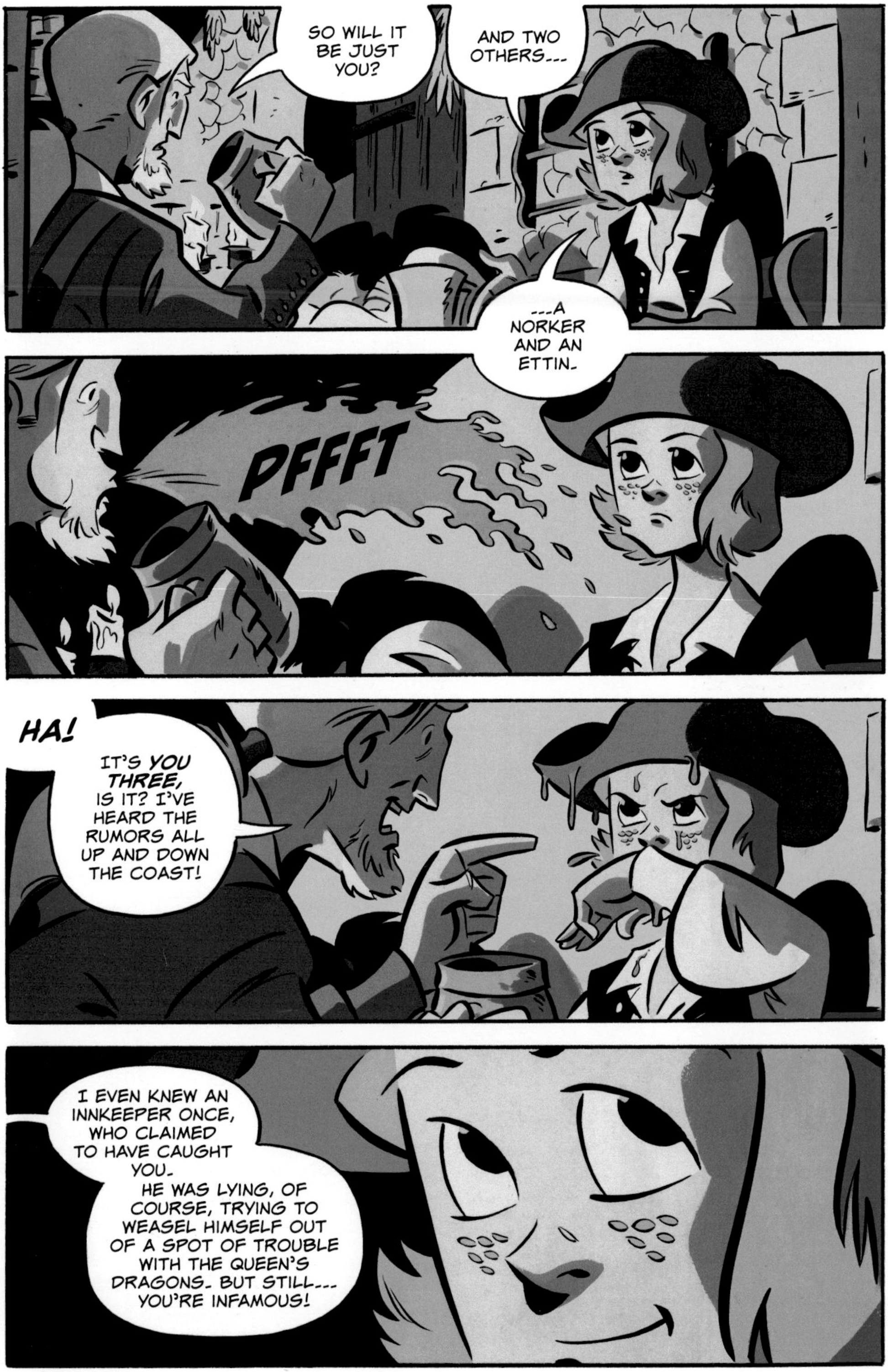
SO WILL IT BE JUST YOU?
AND TWO OTHERS...
...A NORKER AND AN ETTIN.
PFFFT
HA!
IT'S *YOU THREE,* IS IT? I'VE HEARD THE RUMORS ALL UP AND DOWN THE COAST!
I EVEN KNEW AN INNKEEPER ONCE, WHO CLAIMED TO HAVE CAUGHT YOU.
HE WAS LYING, OF COURSE, TRYING TO WEASEL HIMSELF OUT OF A SPOT OF TROUBLE WITH THE QUEEN'S DRAGONS. BUT STILL... YOU'RE INFAMOUS!

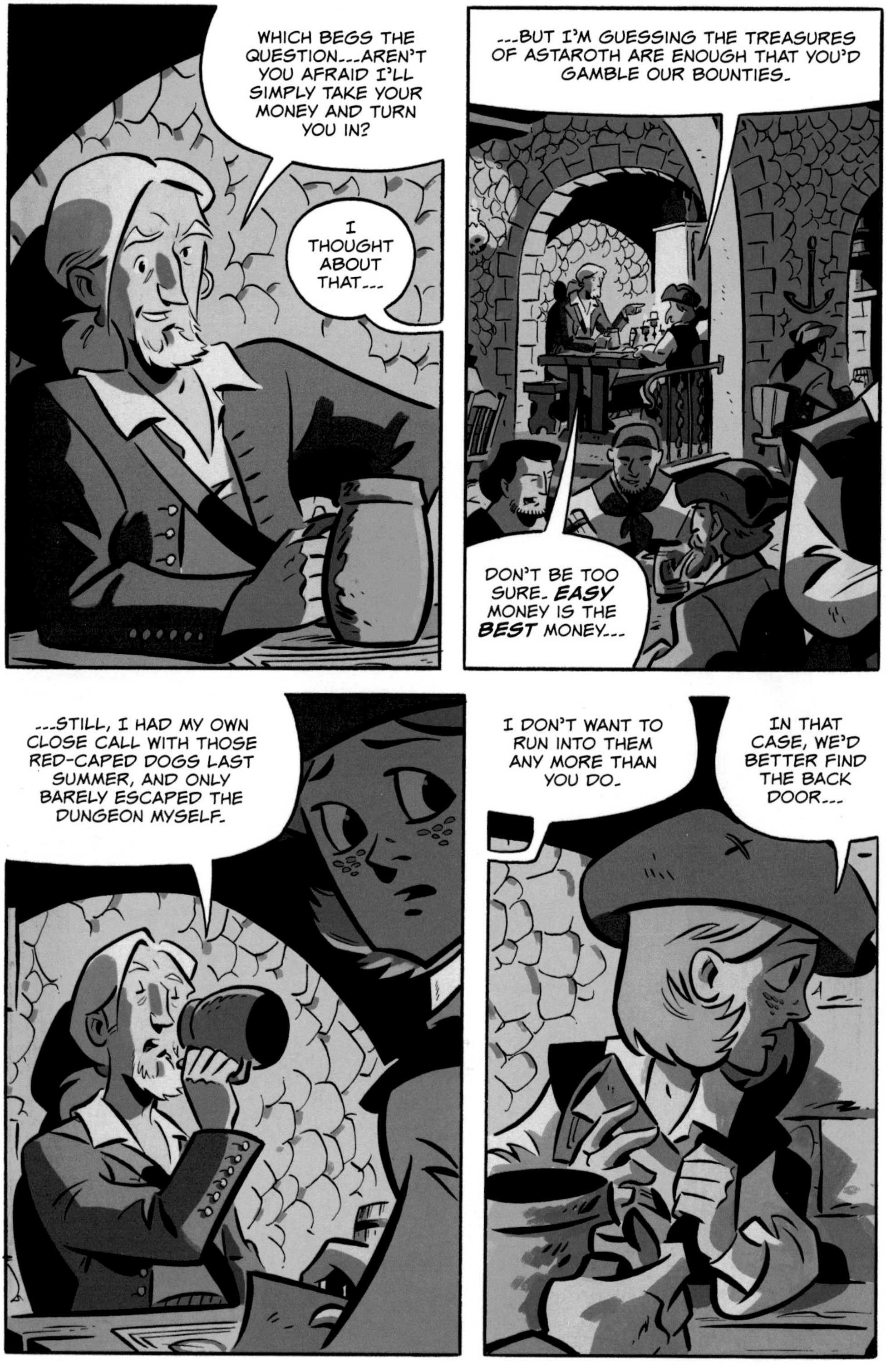
WHICH BEGS THE QUESTION...AREN'T YOU AFRAID I'LL SIMPLY TAKE YOUR MONEY AND TURN YOU IN?
I THOUGHT ABOUT THAT...
...BUT I'M GUESSING THE TREASURES OF ASTAROTH ARE ENOUGH THAT YOU'D GAMBLE OUR BOUNTIES.
DON'T BE TOO SURE. EASY MONEY IS THE BEST MONEY...
...STILL, I HAD MY OWN CLOSE CALL WITH THOSE RED-CAPED DOGS LAST SUMMER, AND ONLY BARELY ESCAPED THE DUNGEON MYSELF.
I DON'T WANT TO RUN INTO THEM ANY MORE THAN YOU DO.
IN THAT CASE, WE'D BETTER FIND THE BACK DOOR...

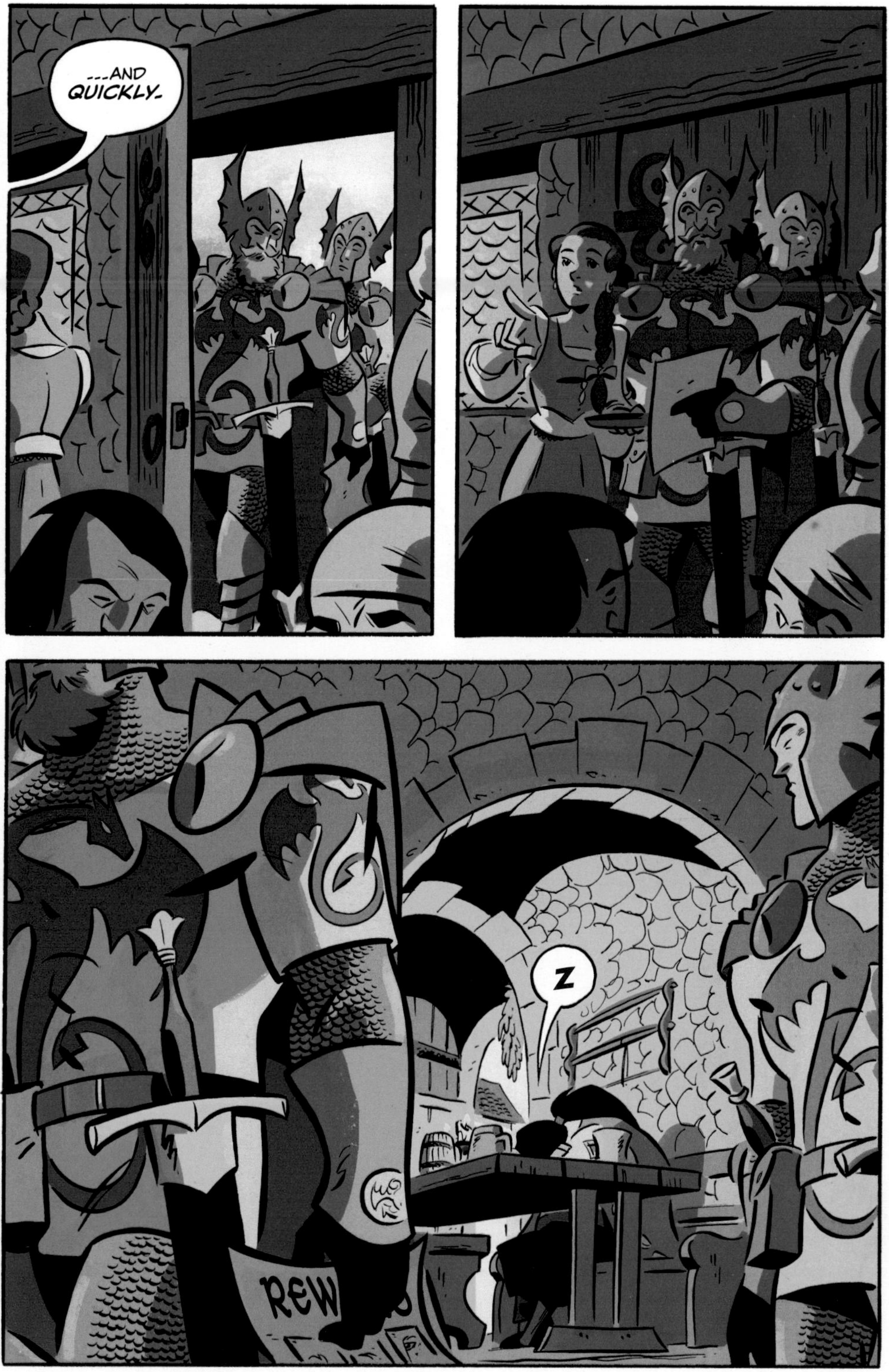

...AND QUICKLY.
Z
REW

ACT TWO

Tribes

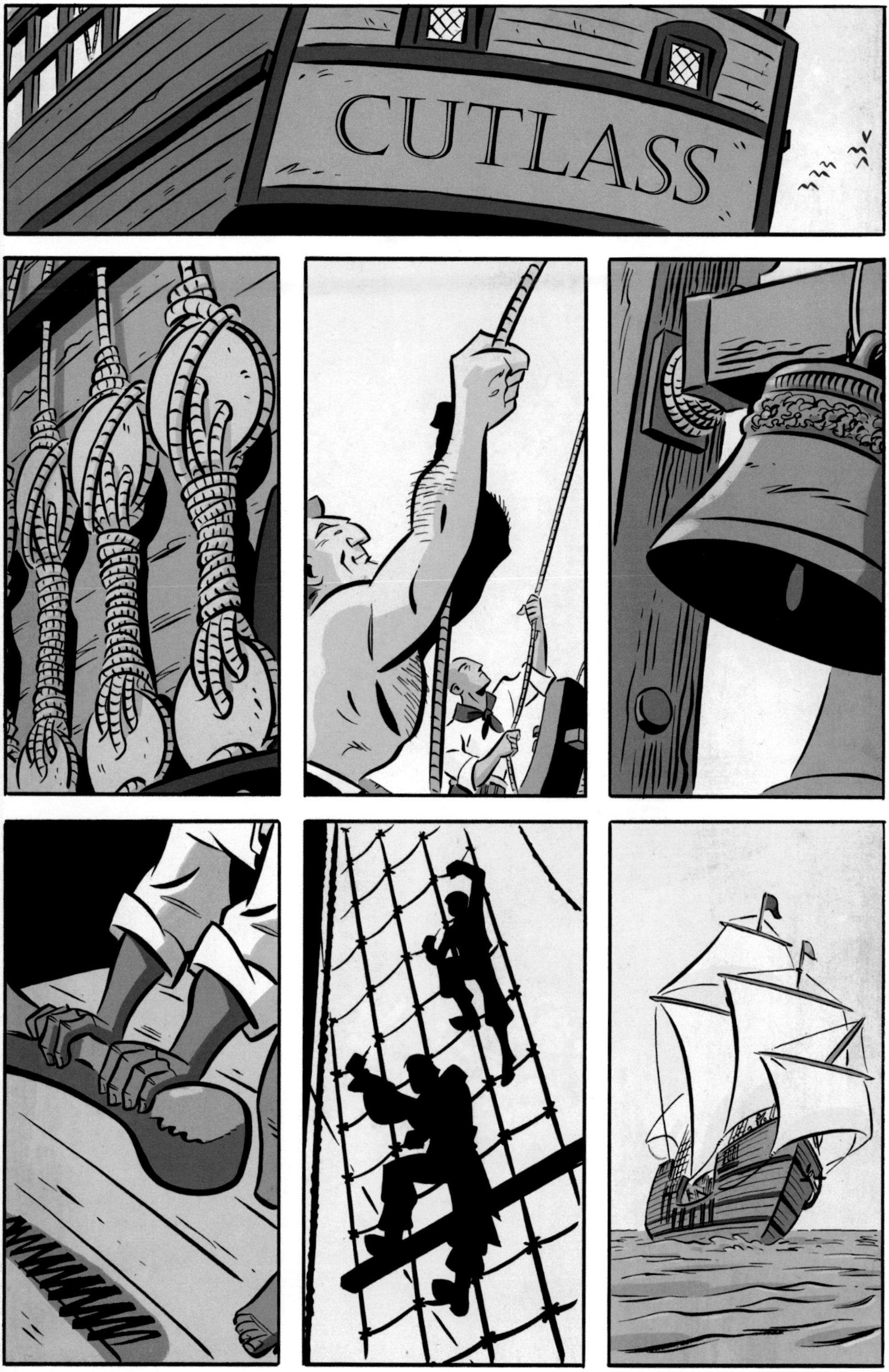
CUTLASS

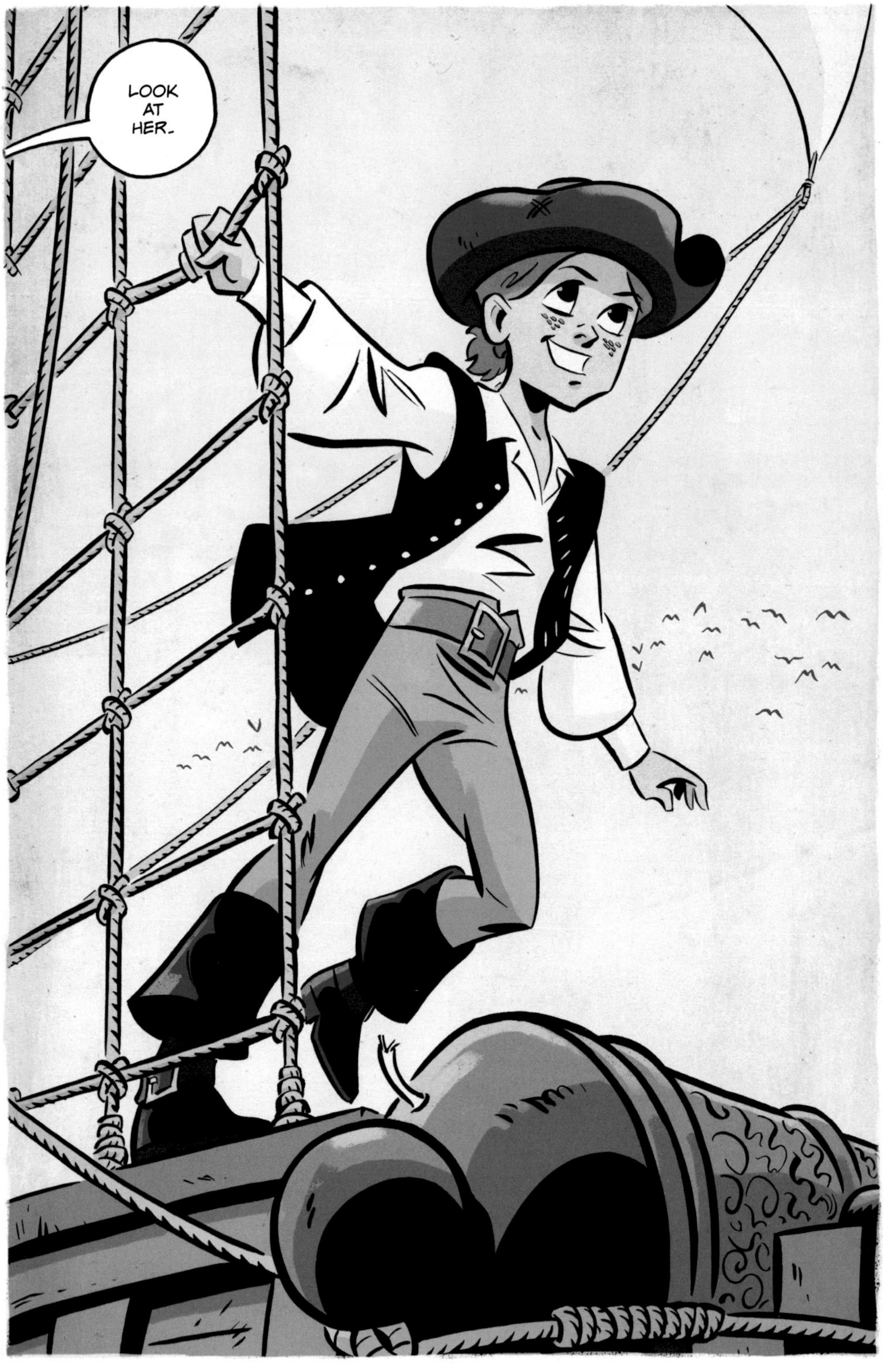
LOOK AT HER...

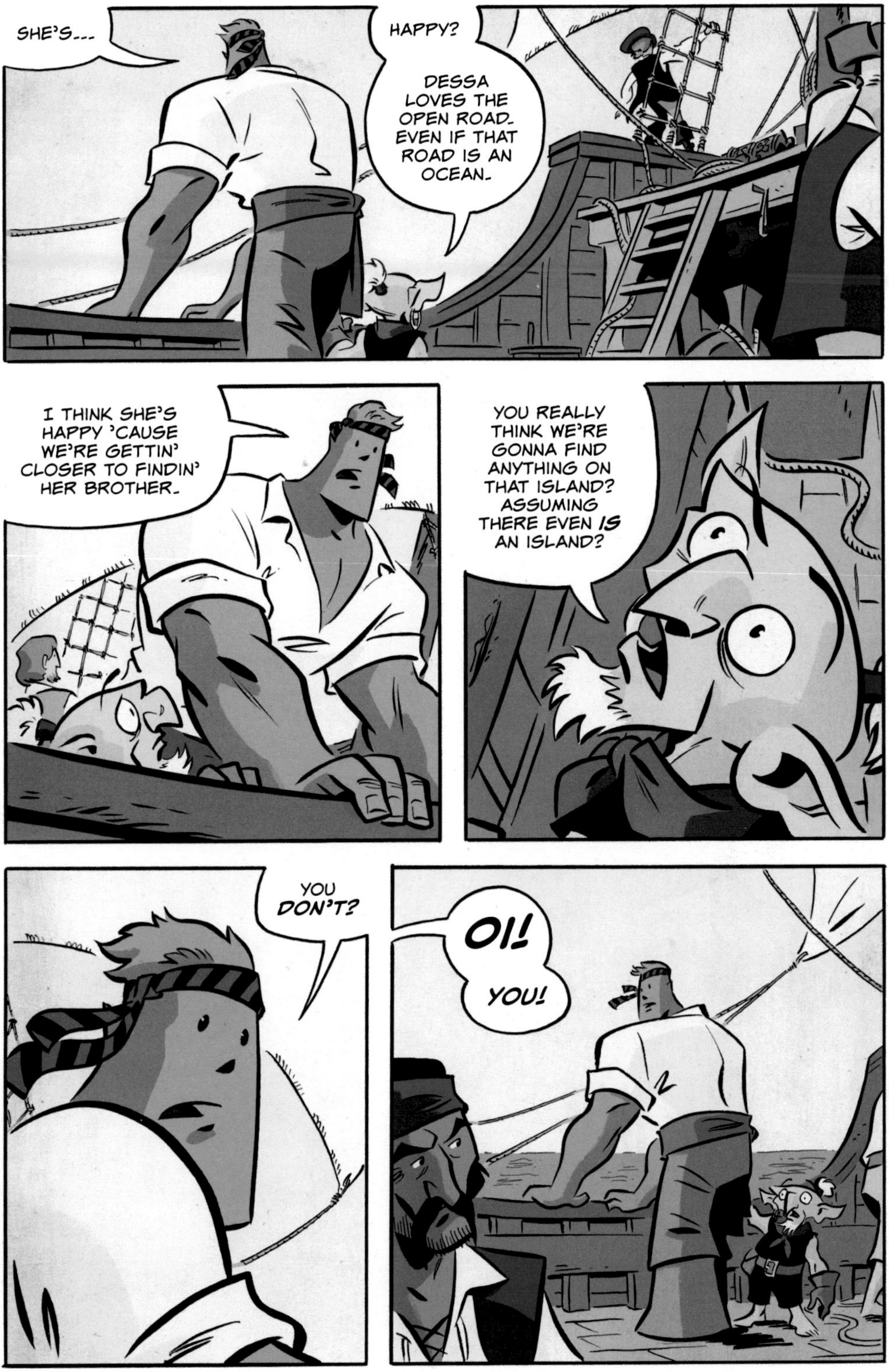
SHE'S...
HAPPY?
DESSA LOVES THE OPEN ROAD. EVEN IF THAT ROAD IS AN OCEAN.
I THINK SHE'S HAPPY 'CAUSE WE'RE GETTIN' CLOSER TO FINDIN' HER BROTHER.
YOU REALLY THINK WE'RE GONNA FIND ANYTHING ON THAT ISLAND? ASSUMING THERE EVEN *IS* AN ISLAND?
YOU *DON'T?*
OI!
YOU!

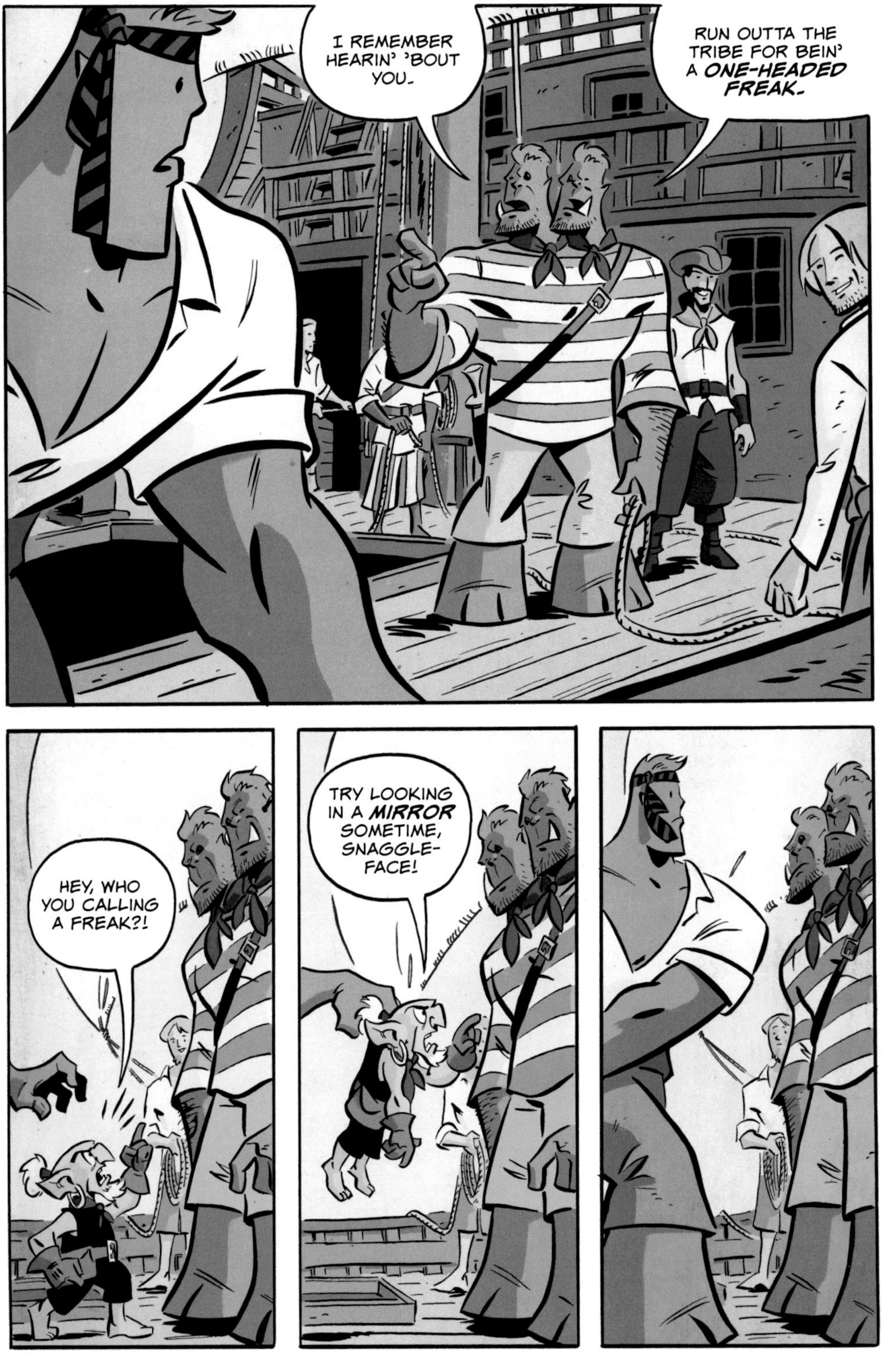
I REMEMBER HEARIN' 'BOUT YOU.
RUN OUTTA THE TRIBE FOR BEIN' A ONE-HEADED FREAK.
HEY, WHO YOU CALLING A FREAK?!
TRY LOOKING IN A MIRROR SOMETIME, SNAGGLE-FACE!

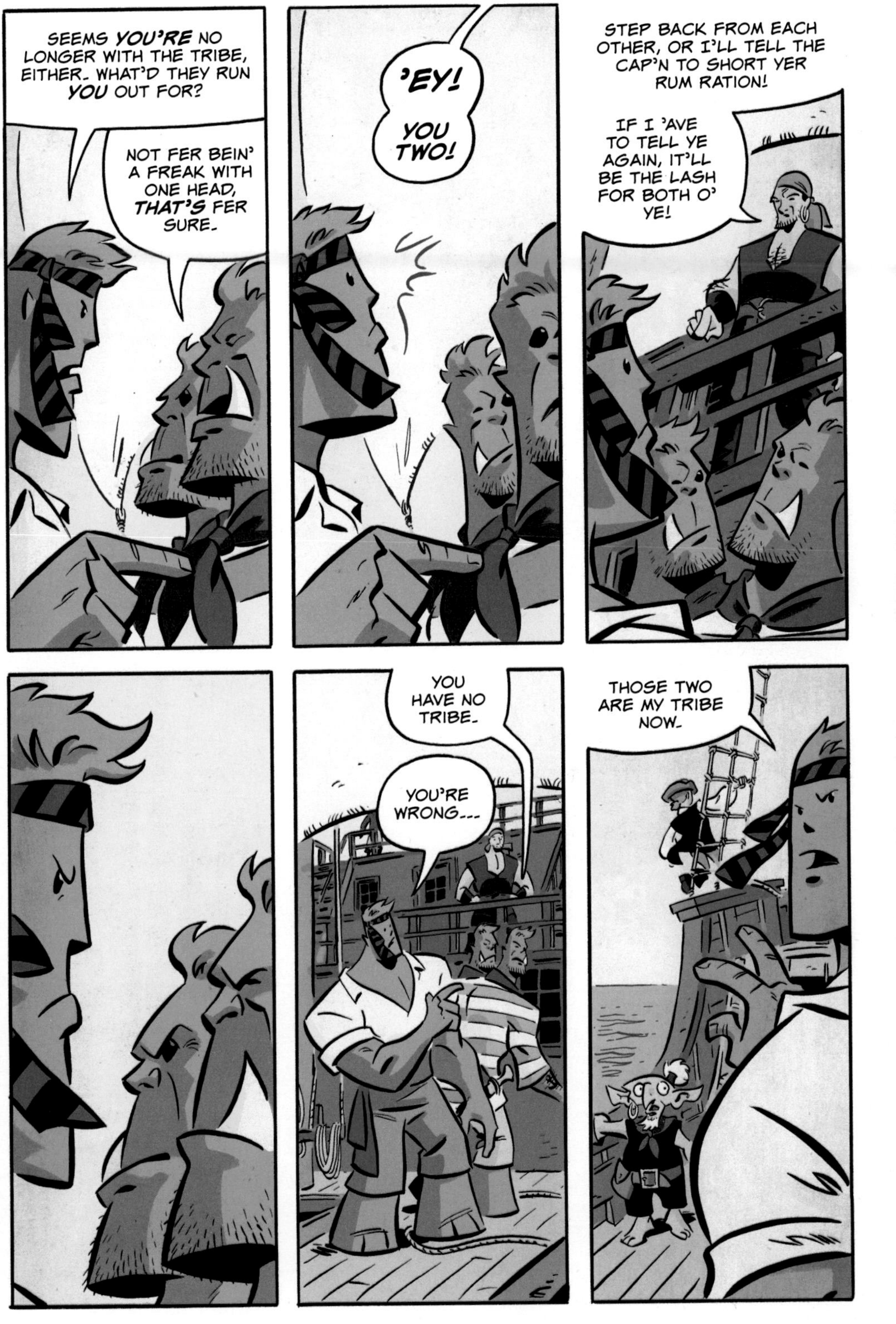

SEEMS YOU'RE NO LONGER WITH THE TRIBE, EITHER. WHAT'D THEY RUN YOU OUT FOR?
NOT FER BEIN' A FREAK WITH ONE HEAD, THAT'S FER SURE.
'EY!
YOU TWO!
STEP BACK FROM EACH OTHER, OR I'LL TELL THE CAP'N TO SHORT YER RUM RATION!
IF I 'AVE TO TELL YE AGAIN, IT'LL BE THE LASH FOR BOTH O' YE!
YOU HAVE NO TRIBE.
YOU'RE WRONG...
THOSE TWO ARE MY TRIBE NOW.

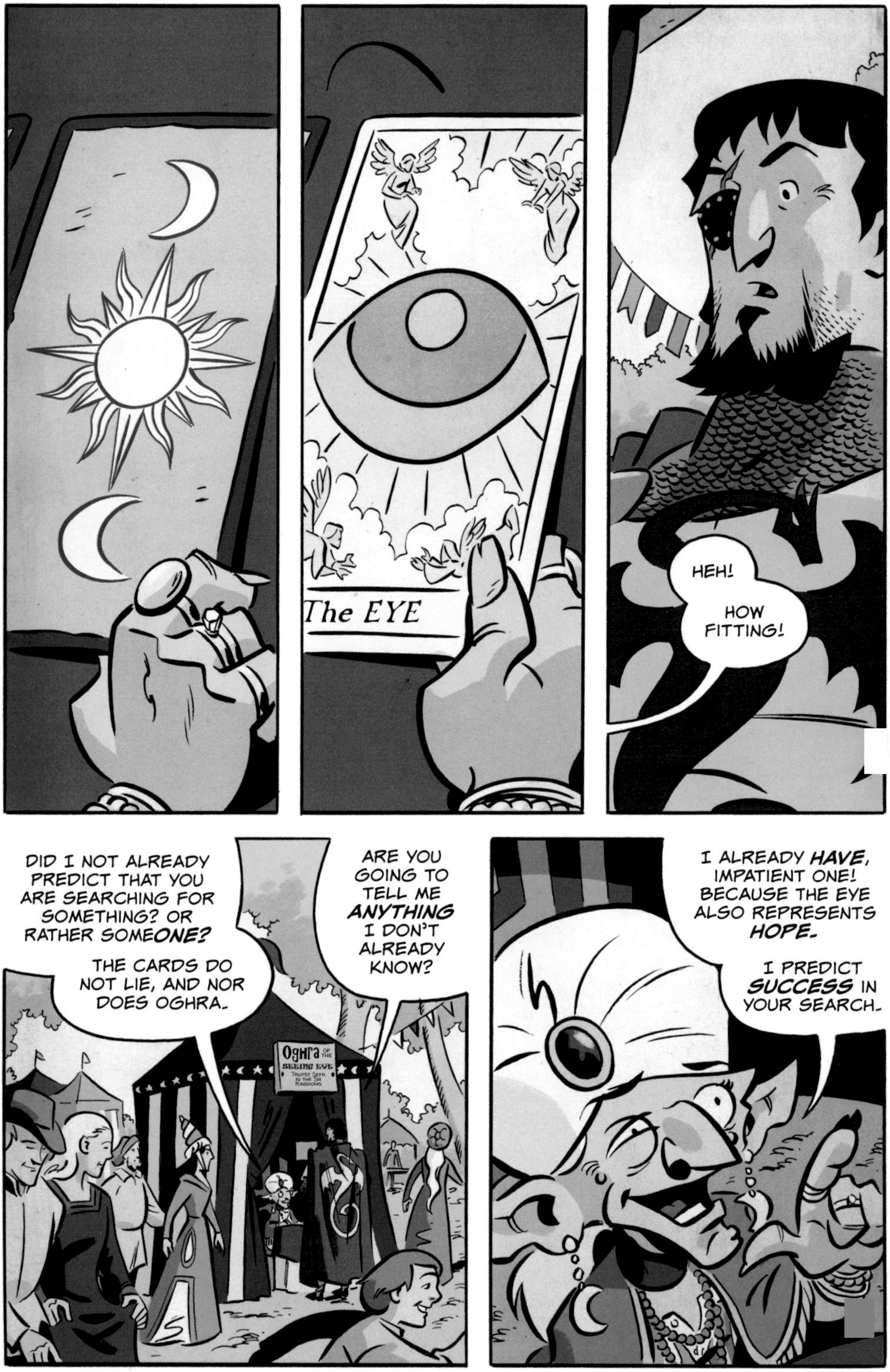
The EYE
HEH!
HOW FITTING!
DID I NOT ALREADY PREDICT THAT YOU ARE SEARCHING FOR SOMETHING? OR RATHER SOMEONE?
THE CARDS DO NOT LIE, AND NOR DOES OGHRA.
ARE YOU GOING TO TELL ME ANYTHING I DON'T ALREADY KNOW?
OGHRA OF THE SEEING EYE
I ALREADY HAVE, IMPATIENT ONE! BECAUSE THE EYE ALSO REPRESENTS HOPE.
I PREDICT SUCCESS IN YOUR SEARCH.

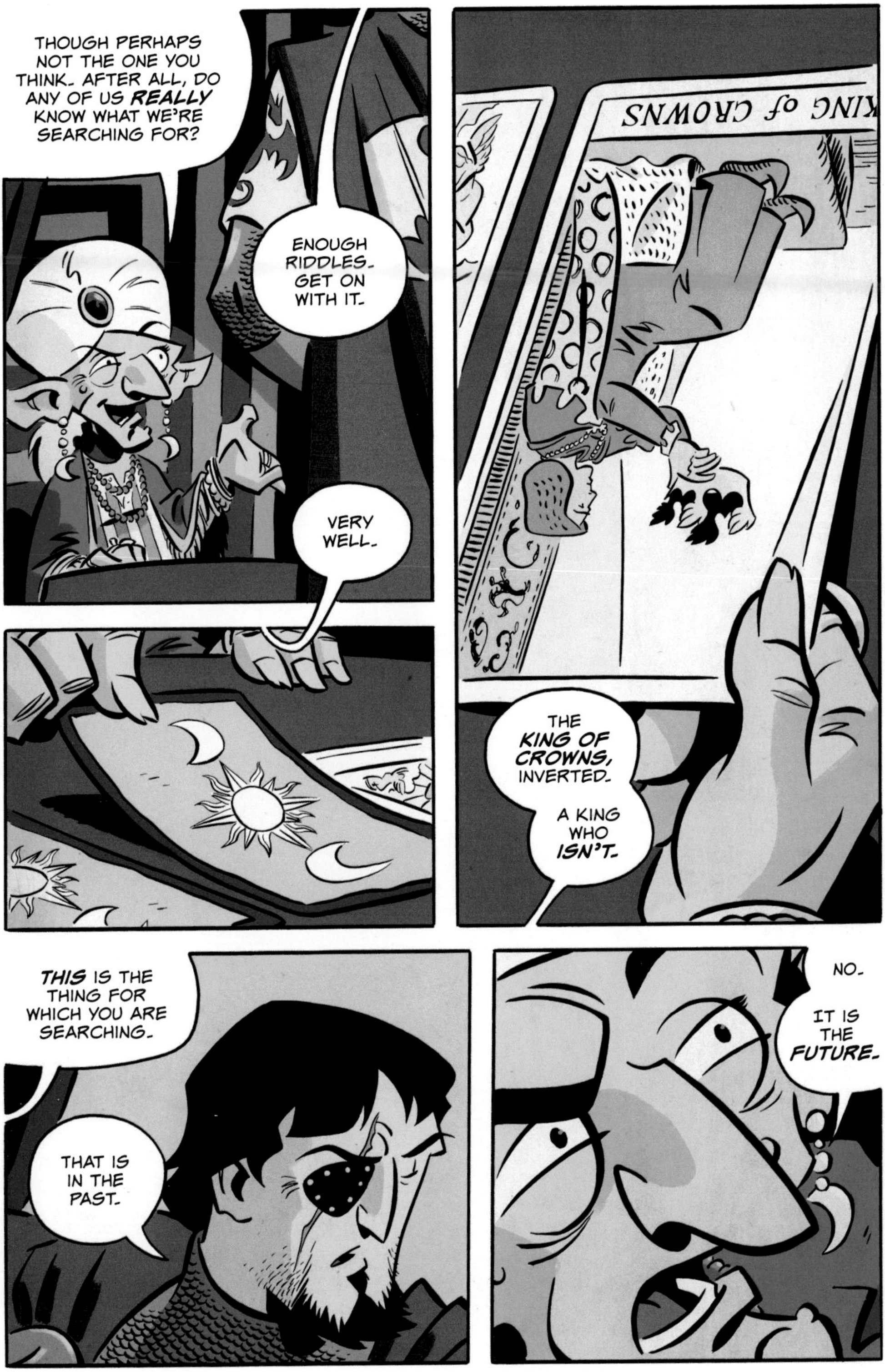
THOUGH PERHAPS NOT THE ONE YOU THINK. AFTER ALL, DO ANY OF US REALLY KNOW WHAT WE'RE SEARCHING FOR?
ENOUGH RIDDLES. GET ON WITH IT.
VERY WELL.
KING of CROWNS
THE KING OF CROWNS, INVERTED.
A KING WHO ISN'T.
THIS IS THE THING FOR WHICH YOU ARE SEARCHING.
THAT IS IN THE PAST.
NO.
IT IS THE FUTURE.

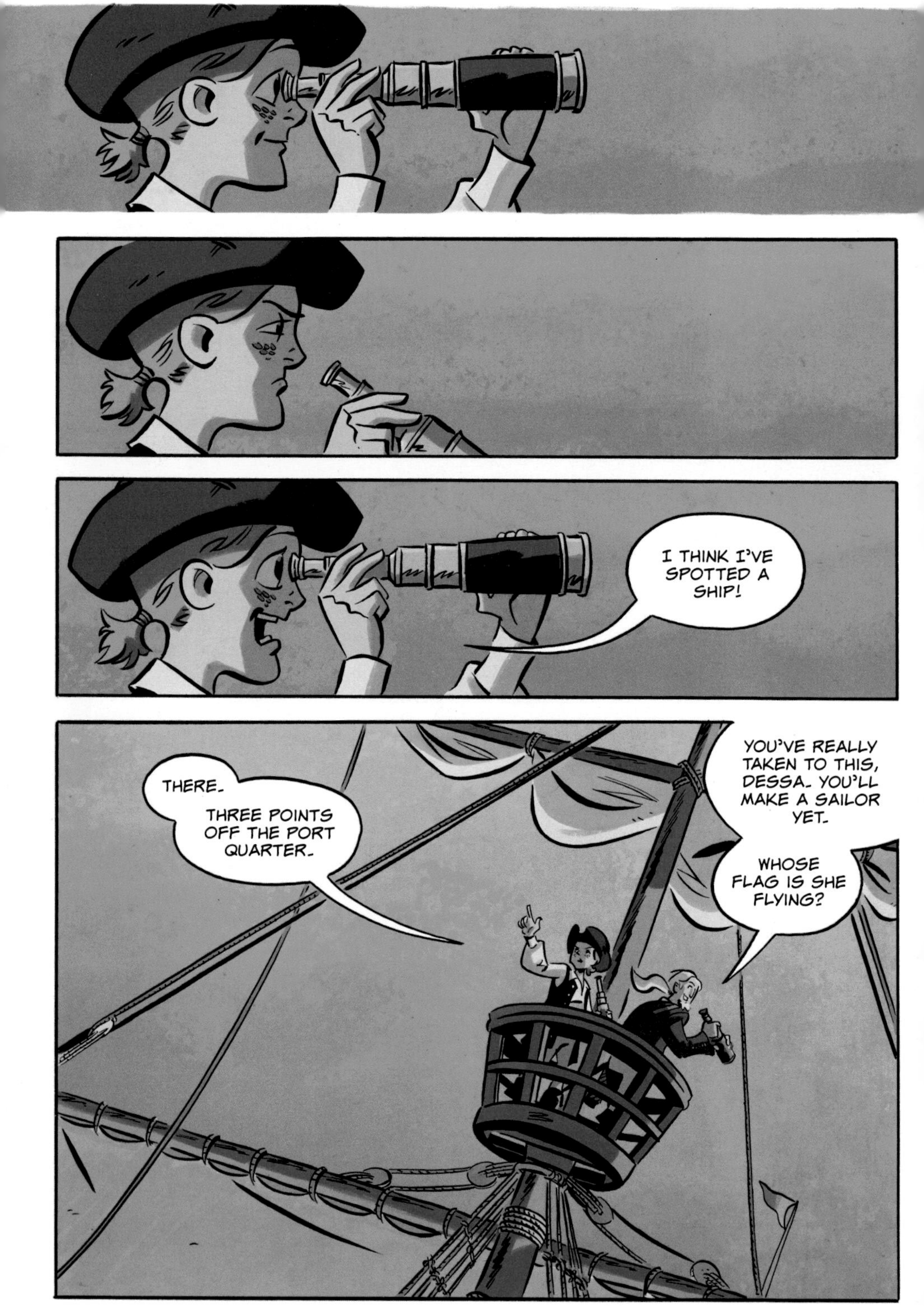
I THINK I'VE SPOTTED A SHIP!
THERE.
THREE POINTS OFF THE PORT QUARTER.
YOU'VE REALLY TAKEN TO THIS, DESSA. YOU'LL MAKE A SAILOR YET.
WHOSE FLAG IS SHE FLYING?

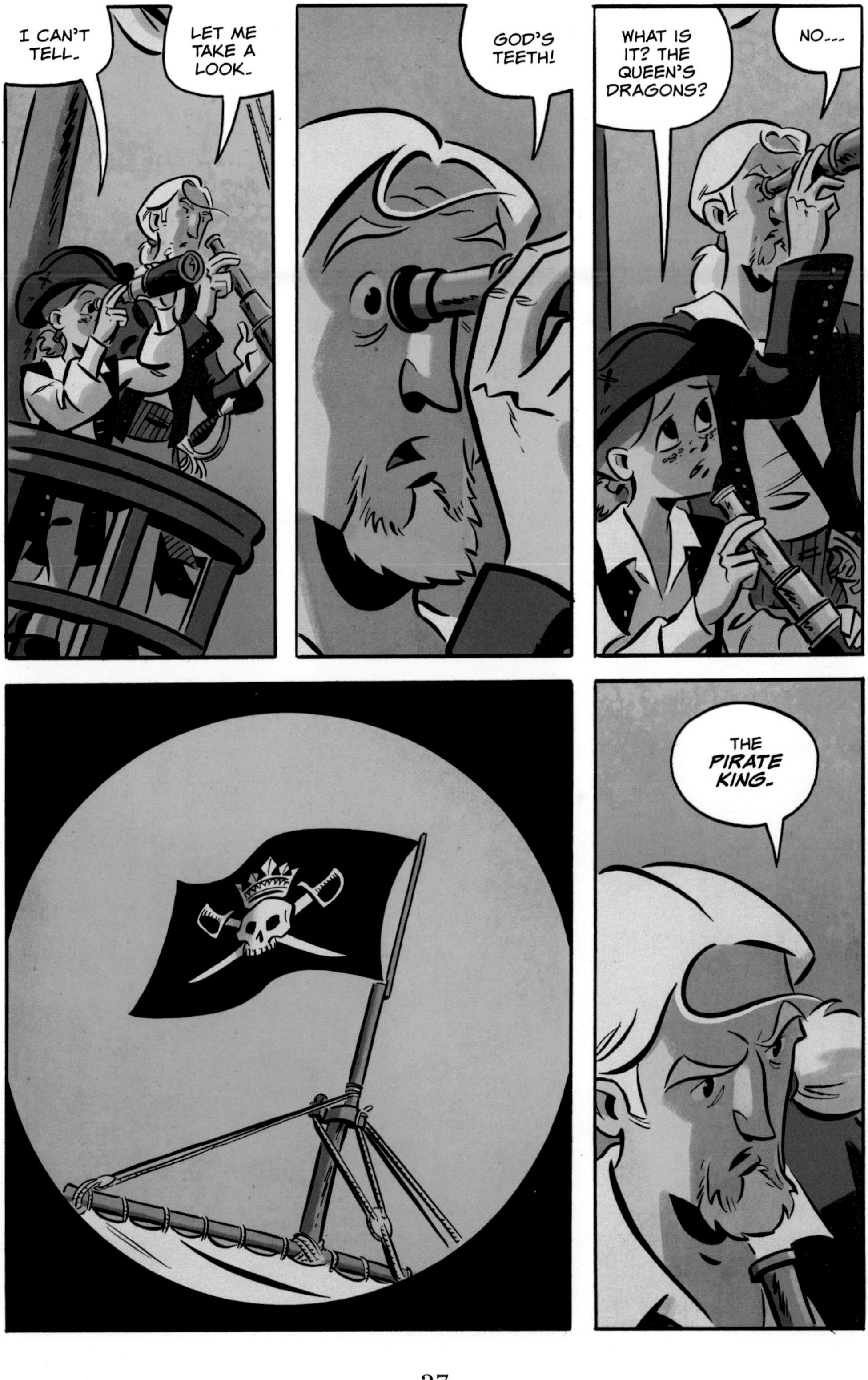
I CAN'T TELL.
LET ME TAKE A LOOK.
GOD'S TEETH!
WHAT IS IT? THE QUEEN'S DRAGONS?
NO...
THE PIRATE KING.

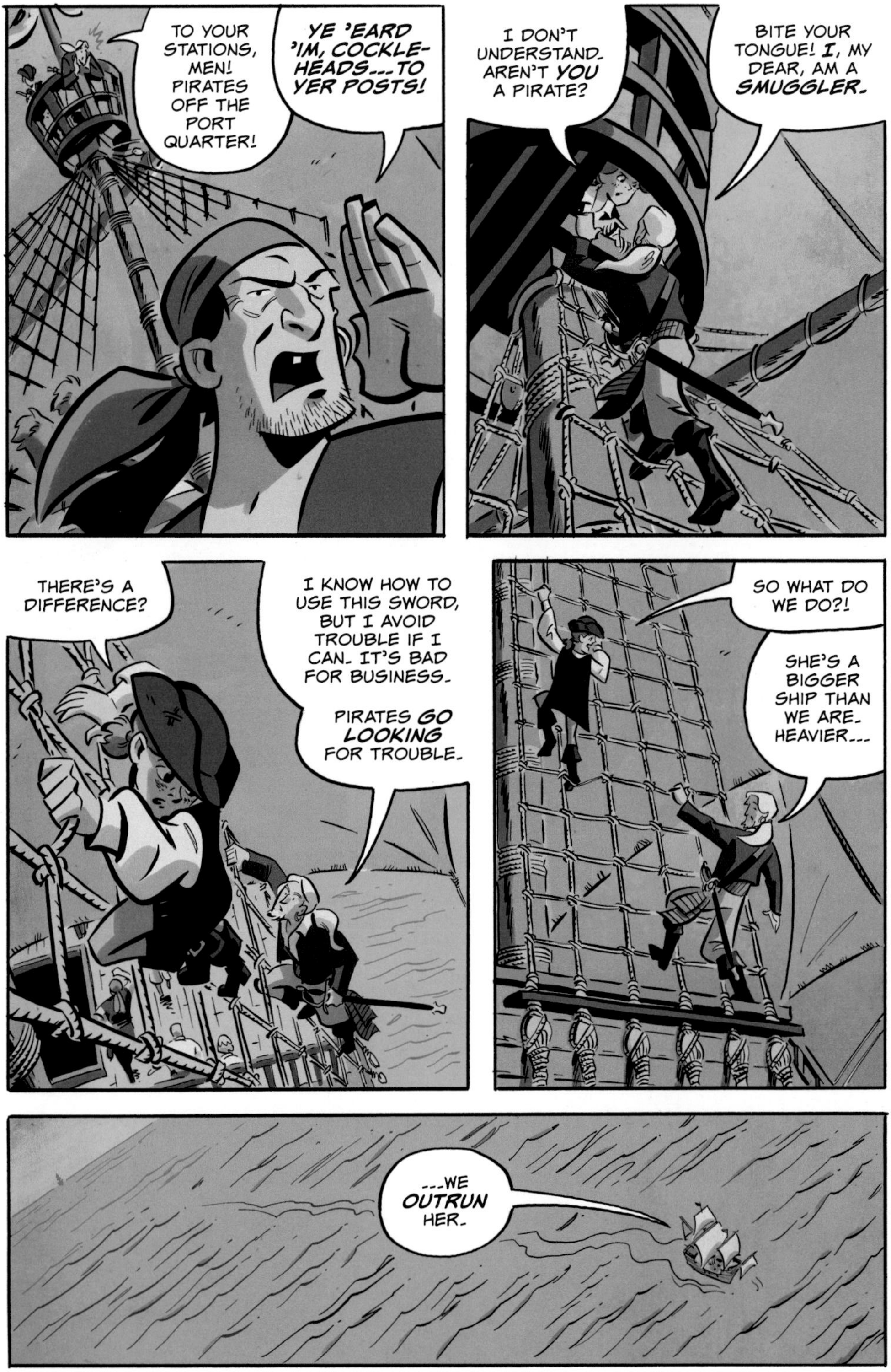
TO YOUR STATIONS, MEN! PIRATES OFF THE PORT QUARTER!
YE 'EARD 'IM, COCKLE-HEADS...TO YER POSTS!
I DON'T UNDERSTAND. AREN'T YOU A PIRATE?
BITE YOUR TONGUE! I, MY DEAR, AM A SMUGGLER.
THERE'S A DIFFERENCE?
I KNOW HOW TO USE THIS SWORD, BUT I AVOID TROUBLE IF I CAN. IT'S BAD FOR BUSINESS.
PIRATES GO LOOKING FOR TROUBLE.
SO WHAT DO WE DO?!
SHE'S A BIGGER SHIP THAN WE ARE. HEAVIER...
...WE OUTRUN HER.

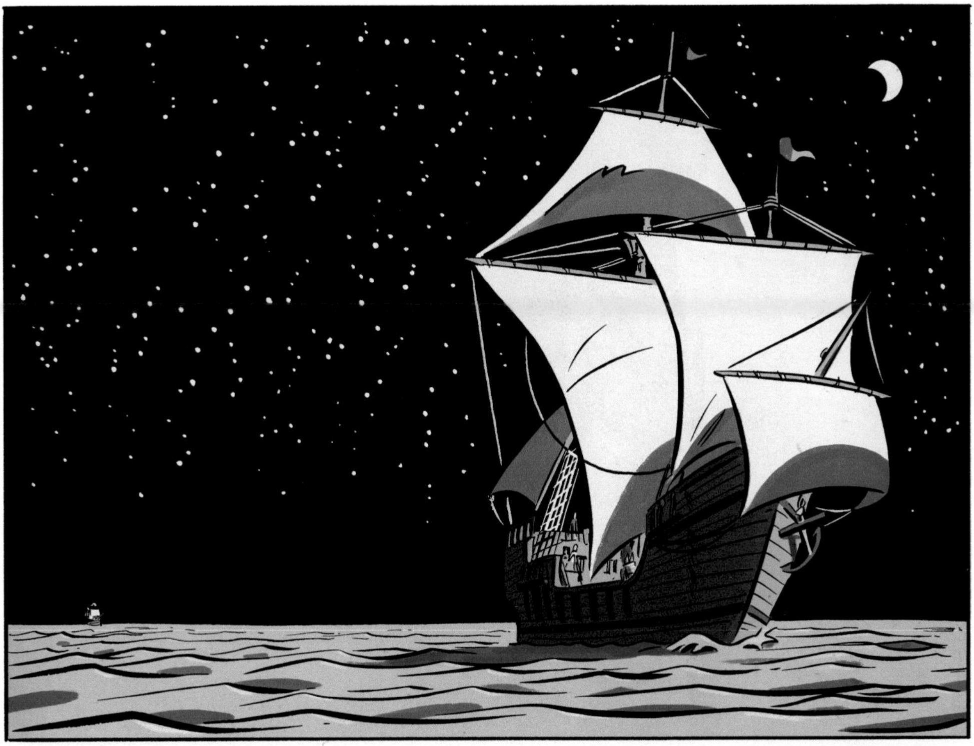

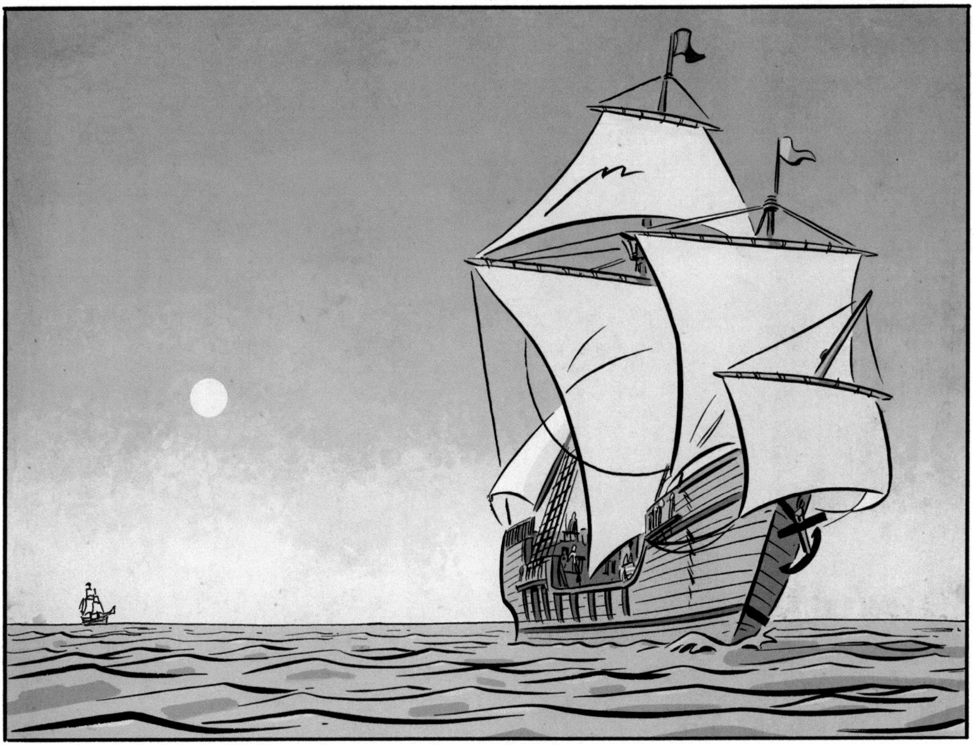

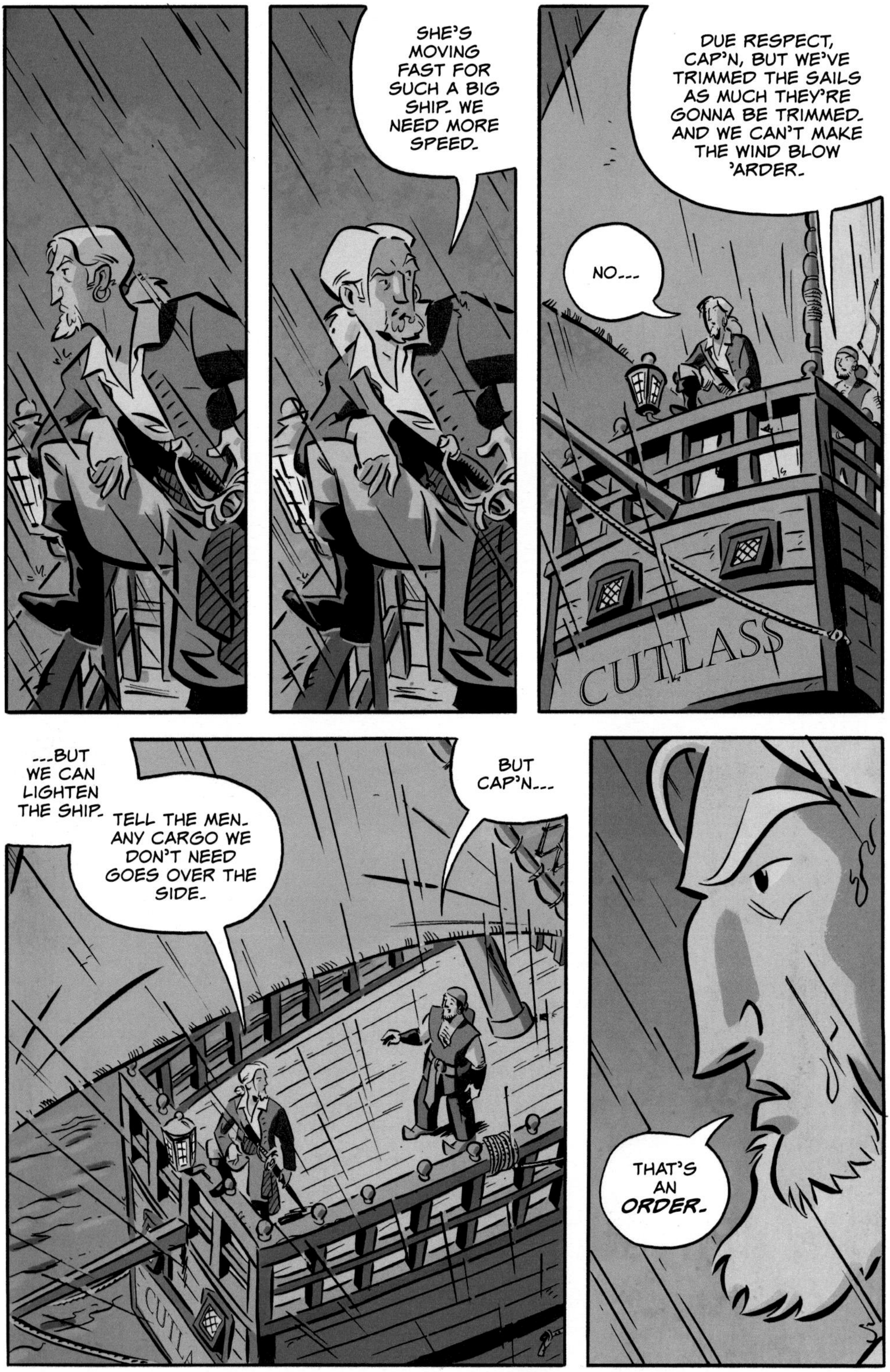
SHE'S MOVING FAST FOR SUCH A BIG SHIP. WE NEED MORE SPEED.
DUE RESPECT, CAP'N, BUT WE'VE TRIMMED THE SAILS AS MUCH THEY'RE GONNA BE TRIMMED. AND WE CAN'T MAKE THE WIND BLOW 'ARDER.
NO...
CUTLASS
...BUT WE CAN LIGHTEN THE SHIP.
TELL THE MEN. ANY CARGO WE DON'T NEED GOES OVER THE SIDE.
BUT CAP'N...
THAT'S AN ORDER.

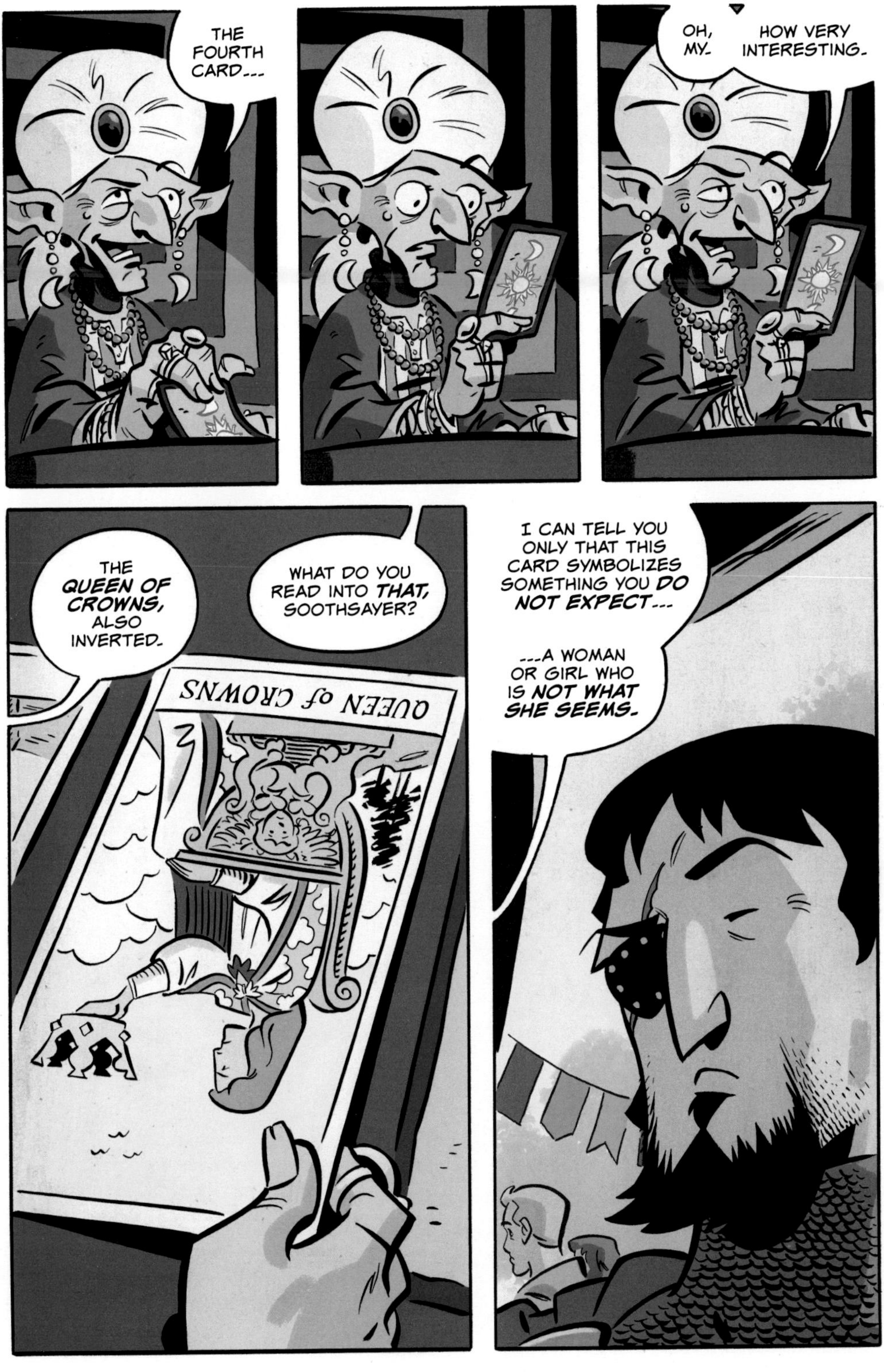
THE FOURTH CARD...
OH, MY.
HOW VERY INTERESTING.
THE QUEEN OF CROWNS, ALSO INVERTED.
WHAT DO YOU READ INTO THAT, SOOTHSAYER?
QUEEN of CROWNS
I CAN TELL YOU ONLY THAT THIS CARD SYMBOLIZES SOMETHING YOU DO NOT EXPECT...
...A WOMAN OR GIRL WHO IS NOT WHAT SHE SEEMS.

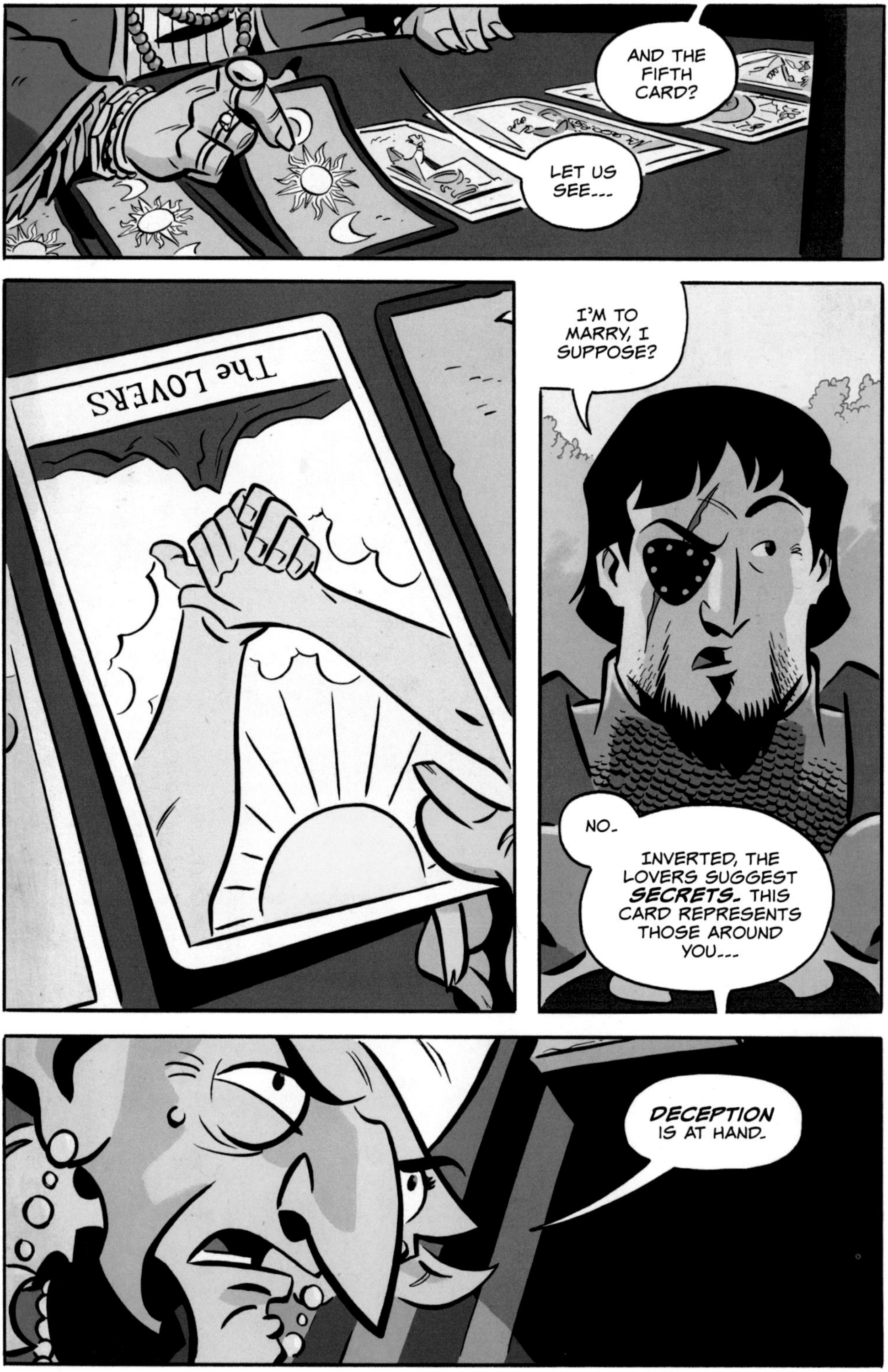
AND THE FIFTH CARD?
LET US SEE...
The LOVERS
I'M TO MARRY, I SUPPOSE?
NO.
INVERTED, THE LOVERS SUGGEST **SECRETS.** THIS CARD REPRESENTS THOSE AROUND YOU...
DECEPTION IS AT HAND.

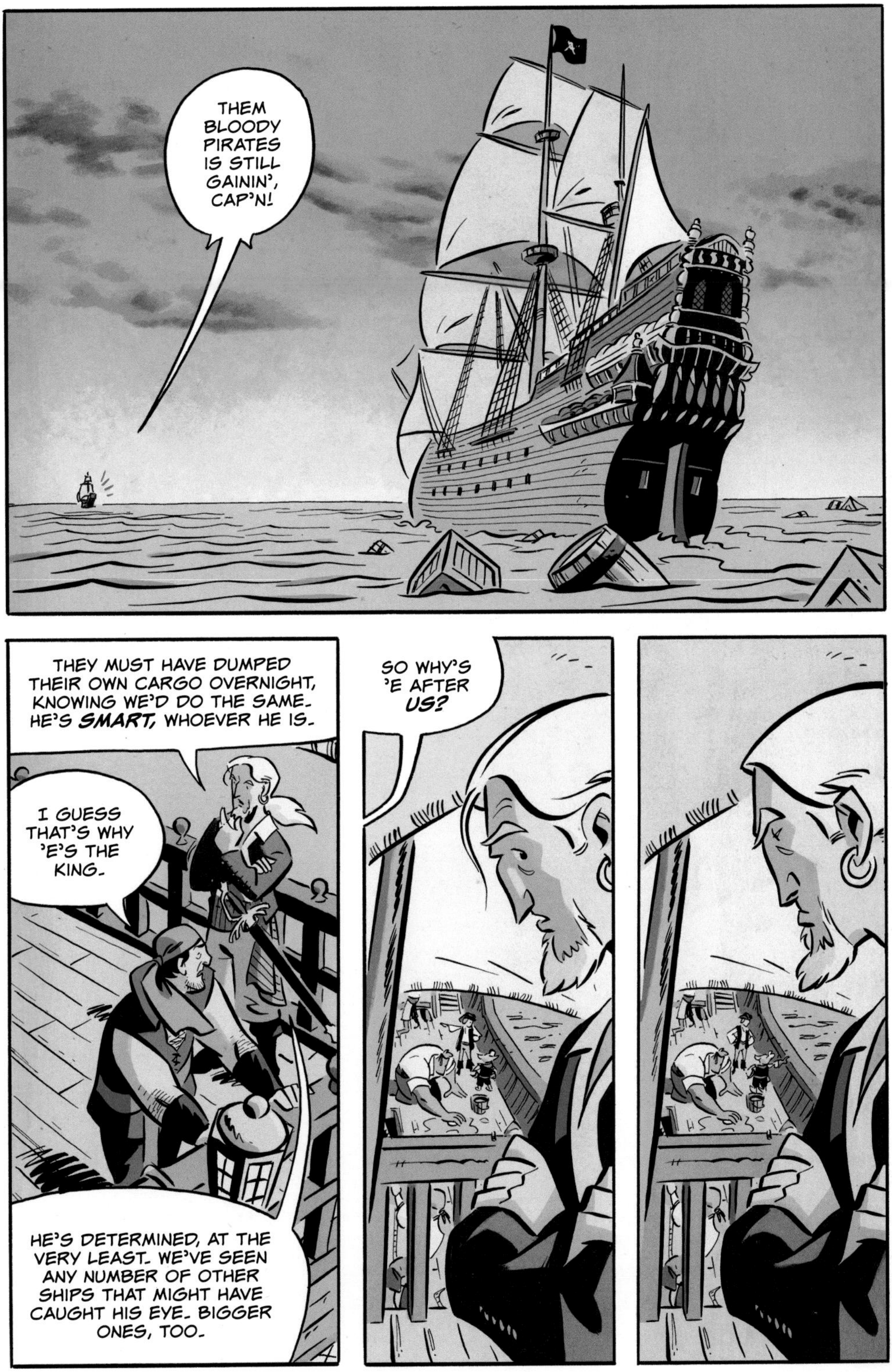

THEM BLOODY PIRATES IS STILL GAININ', CAP'N!
THEY MUST HAVE DUMPED THEIR OWN CARGO OVERNIGHT, KNOWING WE'D DO THE SAME. HE'S SMART, WHOEVER HE IS.
I GUESS THAT'S WHY 'E'S THE KING.
HE'S DETERMINED, AT THE VERY LEAST. WE'VE SEEN ANY NUMBER OF OTHER SHIPS THAT MIGHT HAVE CAUGHT HIS EYE. BIGGER ONES, TOO.
SO WHY'S 'E AFTER US?

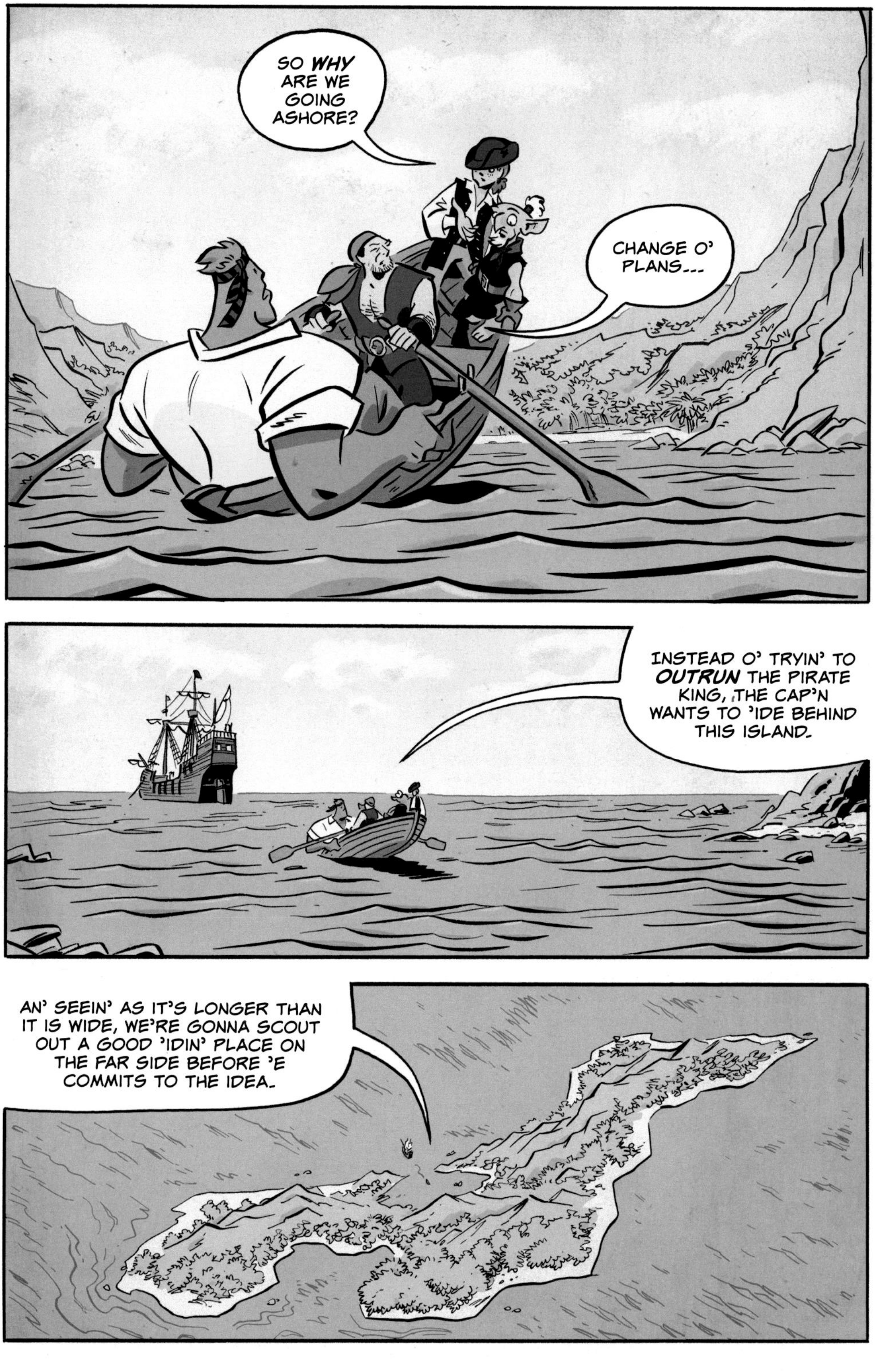
SO WHY ARE WE GOING ASHORE?
CHANGE O' PLANS...
INSTEAD O' TRYIN' TO OUTRUN THE PIRATE KING, THE CAP'N WANTS TO 'IDE BEHIND THIS ISLAND.
AN' SEEIN' AS IT'S LONGER THAN IT IS WIDE, WE'RE GONNA SCOUT OUT A GOOD 'IDIN' PLACE ON THE FAR SIDE BEFORE 'E COMMITS TO THE IDEA.

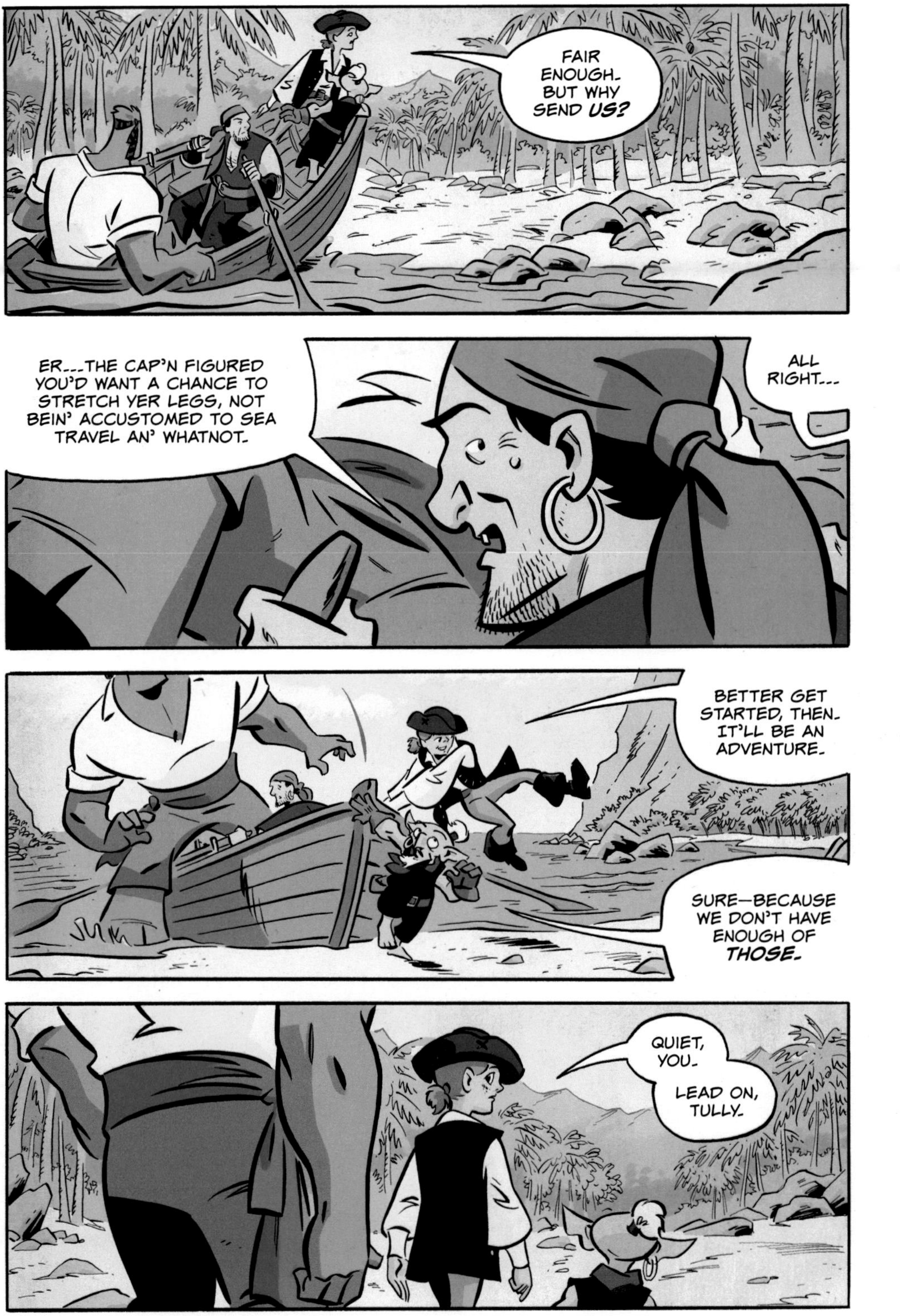
FAIR ENOUGH. BUT WHY SEND *US?*
ER...THE CAP'N FIGURED YOU'D WANT A CHANCE TO STRETCH YER LEGS, NOT BEIN' ACCUSTOMED TO SEA TRAVEL AN' WHATNOT.
ALL RIGHT...
BETTER GET STARTED, THEN. IT'LL BE AN ADVENTURE.
SURE—BECAUSE WE DON'T HAVE ENOUGH OF *THOSE.*
QUIET, YOU.
LEAD ON, TULLY.

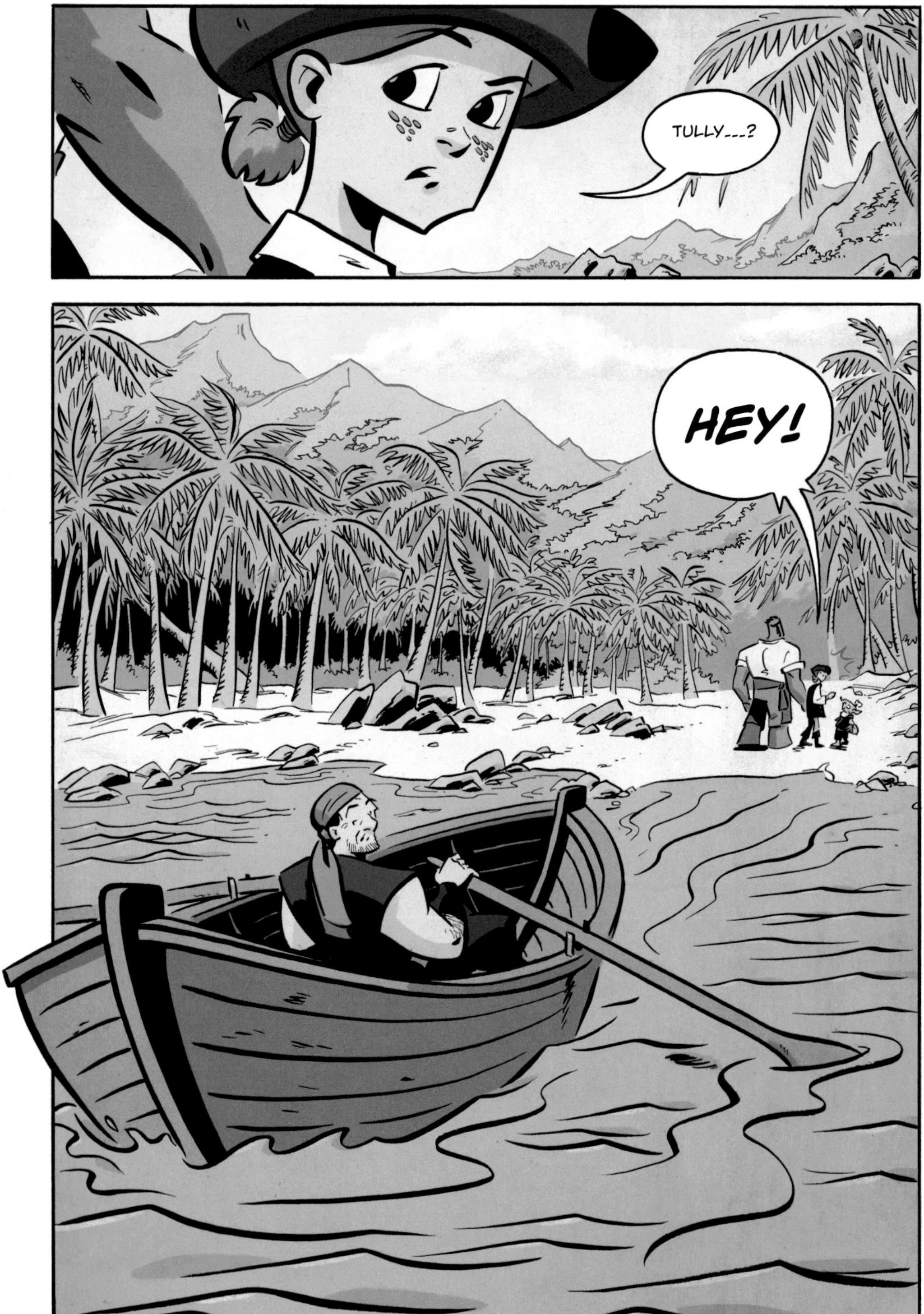
TULLY...?
HEY!

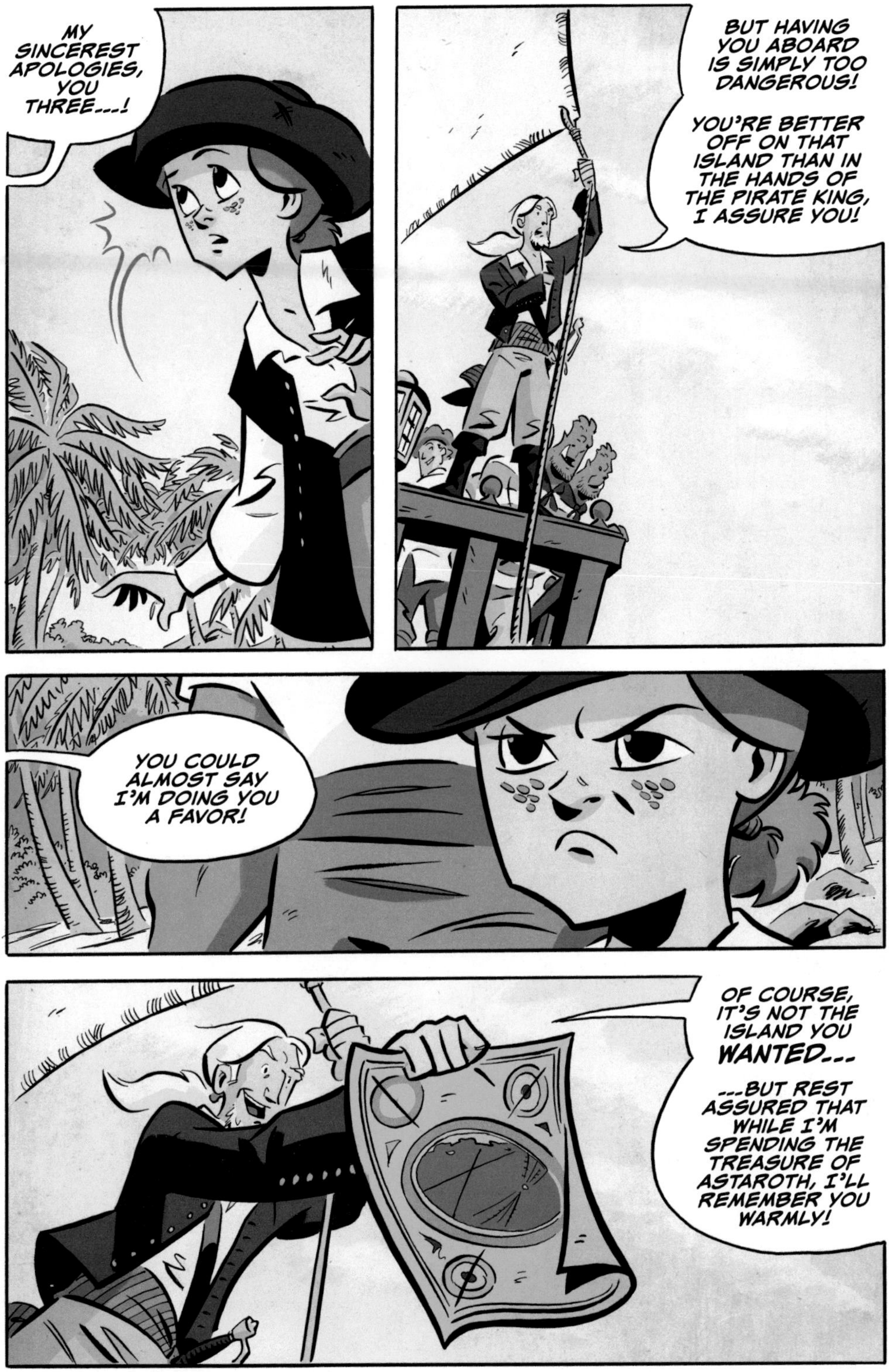
MY SINCEREST APOLOGIES, YOU THREE...!
BUT HAVING YOU ABOARD IS SIMPLY TOO DANGEROUS!
YOU'RE BETTER OFF ON THAT ISLAND THAN IN THE HANDS OF THE PIRATE KING, I ASSURE YOU!
YOU COULD ALMOST SAY I'M DOING YOU A FAVOR!
OF COURSE, IT'S NOT THE ISLAND YOU WANTED...
...BUT REST ASSURED THAT WHILE I'M SPENDING THE TREASURE OF ASTAROTH, I'LL REMEMBER YOU WARMLY!

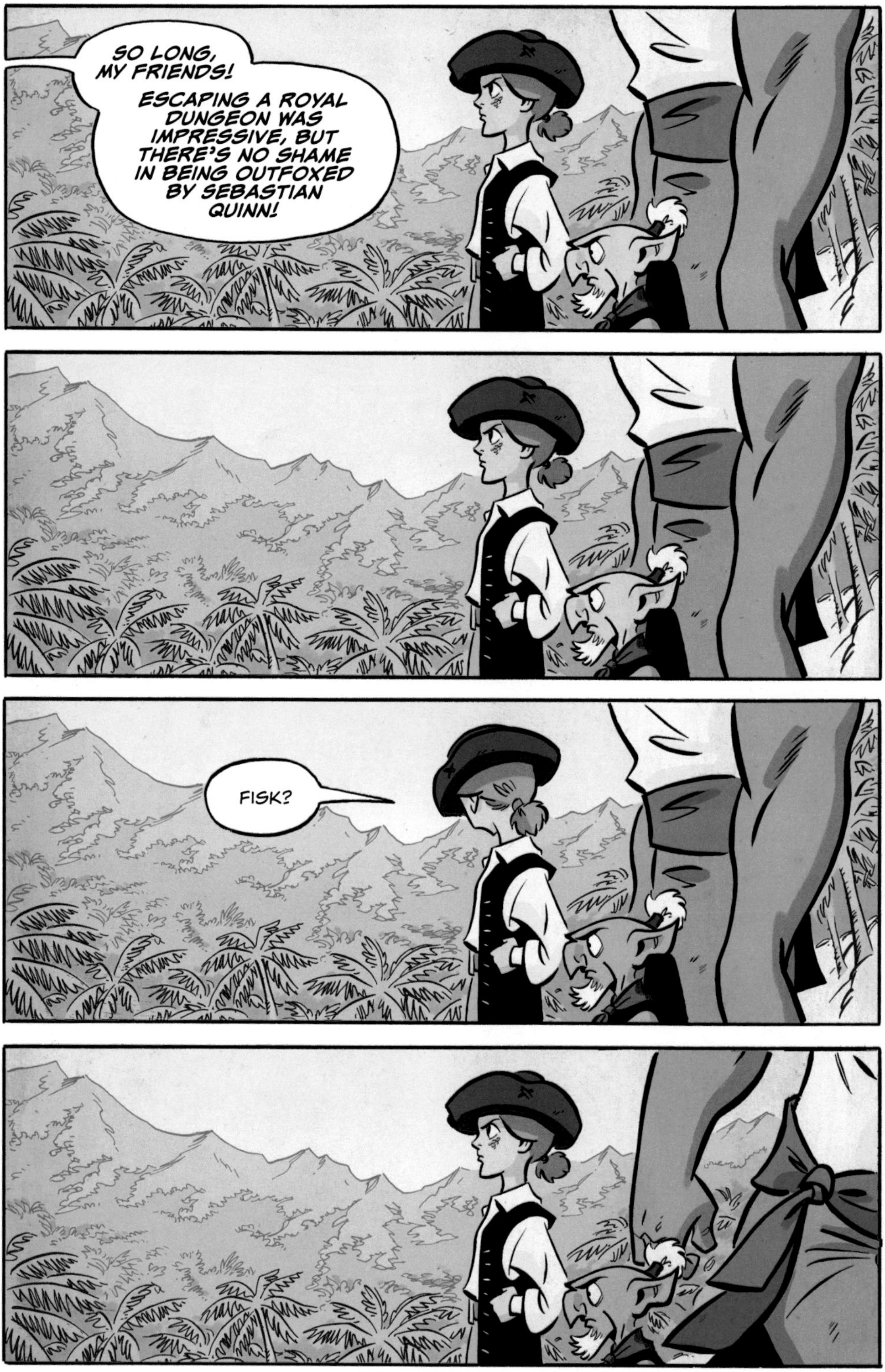
SO LONG, MY FRIENDS!
ESCAPING A ROYAL DUNGEON WAS IMPRESSIVE, BUT THERE'S NO SHAME IN BEING OUTFOXED BY SEBASTIAN QUINN!
FISK?

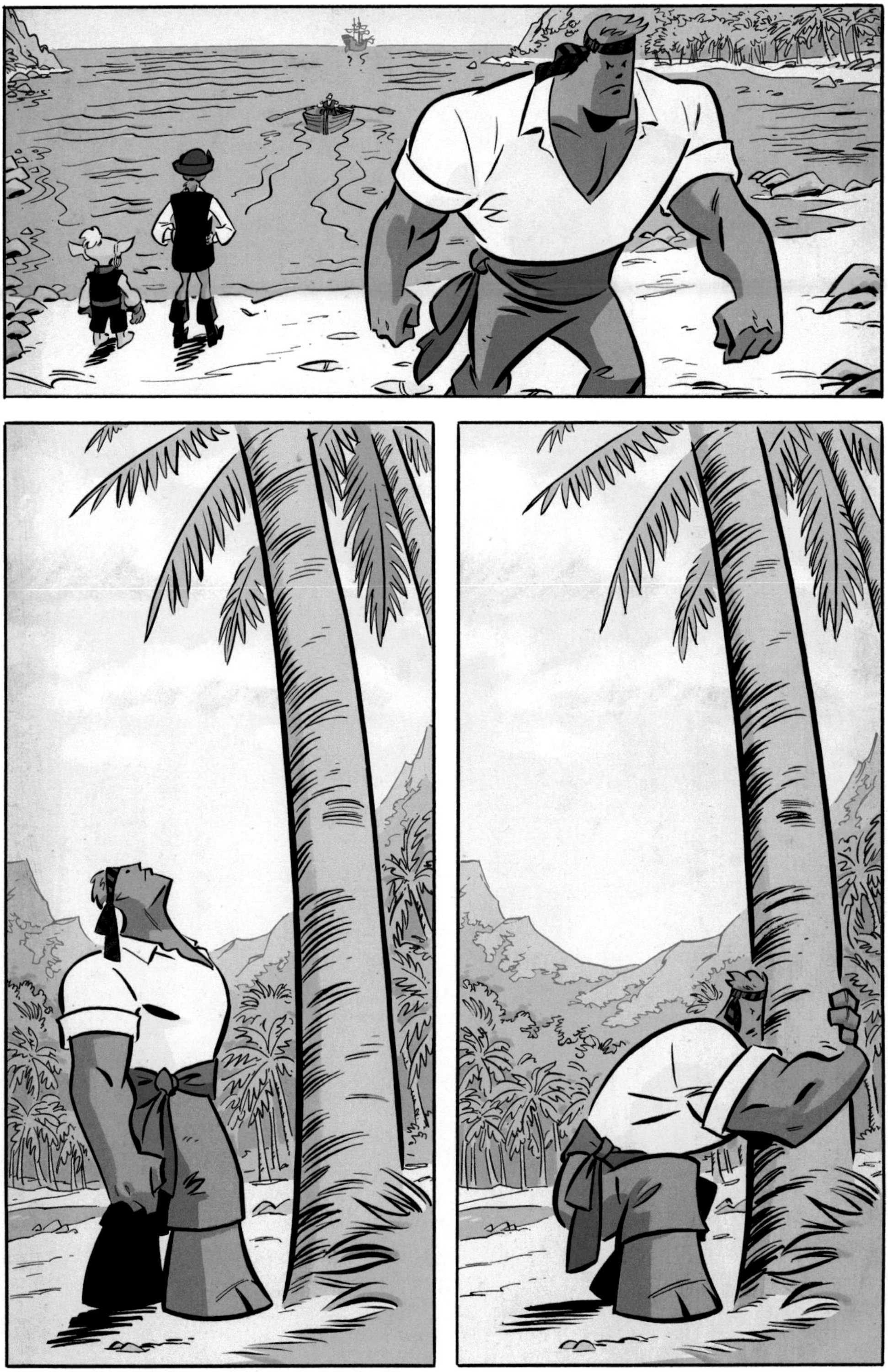

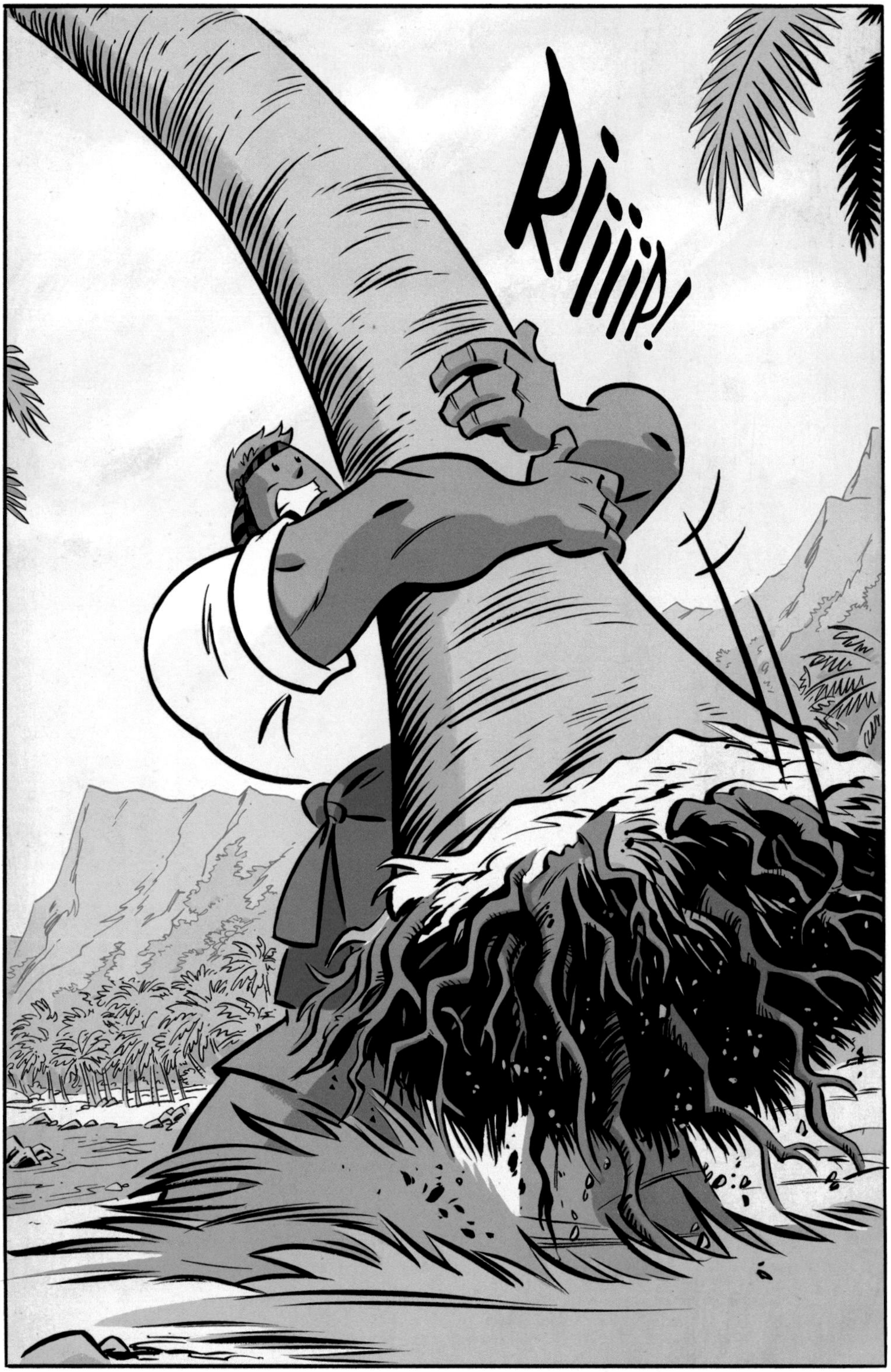
RIIIIP!

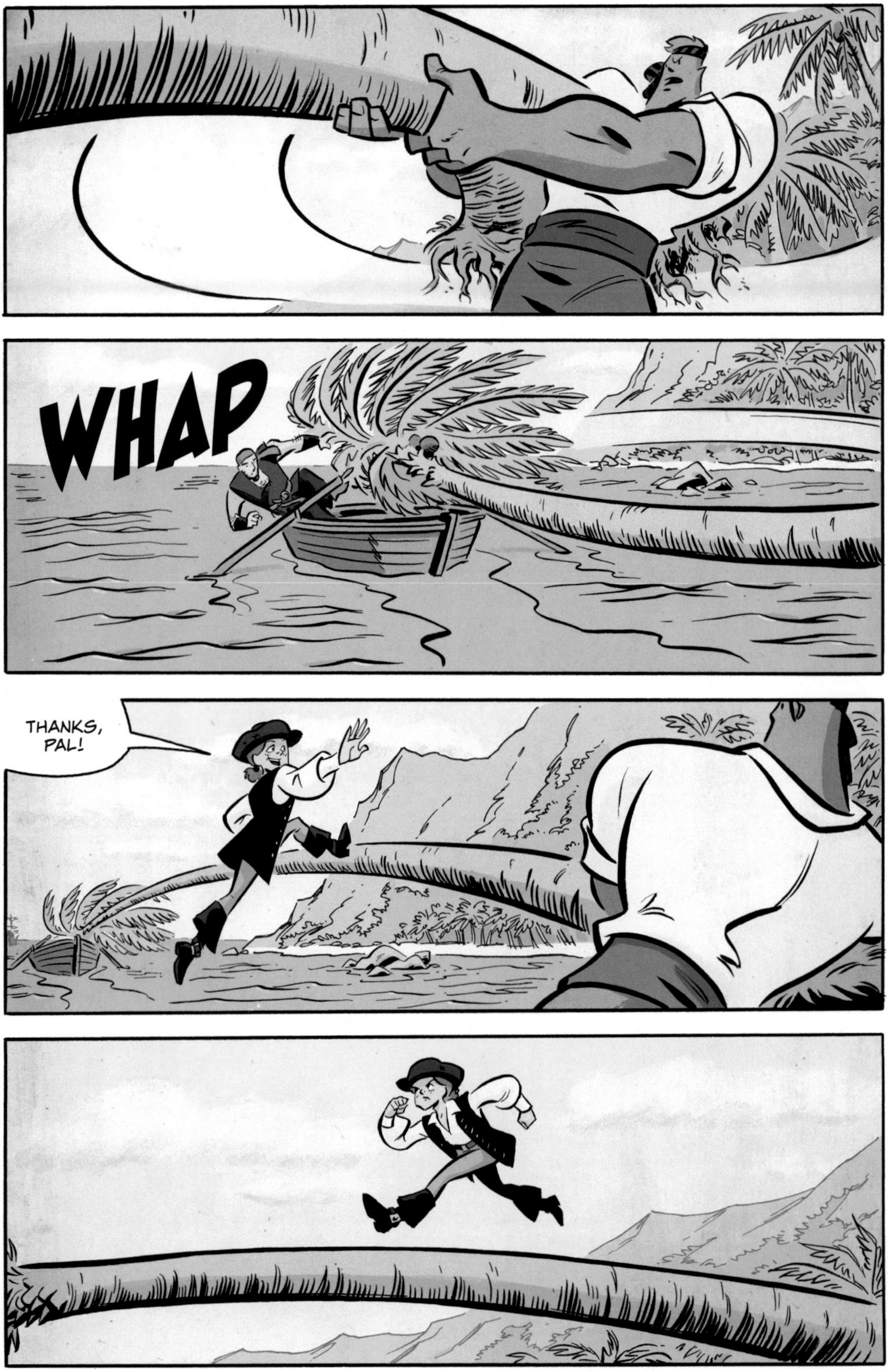
WHAP
THANKS, PAL!

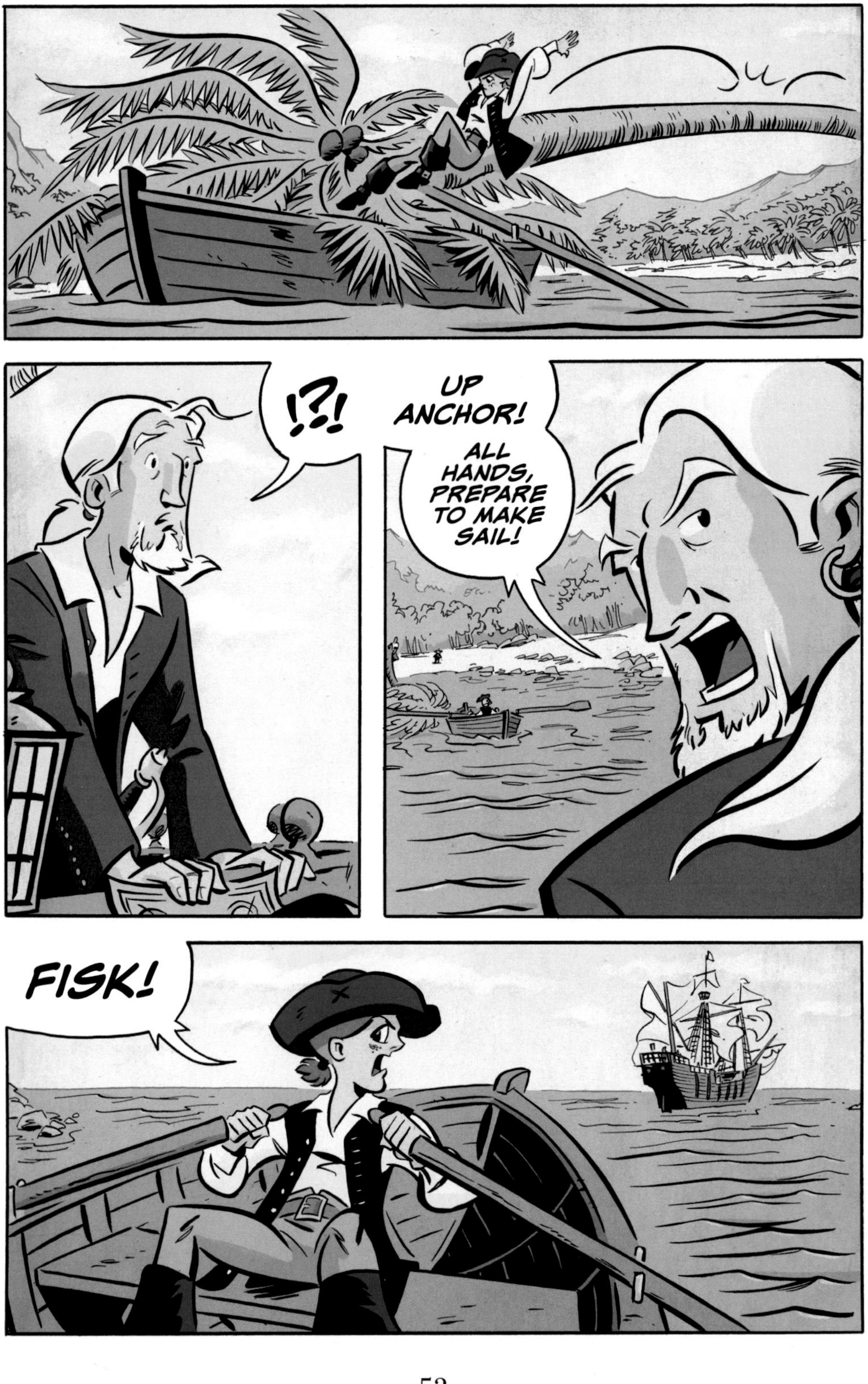

!?!
UP ANCHOR!
ALL HANDS, PREPARE TO MAKE SAIL!
FISK!

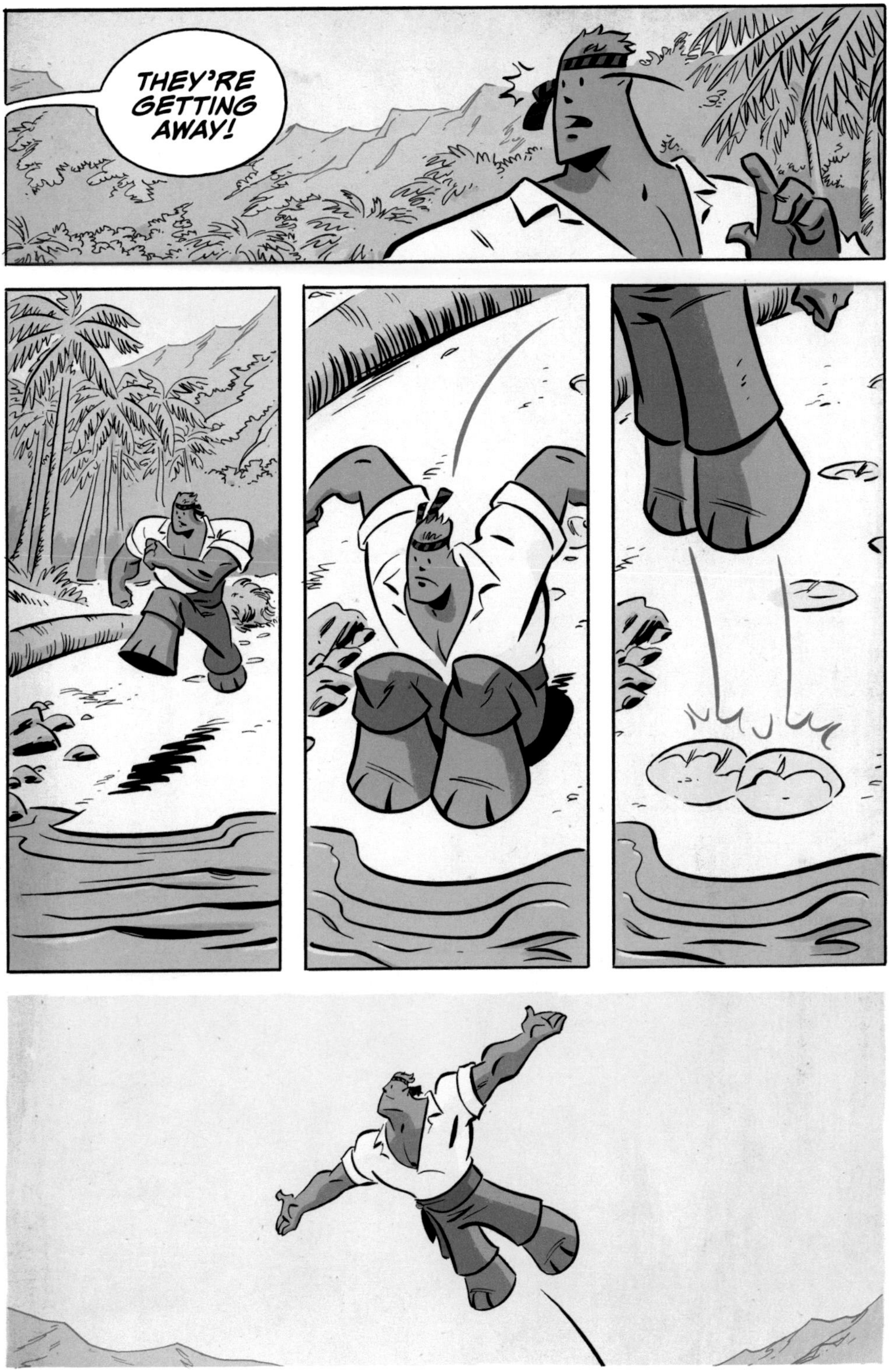
THEY'RE GETTING AWAY!

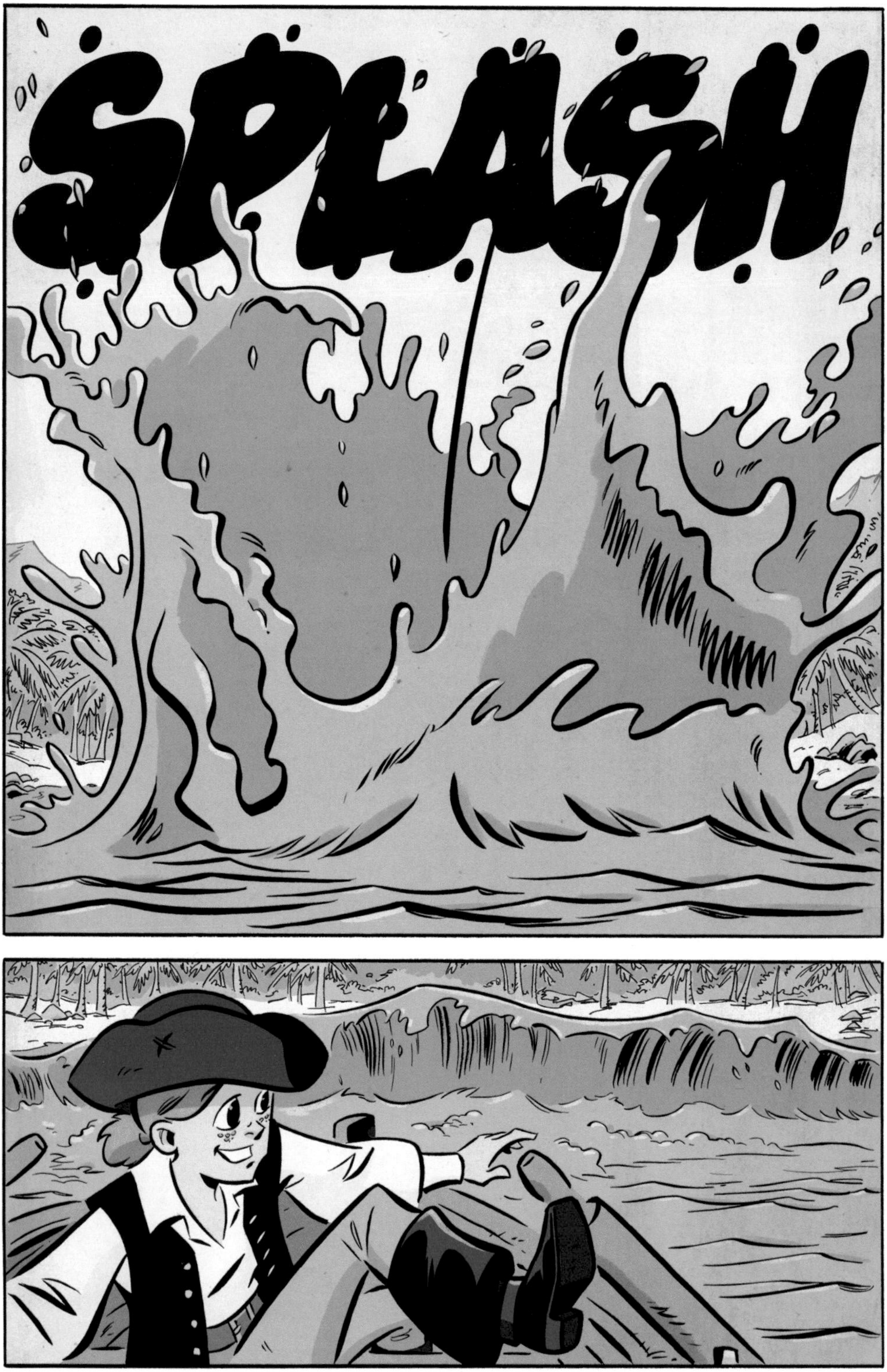
SPLASH

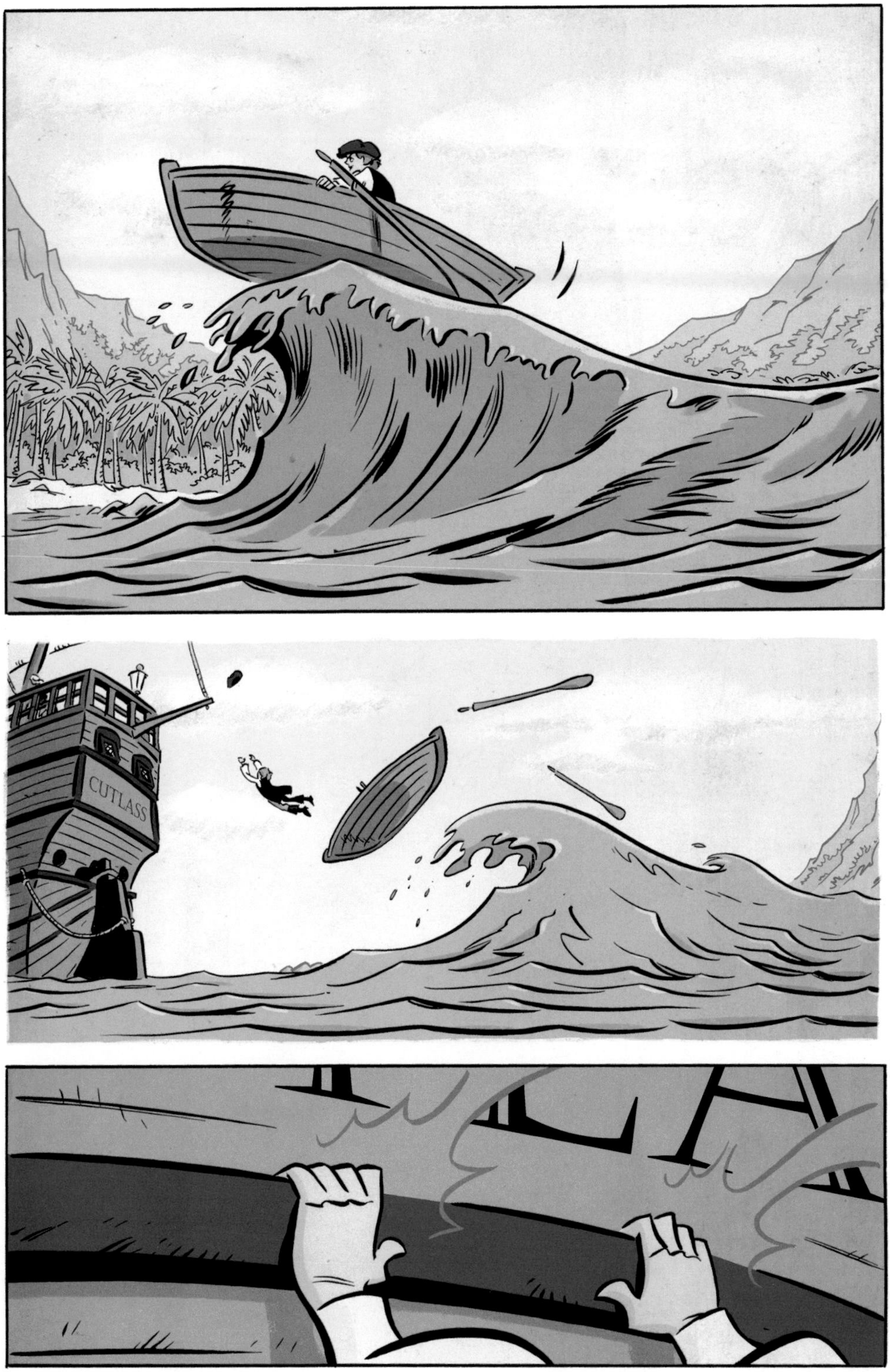
CUTLASS

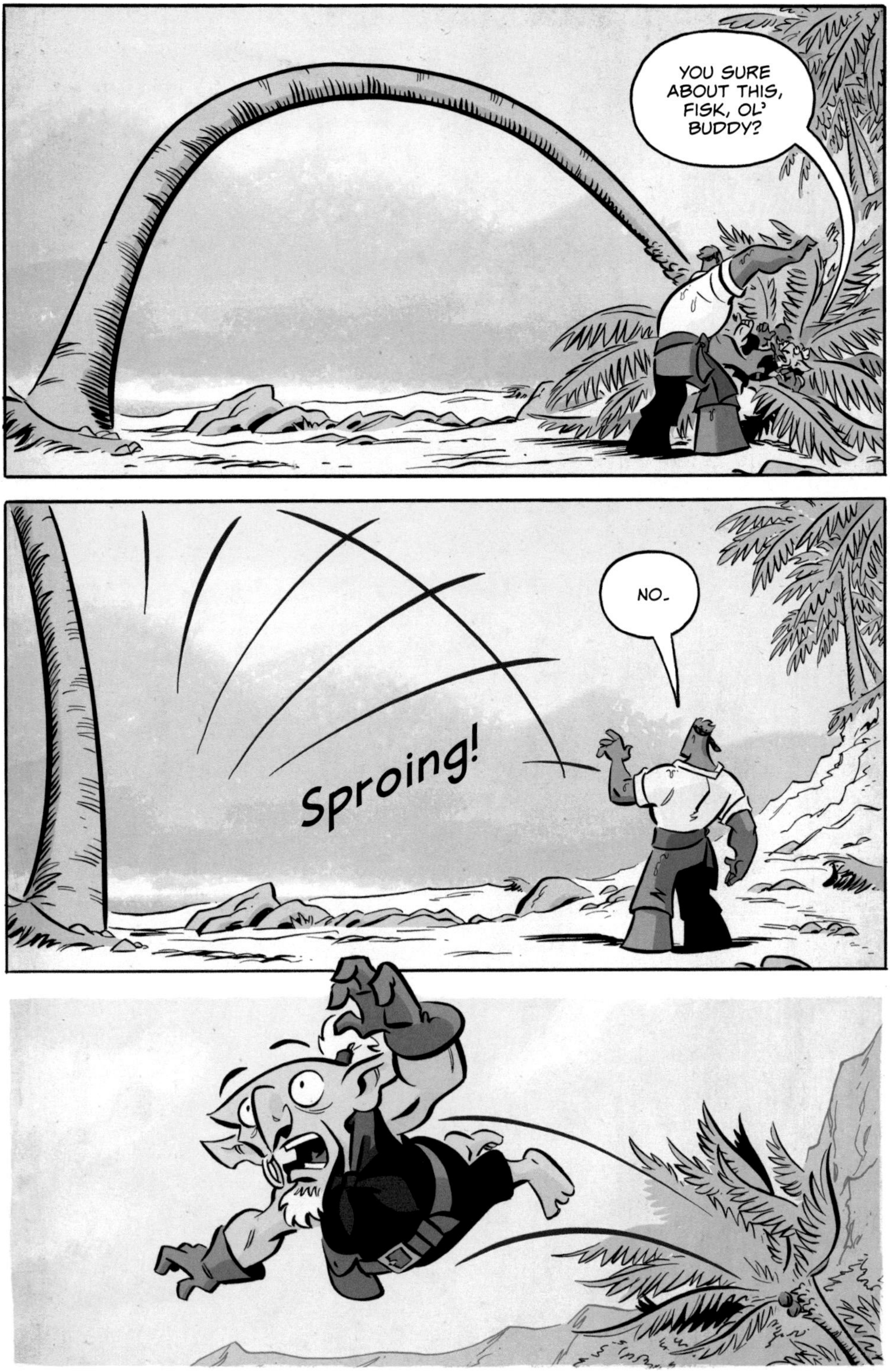
YOU SURE ABOUT THIS, FISK, OL' BUDDY?
NO.
Sproing!

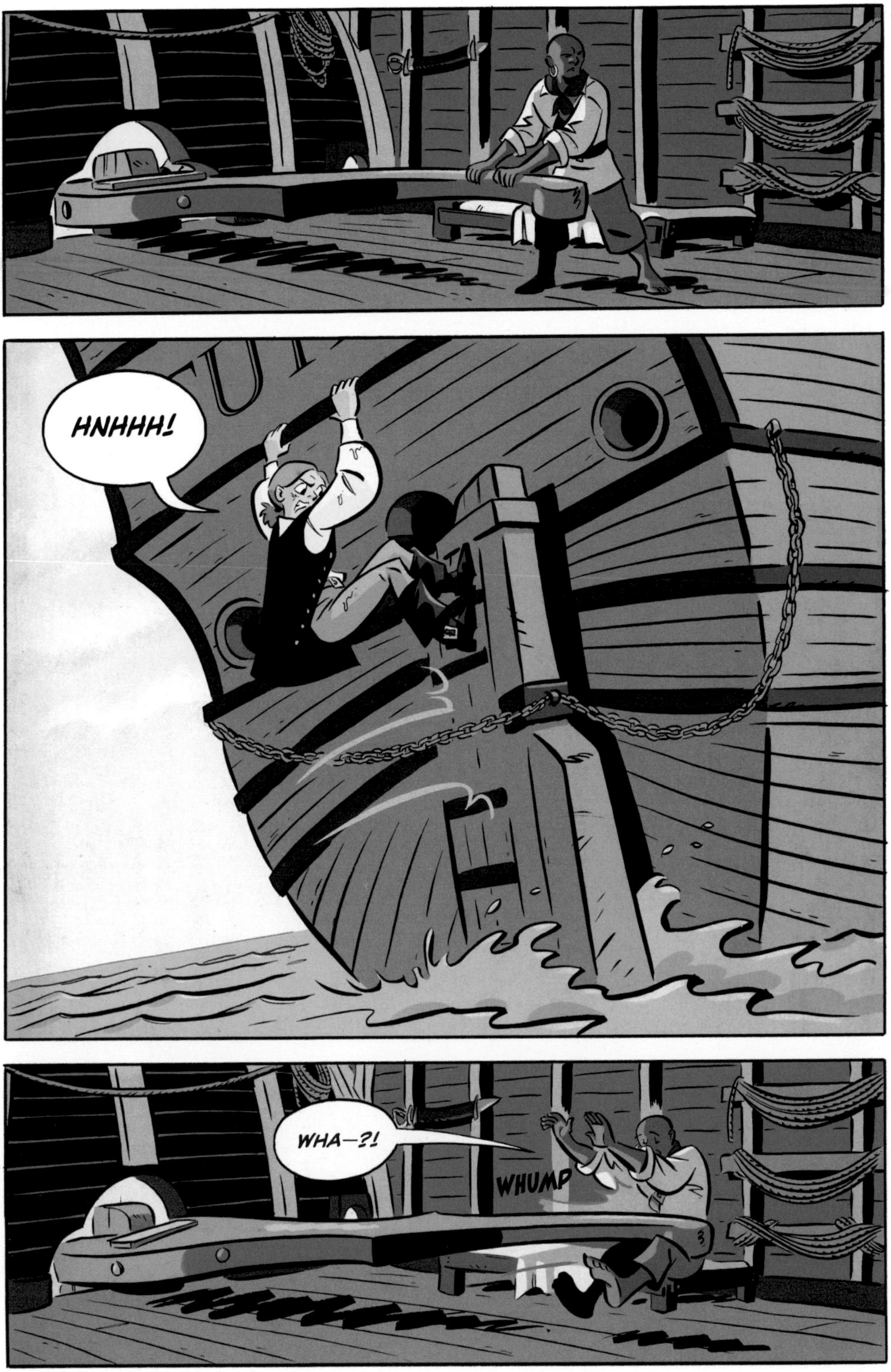
HNHHH!
WHA—?!
WHUMP

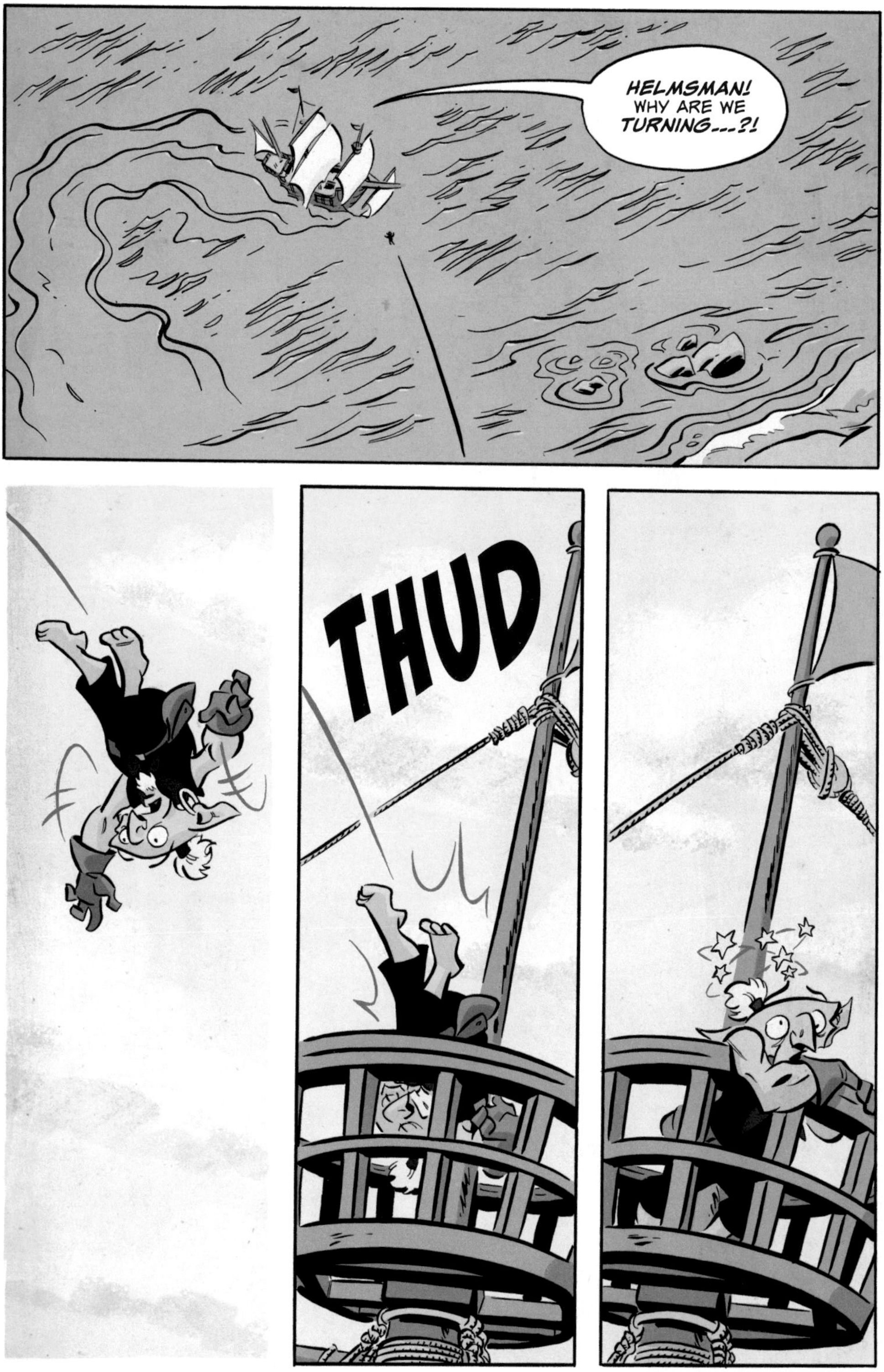
HELMSMAN! WHY ARE WE TURNING---?!
THUD

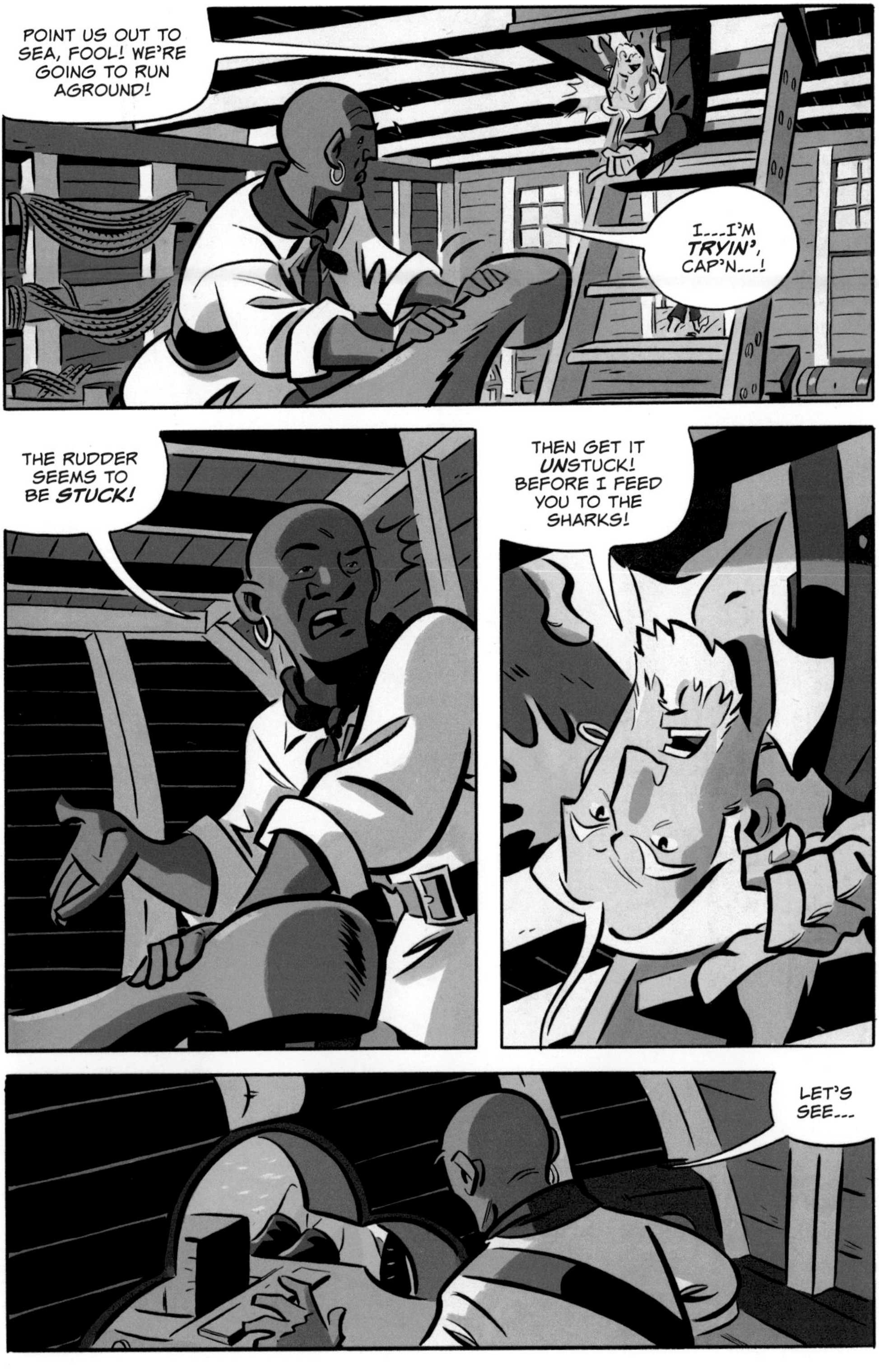
POINT US OUT TO SEA, FOOL! WE'RE GOING TO RUN AGROUND!
I---I'M TRYIN', CAP'N---!
THE RUDDER SEEMS TO BE STUCK!
THEN GET IT UNSTUCK! BEFORE I FEED YOU TO THE SHARKS!
LET'S SEE---

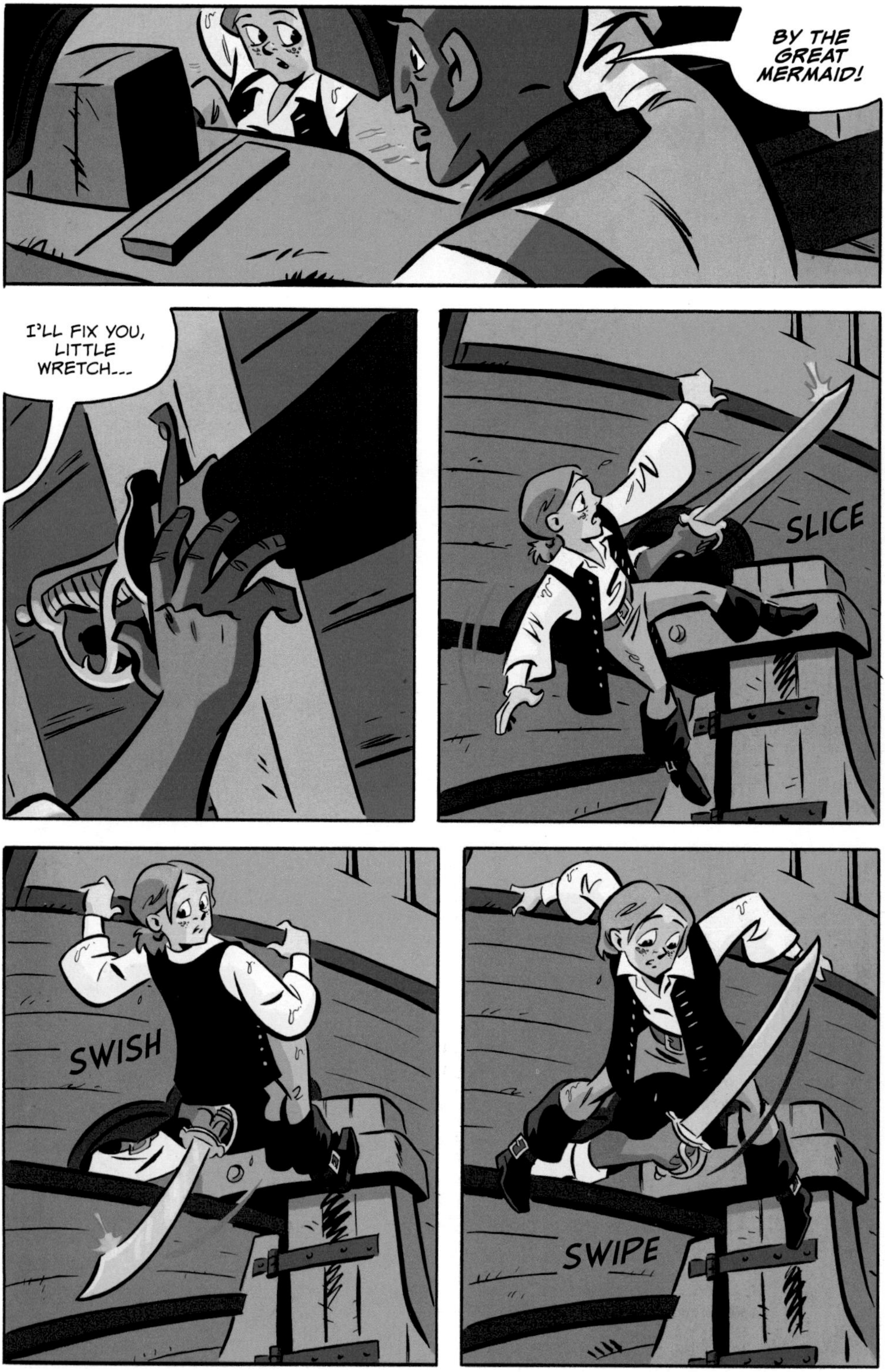
BY THE GREAT MERMAID!
I'LL FIX YOU, LITTLE WRETCH...
SLICE
SWISH
SWIPE

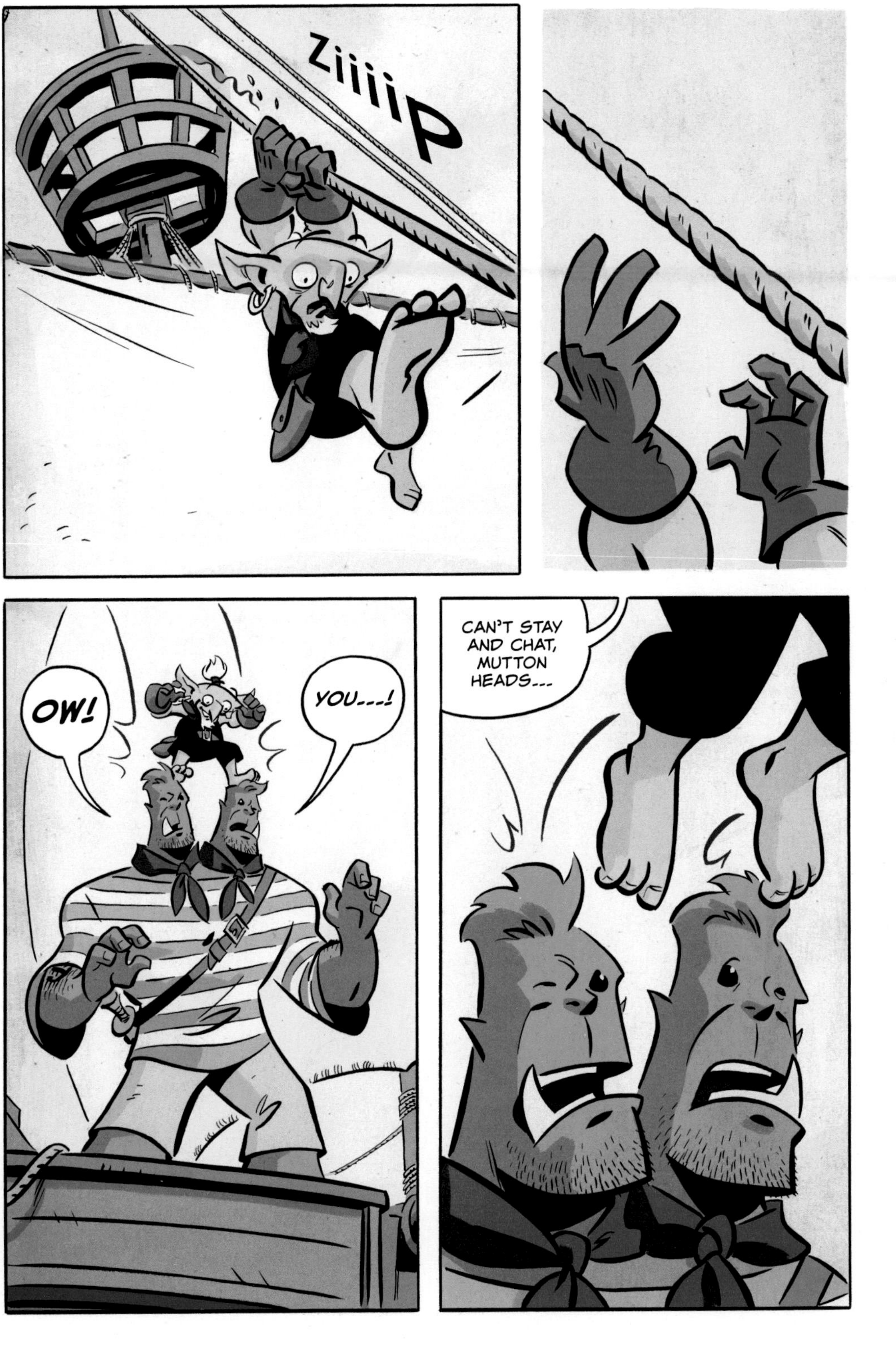
ZiiiiP
OW!
YOU...!
CAN'T STAY AND CHAT, MUTTON HEADS...

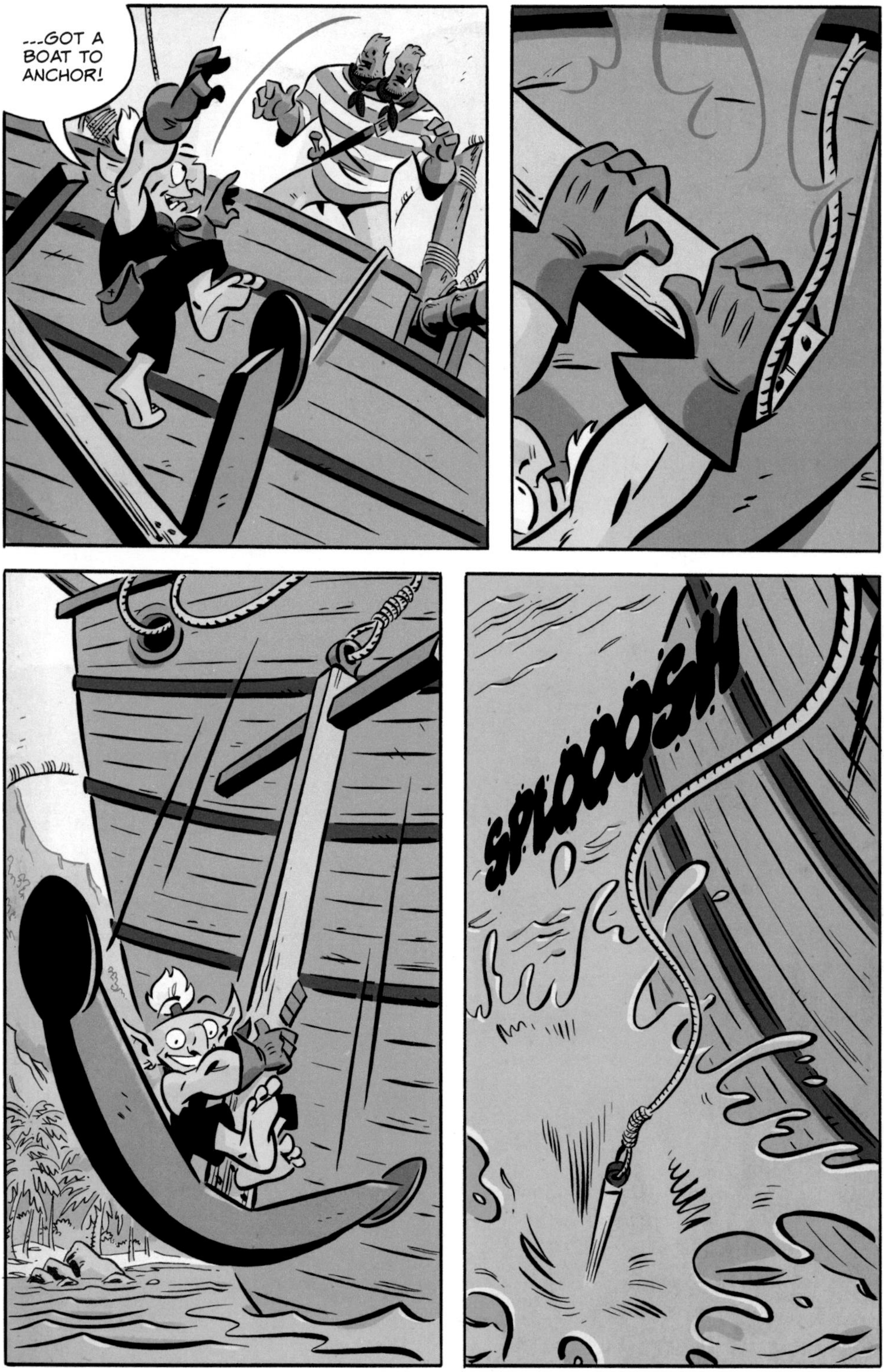
...GOT A BOAT TO ANCHOR!
SPLOOOSH

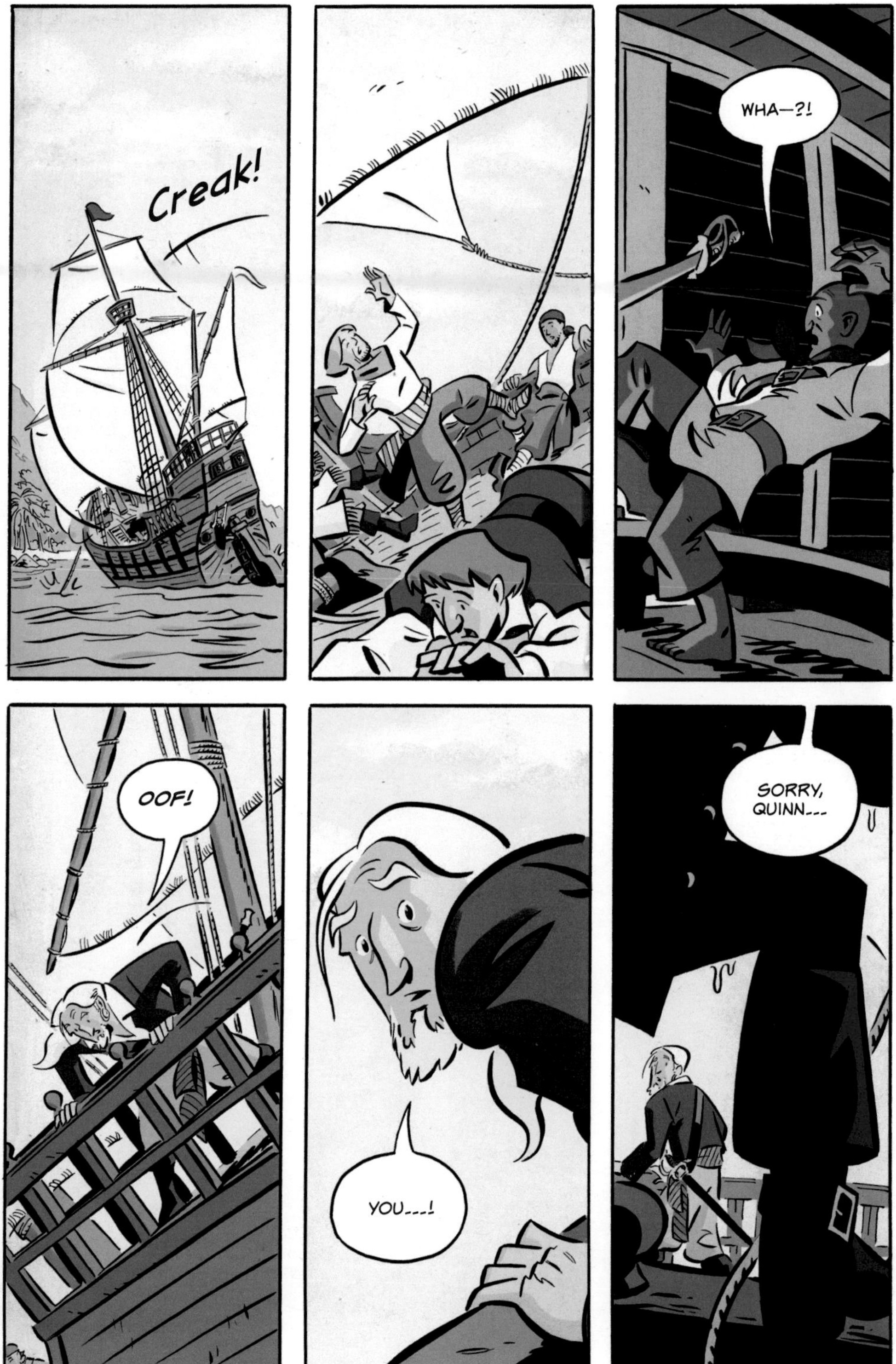
Creak!
WHA—?!
OOF!
YOU...!
SORRY, QUINN...

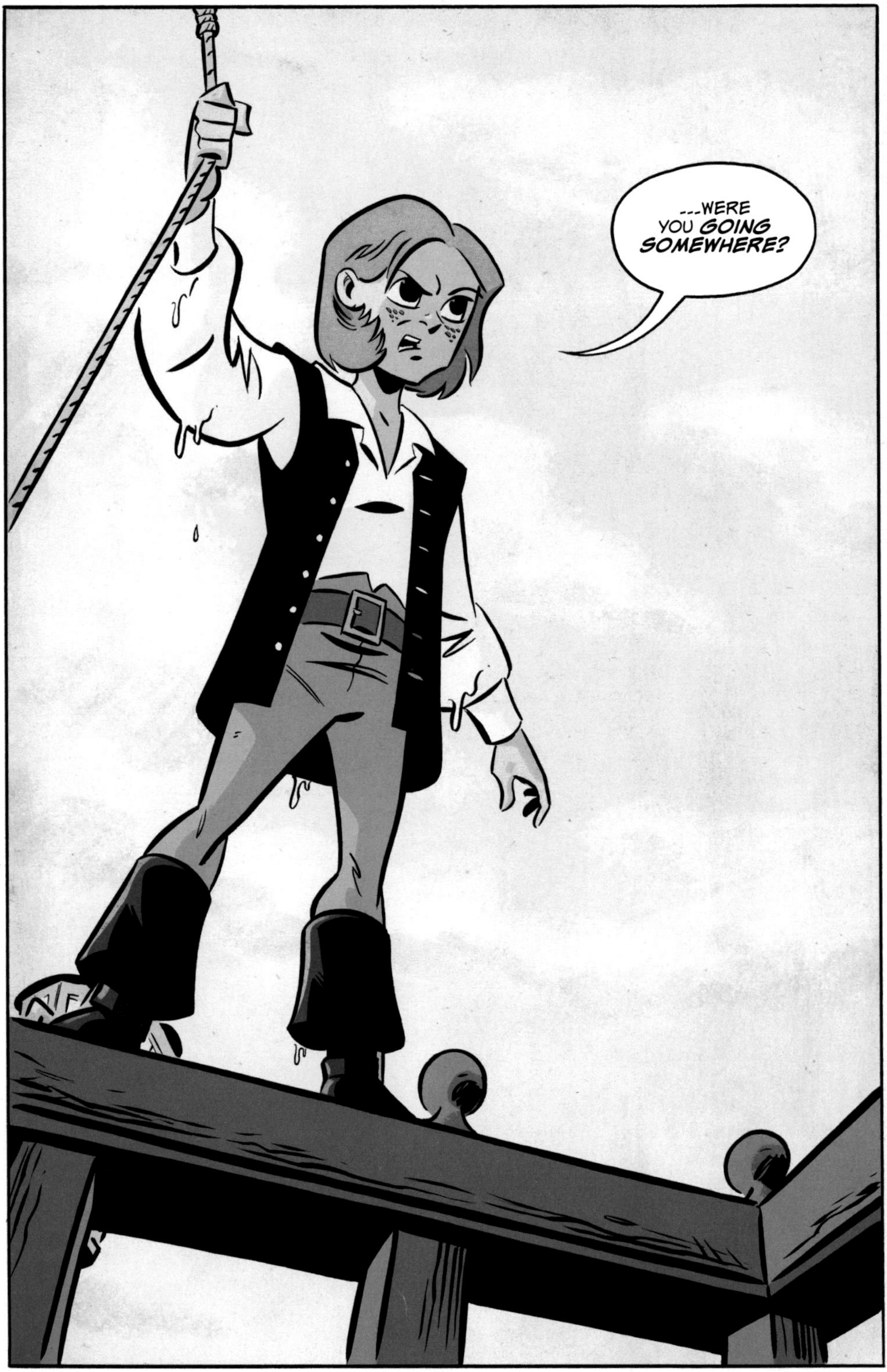
---WERE YOU *GOING* *SOMEWHERE?*

ACT THREE

The King
Who Isn't

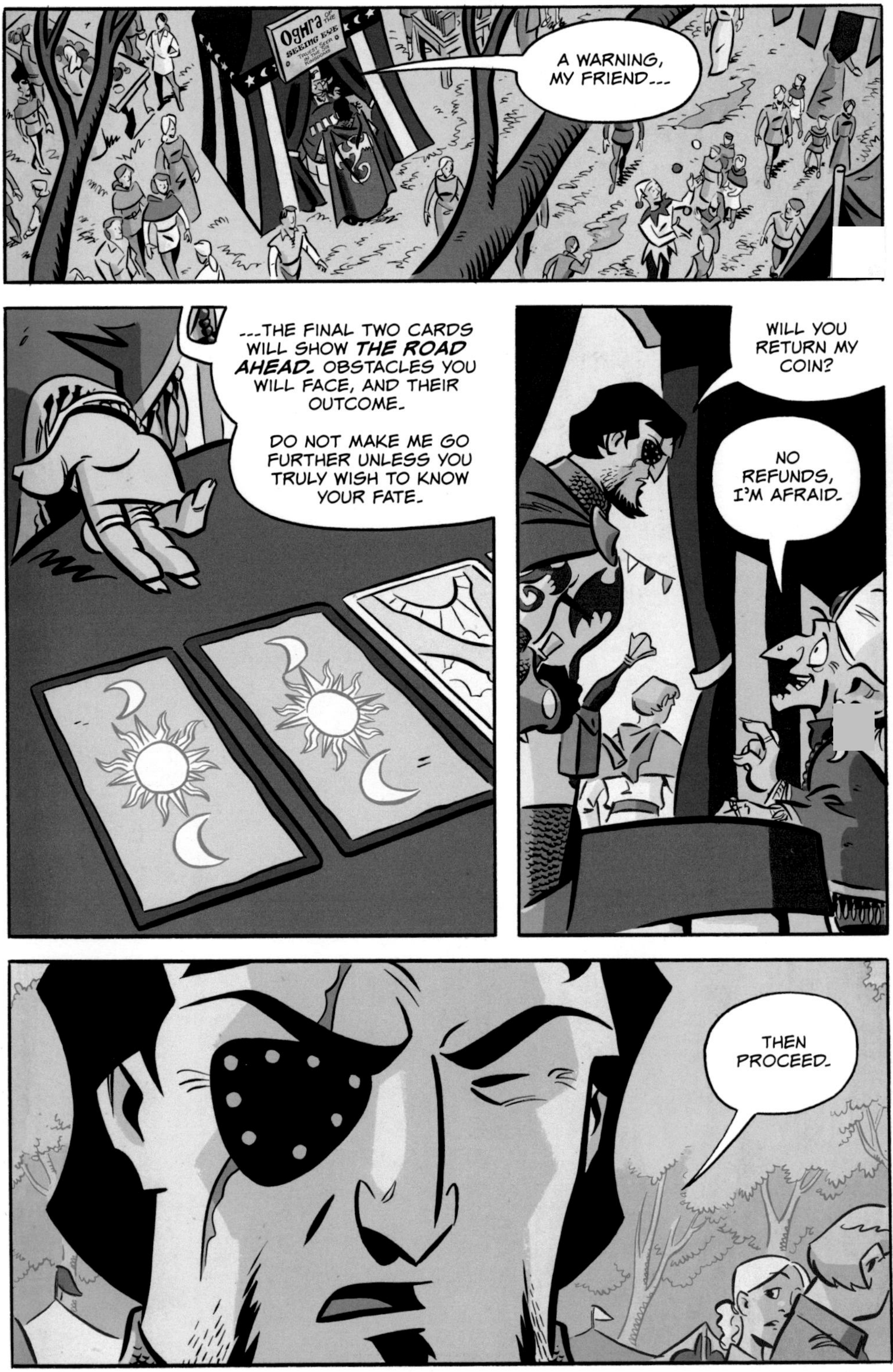
OGHRA OF THE SEEING EYE
A WARNING, MY FRIEND...
...THE FINAL TWO CARDS WILL SHOW ***THE ROAD AHEAD.*** OBSTACLES YOU WILL FACE, AND THEIR OUTCOME.
DO NOT MAKE ME GO FURTHER UNLESS YOU TRULY WISH TO KNOW YOUR FATE.
WILL YOU RETURN MY COIN?
NO REFUNDS, I'M AFRAID.
THEN PROCEED.

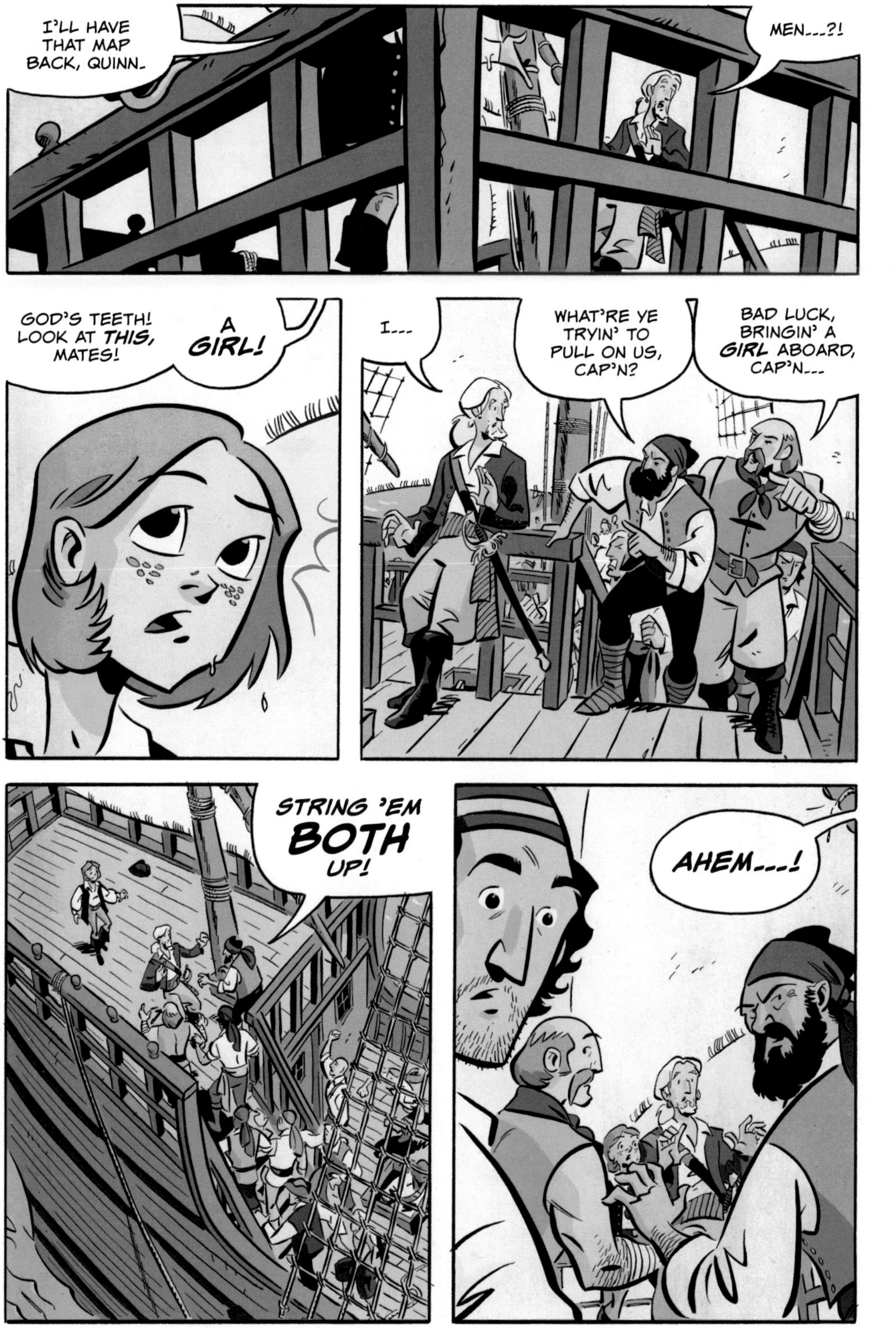
I'LL HAVE THAT MAP BACK, QUINN.
MEN...?!
GOD'S TEETH! LOOK AT *THIS*, MATES!
A *GIRL!*
I...
WHAT'RE YE TRYIN' TO PULL ON US, CAP'N?
BAD LUCK, BRINGIN' A *GIRL* ABOARD, CAP'N...
STRING 'EM *BOTH* UP!
AHEM...!

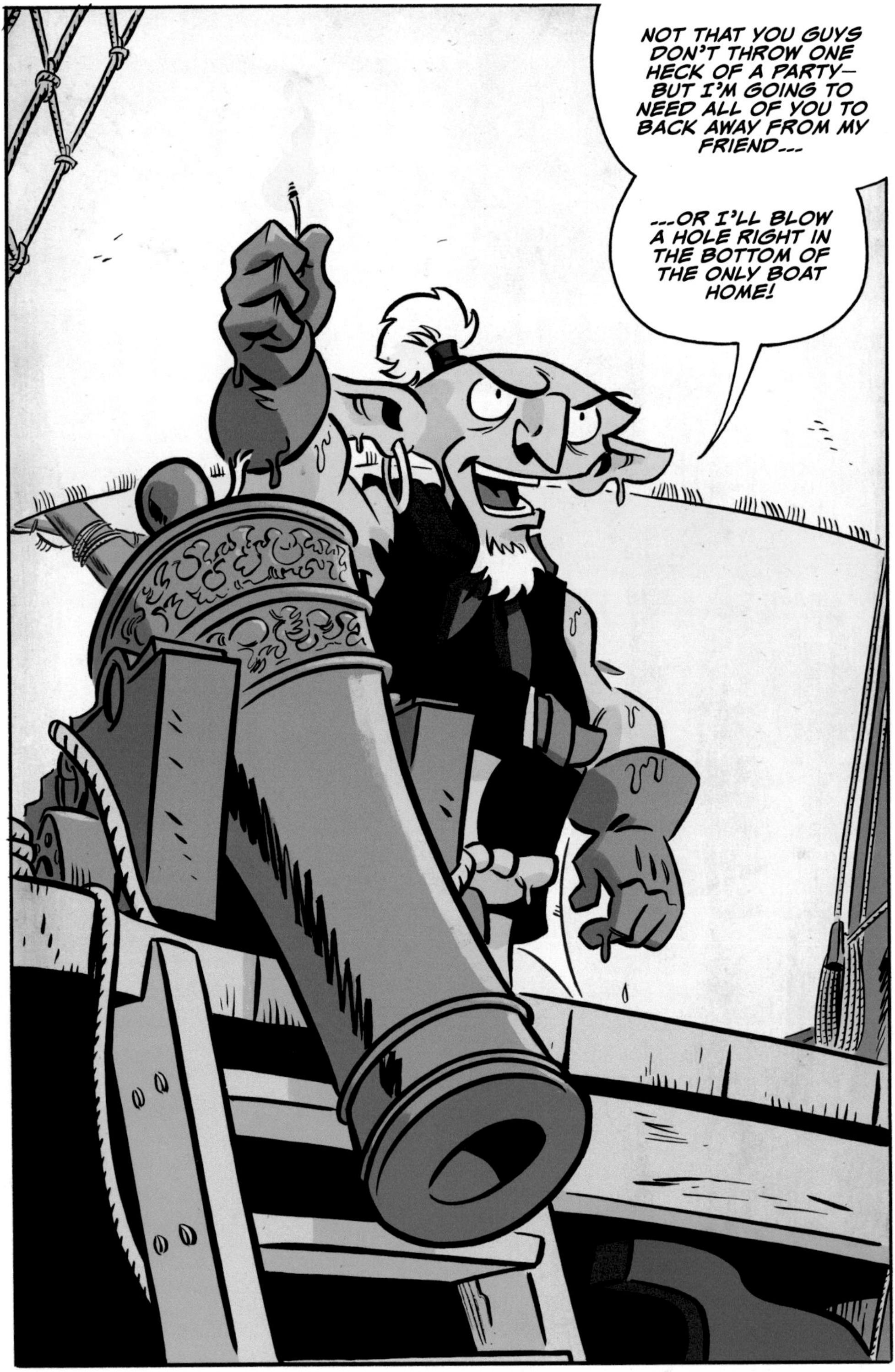
NOT THAT YOU GUYS DON'T THROW ONE HECK OF A PARTY— BUT I'M GOING TO NEED ALL OF YOU TO BACK AWAY FROM MY FRIEND---
---OR I'LL BLOW A HOLE RIGHT IN THE BOTTOM OF THE ONLY BOAT HOME!

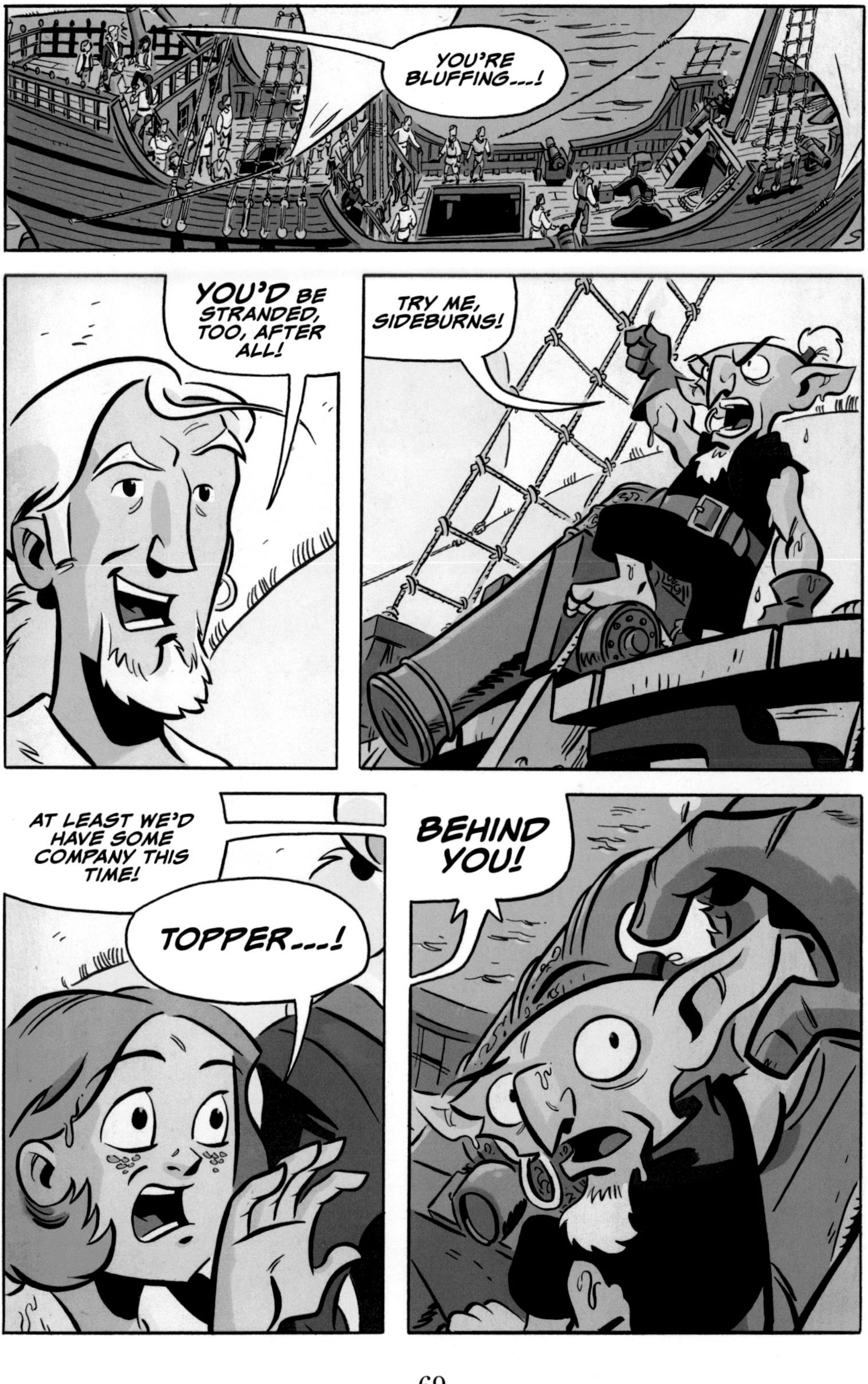
YOU'RE BLUFFING...!
YOU'D BE STRANDED, TOO, AFTER ALL!
TRY ME, SIDEBURNS!
AT LEAST WE'D HAVE SOME COMPANY THIS TIME!
TOPPER...!
BEHIND YOU!

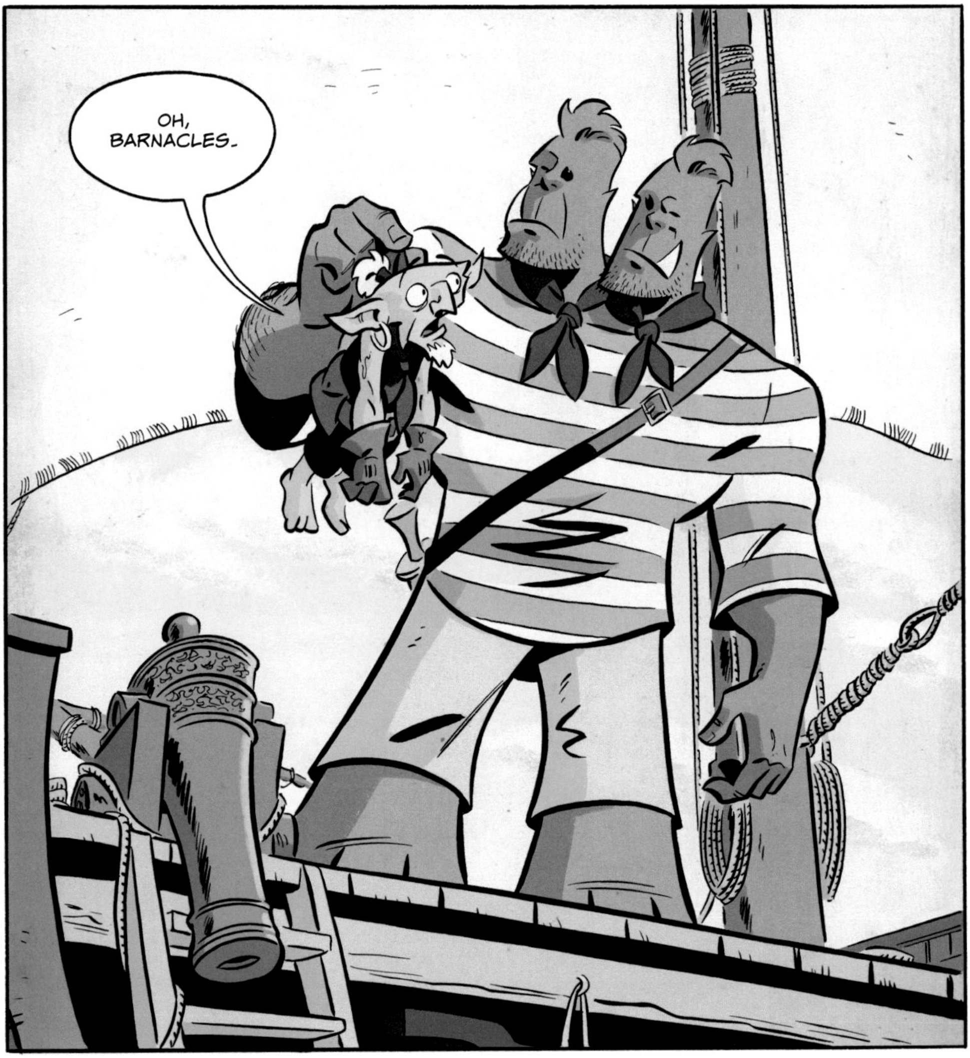
OH, BARNACLES.

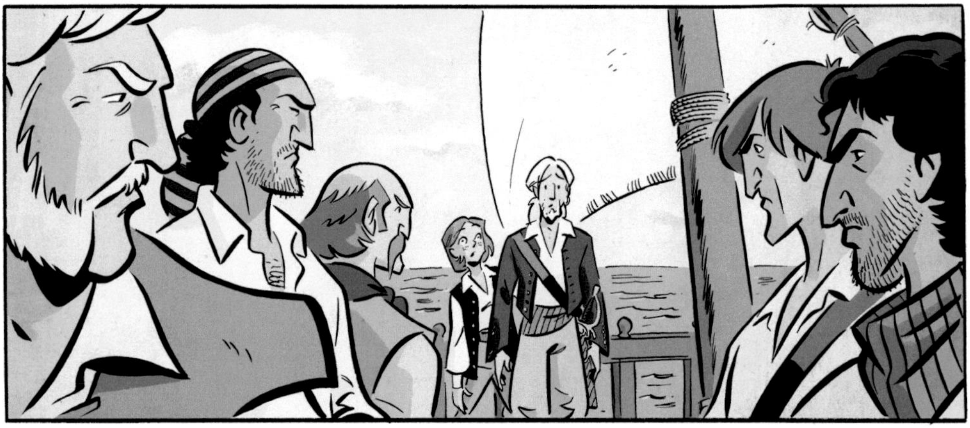

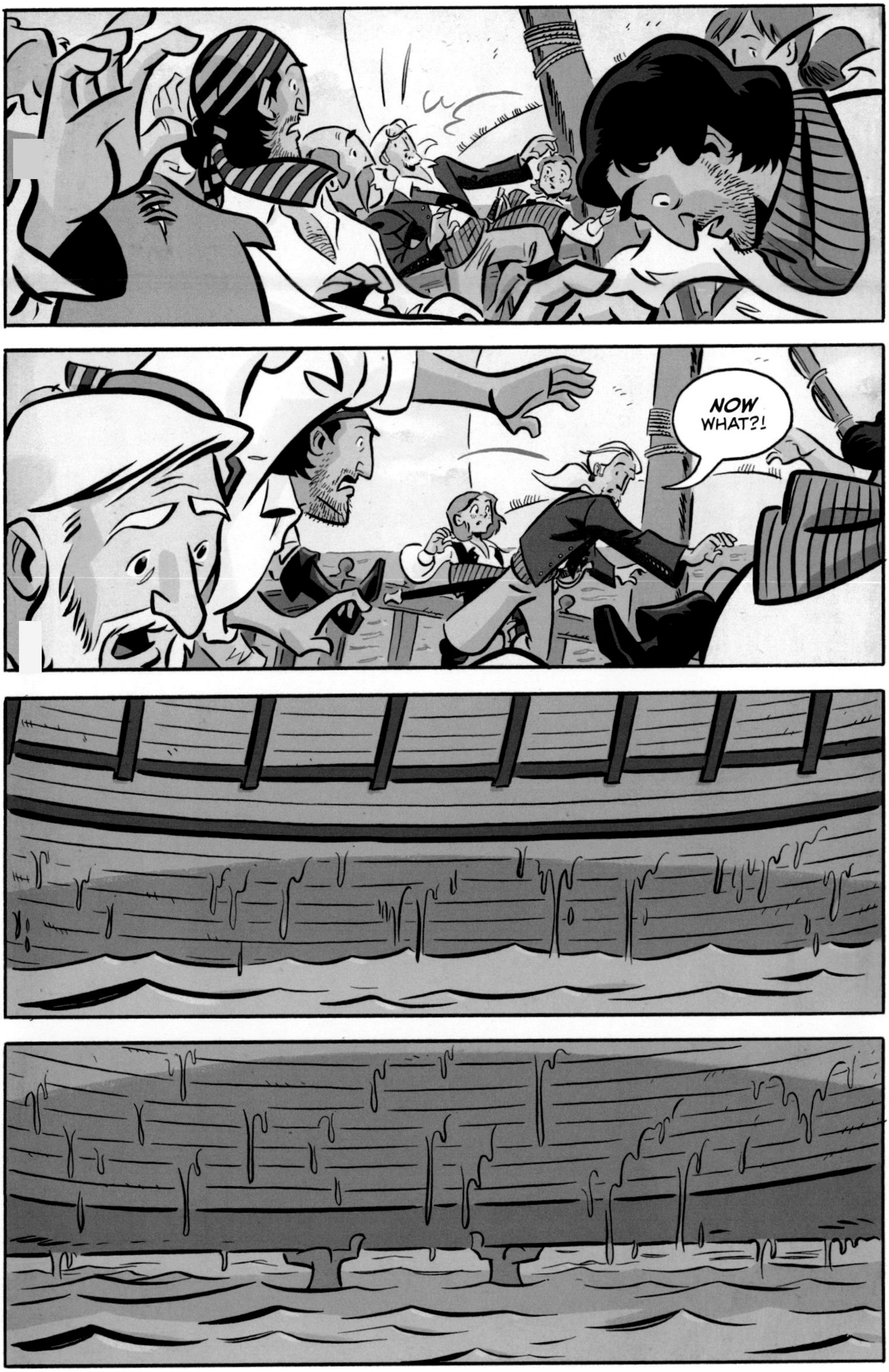
NOW WHAT?!

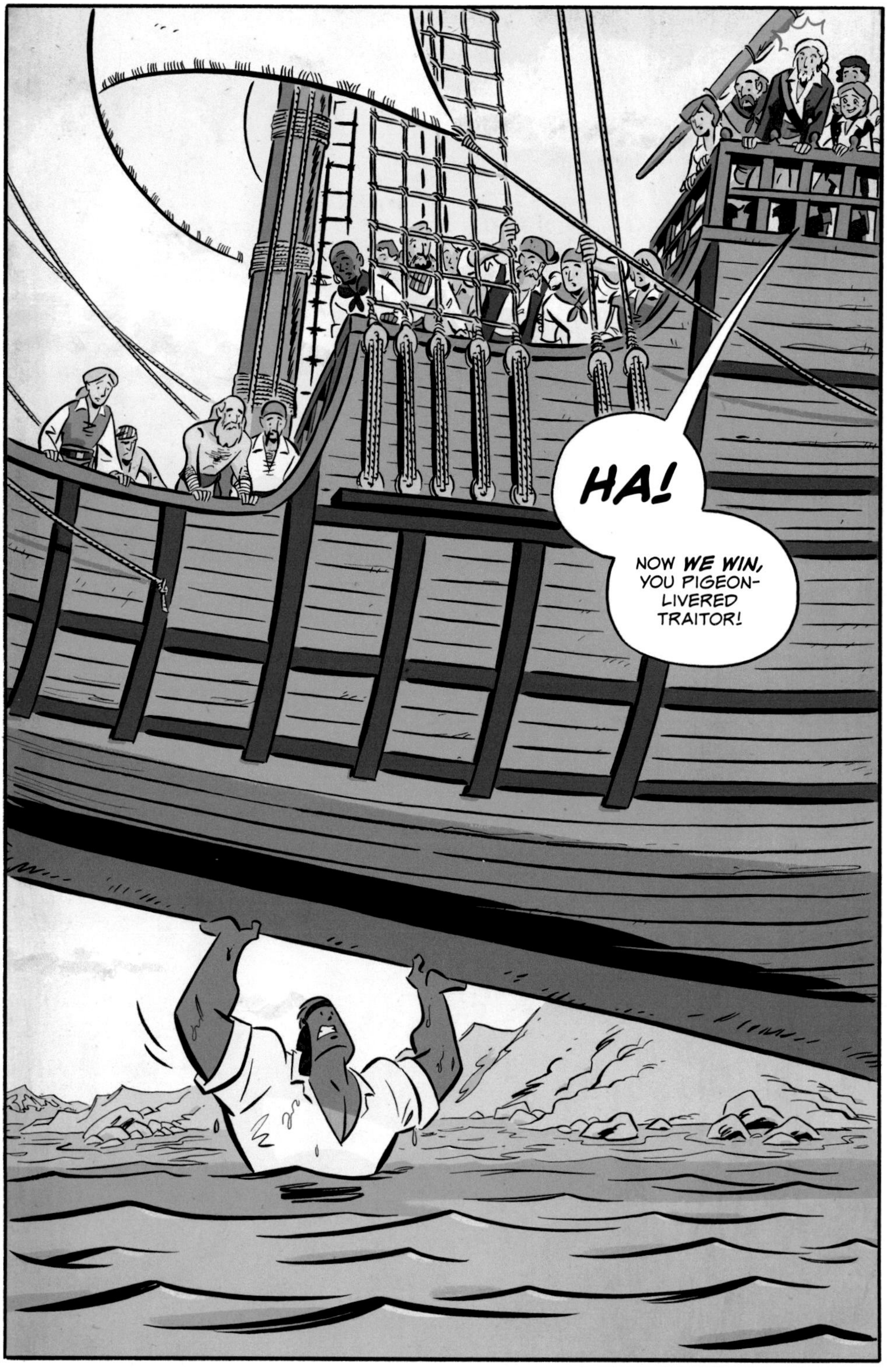
HA!
NOW WE WIN, YOU PIGEON-LIVERED TRAITOR!

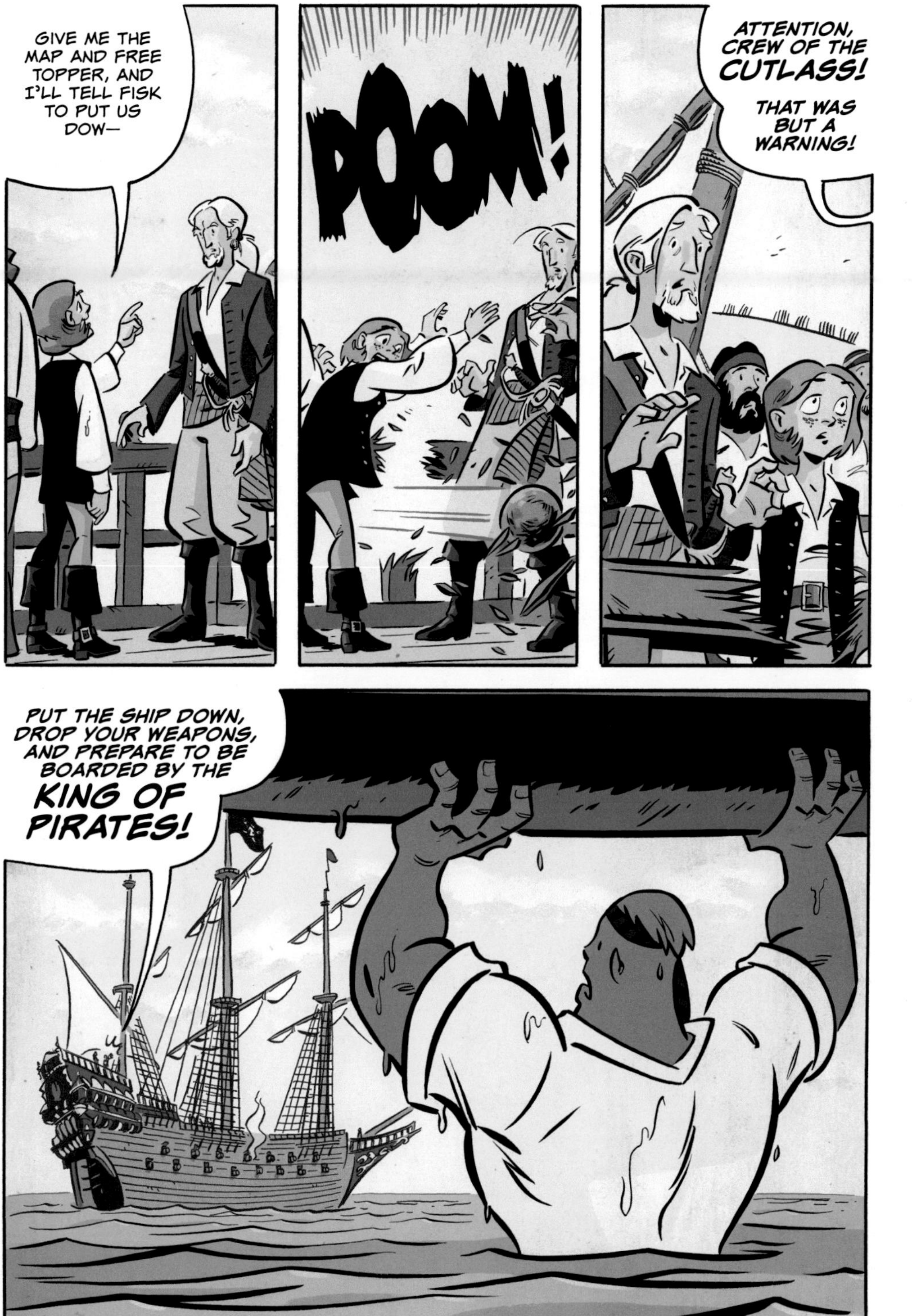
GIVE ME THE MAP AND FREE TOPPER, AND I'LL TELL FISK TO PUT US DOW—
POOM!
ATTENTION, CREW OF THE CUTLASS!
THAT WAS BUT A WARNING!
PUT THE SHIP DOWN, DROP YOUR WEAPONS, AND PREPARE TO BE BOARDED BY THE KING OF PIRATES!

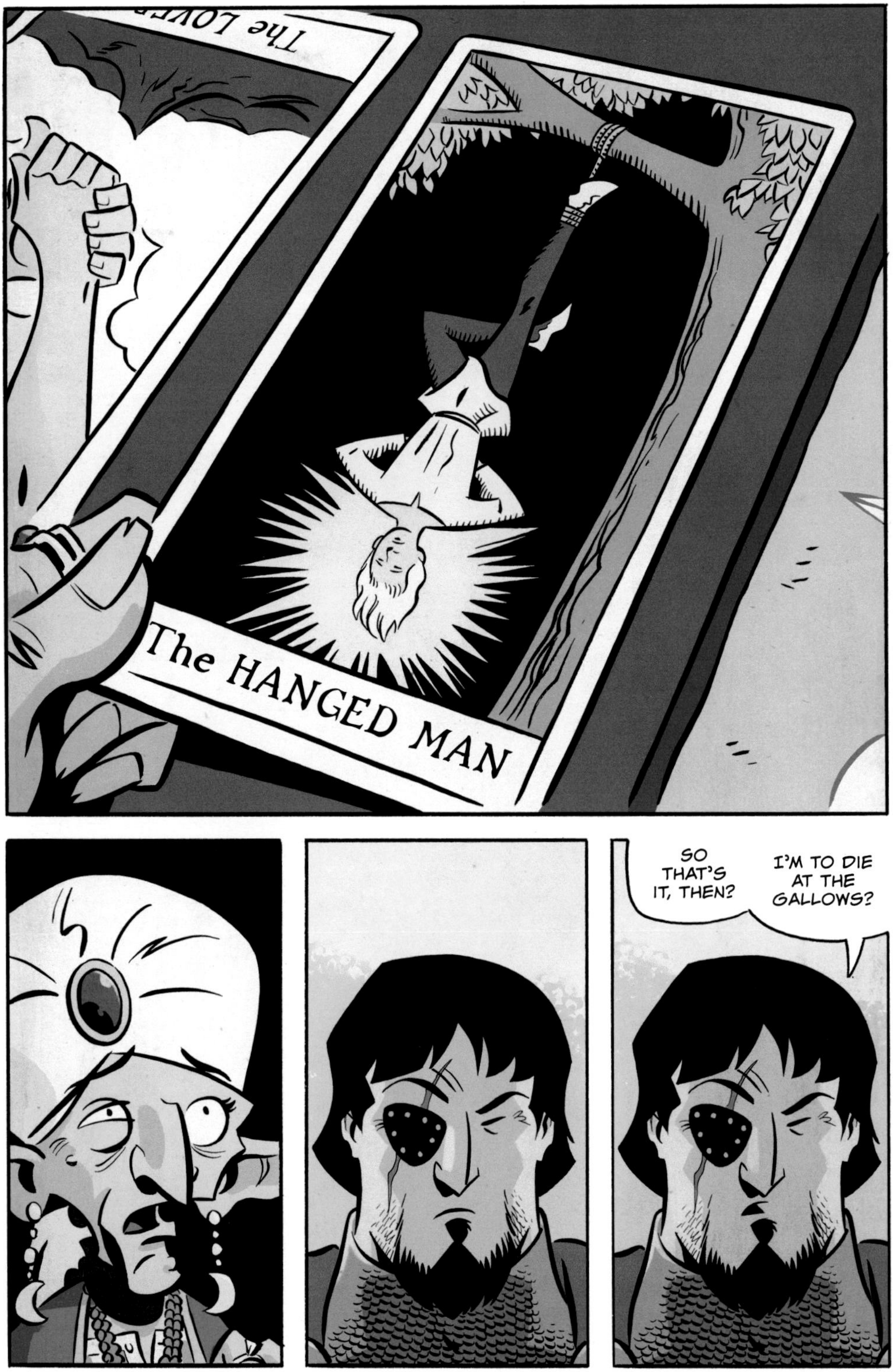
The LOVER
The HANGED MAN
SO THAT'S IT, THEN?
I'M TO DIE AT THE GALLOWS?

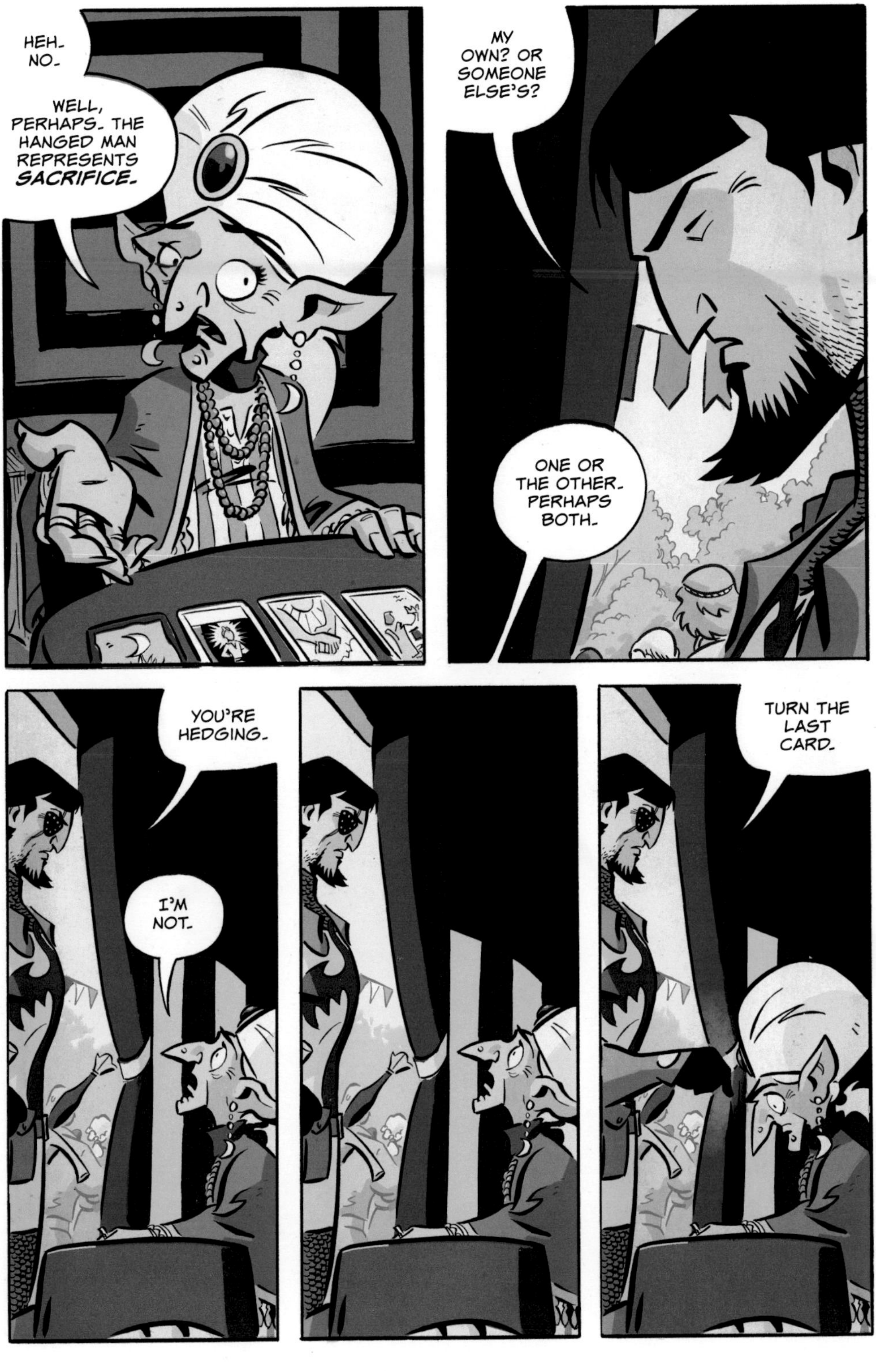
HEH. NO.
WELL, PERHAPS. THE HANGED MAN REPRESENTS *SACRIFICE.*
MY OWN? OR SOMEONE ELSE'S?
ONE OR THE OTHER. PERHAPS BOTH.
YOU'RE HEDGING.
I'M NOT.
TURN THE LAST CARD.

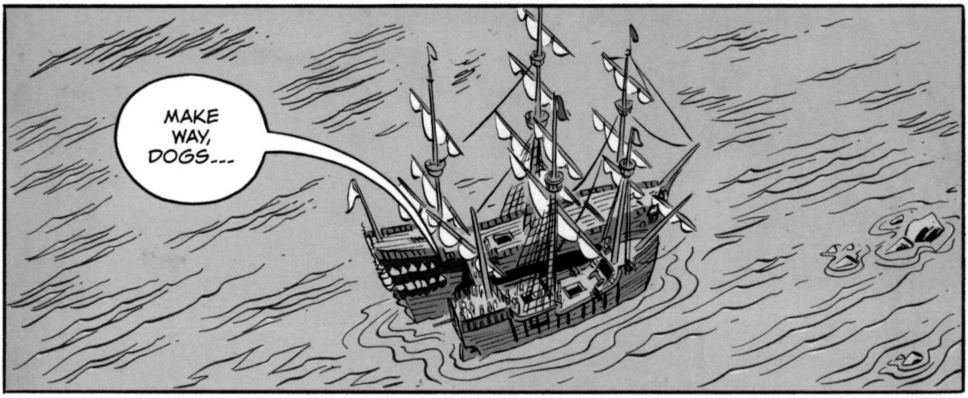
MAKE WAY, DOGS---

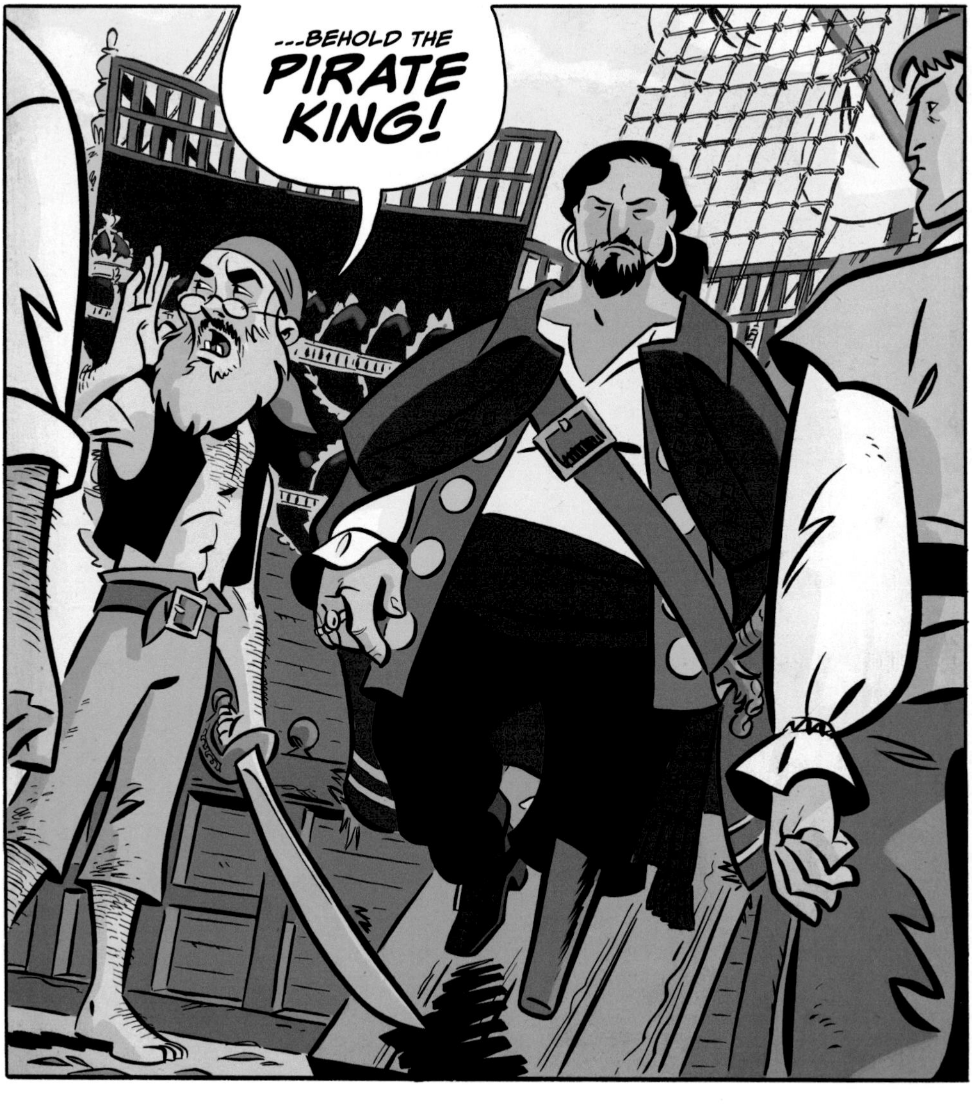
---BEHOLD THE PIRATE KING!

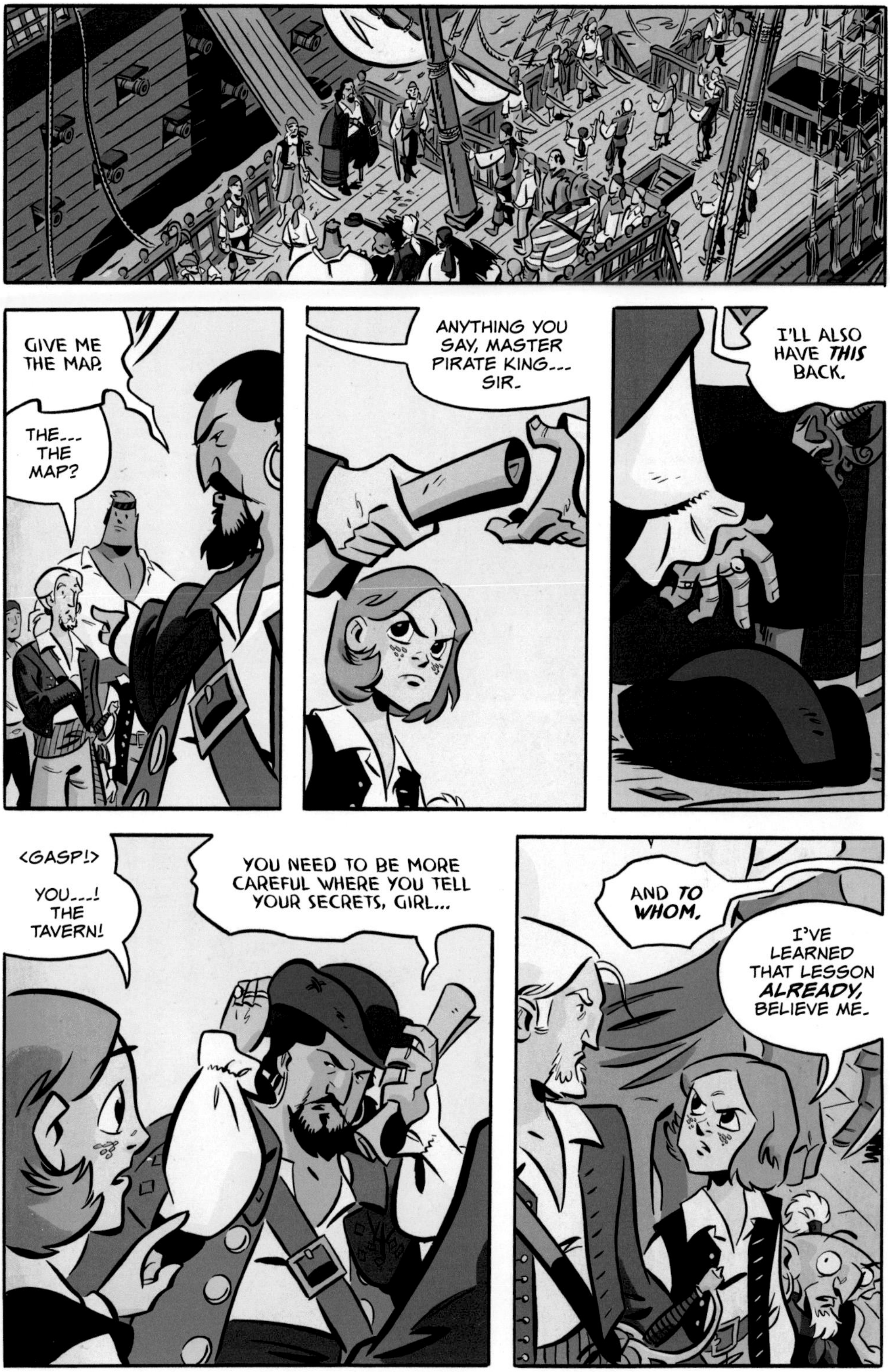
GIVE ME THE MAP.
THE... THE MAP?
ANYTHING YOU SAY, MASTER PIRATE KING... SIR.
I'LL ALSO HAVE THIS BACK.
<GASP!> YOU...! THE TAVERN!
YOU NEED TO BE MORE CAREFUL WHERE YOU TELL YOUR SECRETS, GIRL...
AND TO WHOM.
I'VE LEARNED THAT LESSON ALREADY, BELIEVE ME.

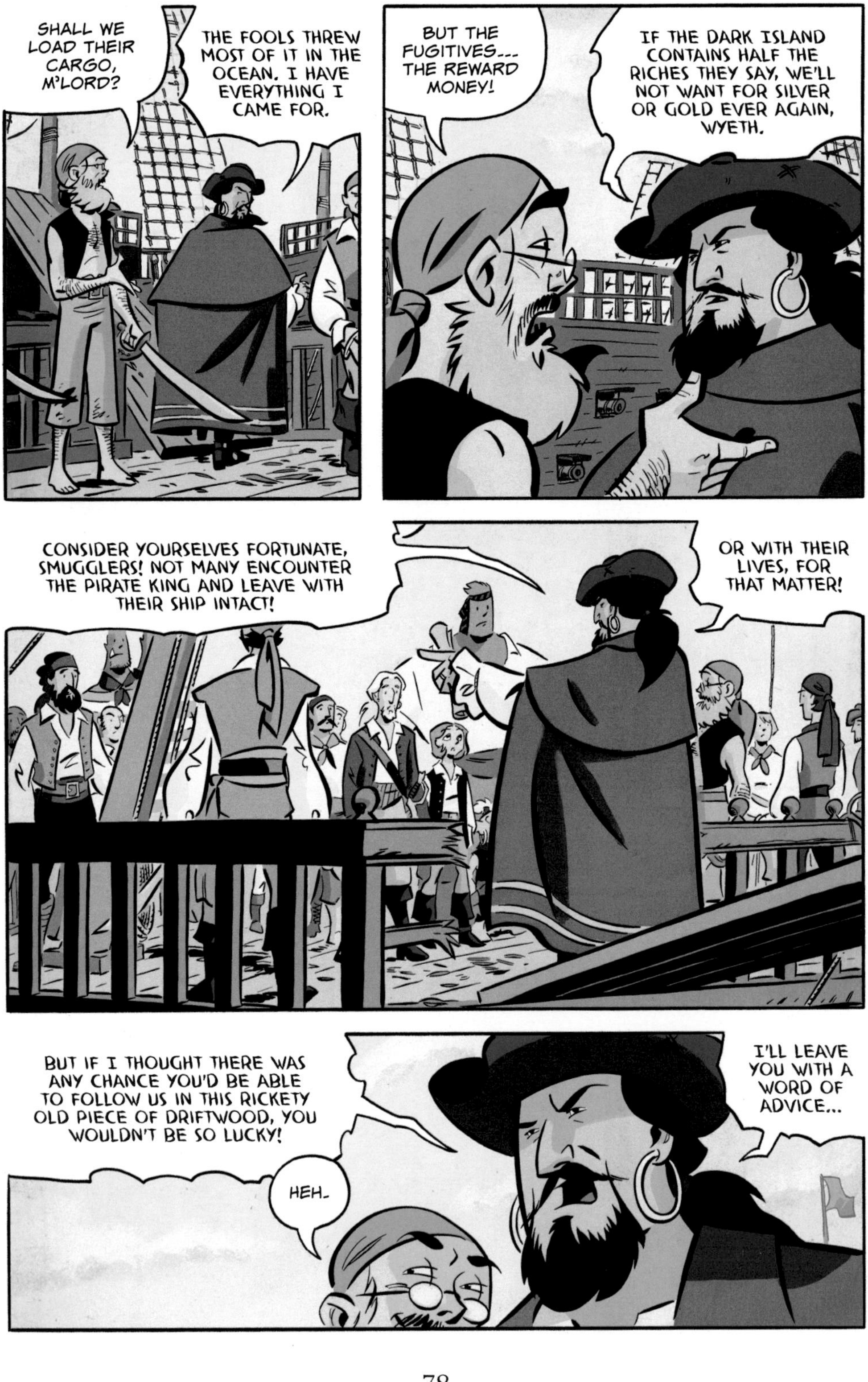
SHALL WE LOAD THEIR CARGO, M'LORD?
THE FOOLS THREW MOST OF IT IN THE OCEAN. I HAVE EVERYTHING I CAME FOR.
BUT THE FUGITIVES... THE REWARD MONEY!
IF THE DARK ISLAND CONTAINS HALF THE RICHES THEY SAY, WE'LL NOT WANT FOR SILVER OR GOLD EVER AGAIN, WYETH.
CONSIDER YOURSELVES FORTUNATE, SMUGGLERS! NOT MANY ENCOUNTER THE PIRATE KING AND LEAVE WITH THEIR SHIP INTACT!
OR WITH THEIR LIVES, FOR THAT MATTER!
BUT IF I THOUGHT THERE WAS ANY CHANCE YOU'D BE ABLE TO FOLLOW US IN THIS RICKETY OLD PIECE OF DRIFTWOOD, YOU WOULDN'T BE SO LUCKY!
HEH.
I'LL LEAVE YOU WITH A WORD OF ADVICE...

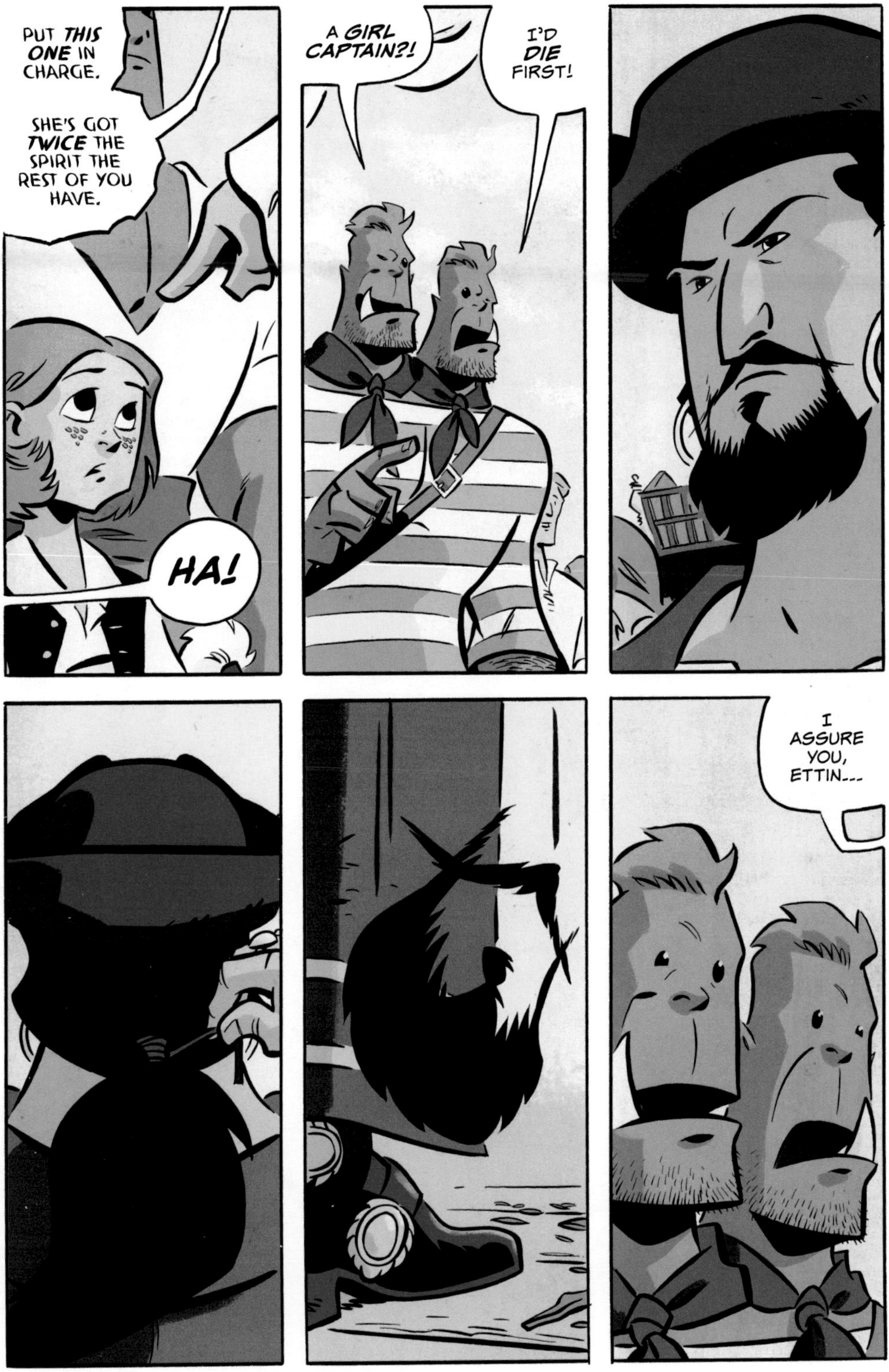
PUT THIS ONE IN CHARGE.
SHE'S GOT TWICE THE SPIRIT THE REST OF YOU HAVE.
HA!
A GIRL CAPTAIN?!
I'D DIE FIRST!
I ASSURE YOU, ETTIN...

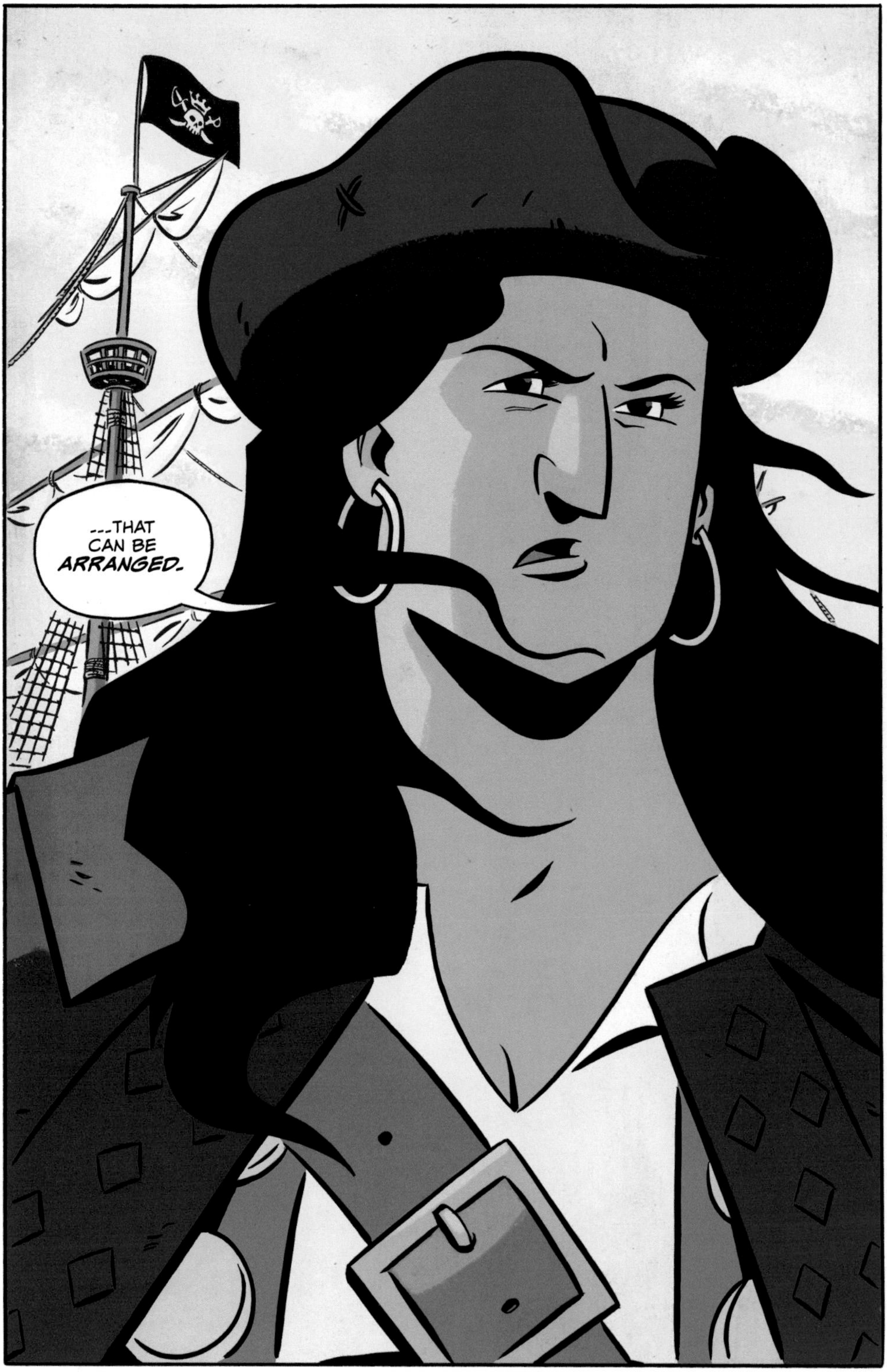
---THAT CAN BE ARRANGED.

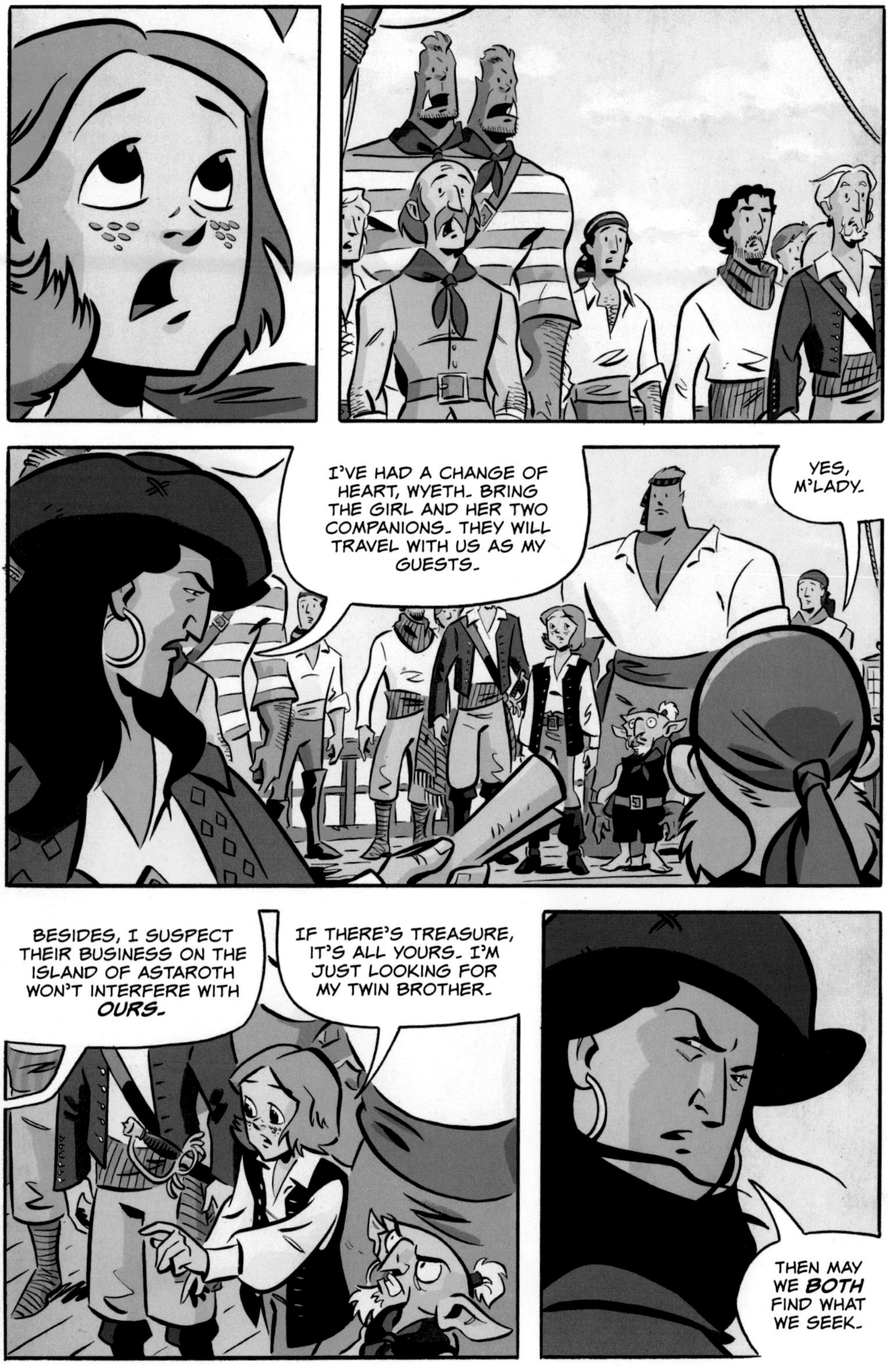
I'VE HAD A CHANGE OF HEART, WYETH. BRING THE GIRL AND HER TWO COMPANIONS. THEY WILL TRAVEL WITH US AS MY GUESTS.
YES, M'LADY.
BESIDES, I SUSPECT THEIR BUSINESS ON THE ISLAND OF ASTAROTH WON'T INTERFERE WITH OURS.
IF THERE'S TREASURE, IT'S ALL YOURS. I'M JUST LOOKING FOR MY TWIN BROTHER.
THEN MAY WE BOTH FIND WHAT WE SEEK.

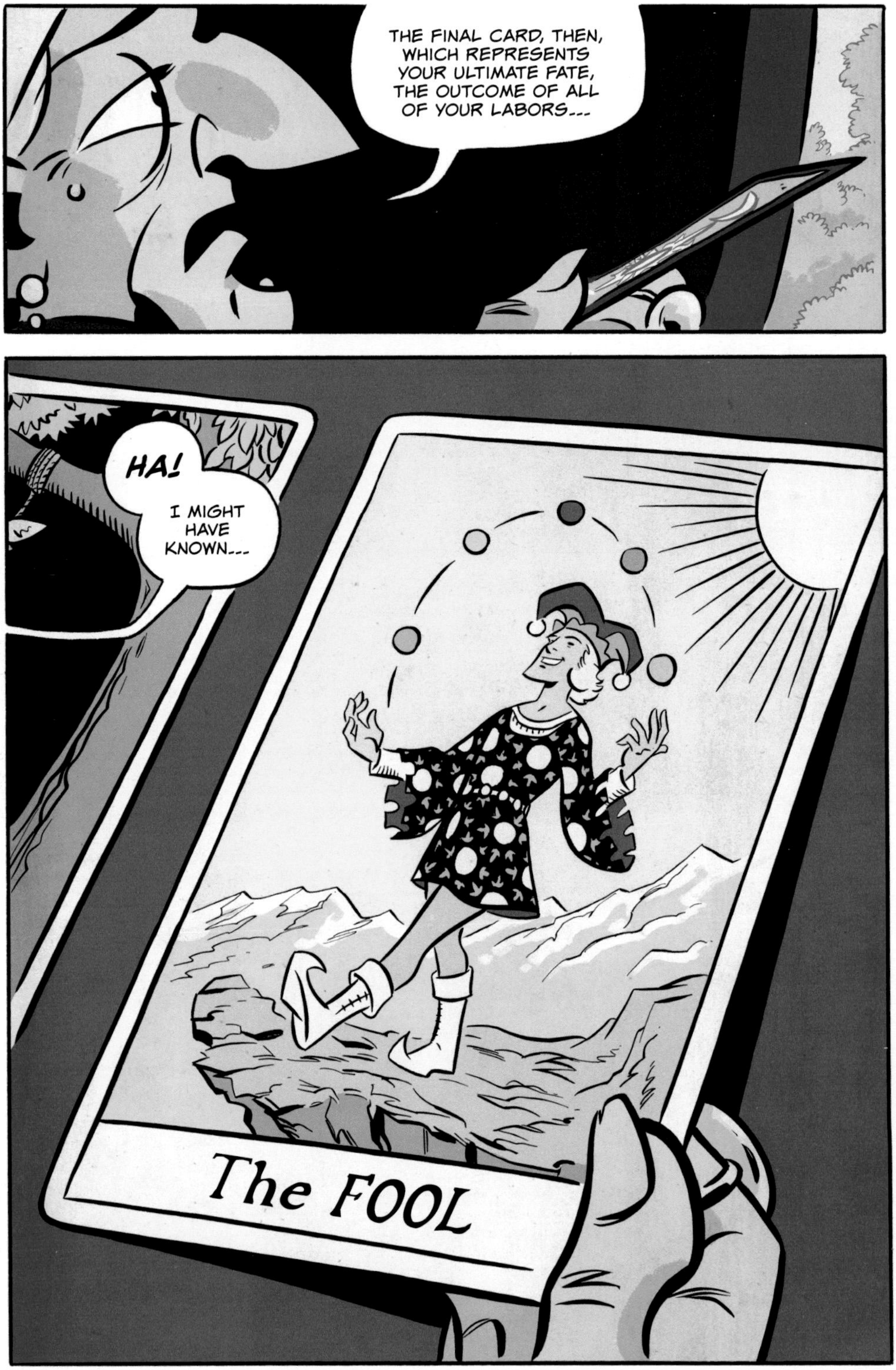
THE FINAL CARD, THEN, WHICH REPRESENTS YOUR ULTIMATE FATE, THE OUTCOME OF ALL OF YOUR LABORS...
HA!
I MIGHT HAVE KNOWN...
The FOOL

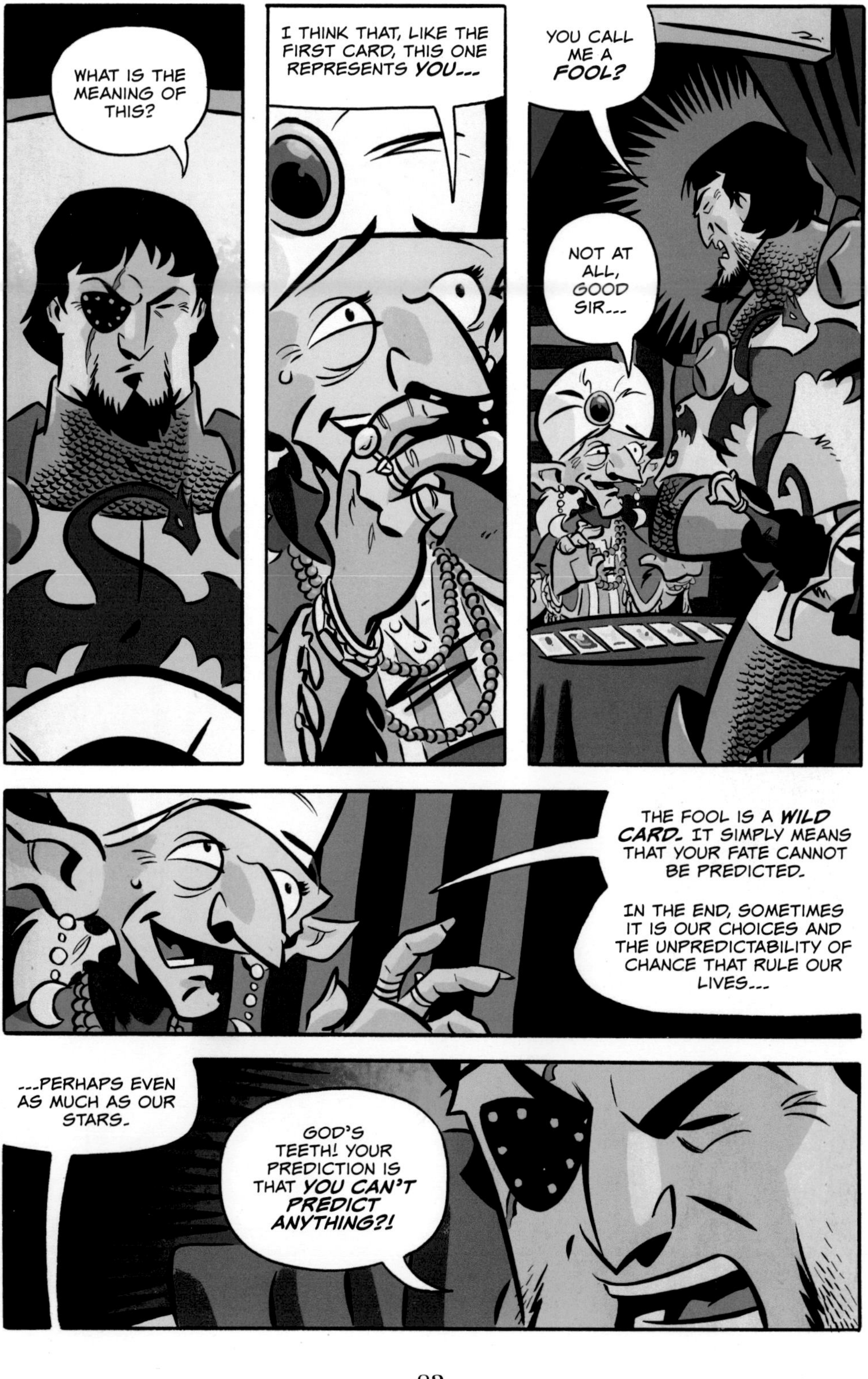
WHAT IS THE MEANING OF THIS?
I THINK THAT, LIKE THE FIRST CARD, THIS ONE REPRESENTS *YOU*...
YOU CALL ME A *FOOL?*
NOT AT ALL, GOOD SIR...
THE FOOL IS A *WILD CARD*. IT SIMPLY MEANS THAT YOUR FATE CANNOT BE PREDICTED.
IN THE END, SOMETIMES IT IS OUR CHOICES AND THE UNPREDICTABILITY OF CHANCE THAT RULE OUR LIVES...
...PERHAPS EVEN AS MUCH AS OUR STARS.
GOD'S TEETH! YOUR PREDICTION IS THAT *YOU CAN'T PREDICT ANYTHING?!*

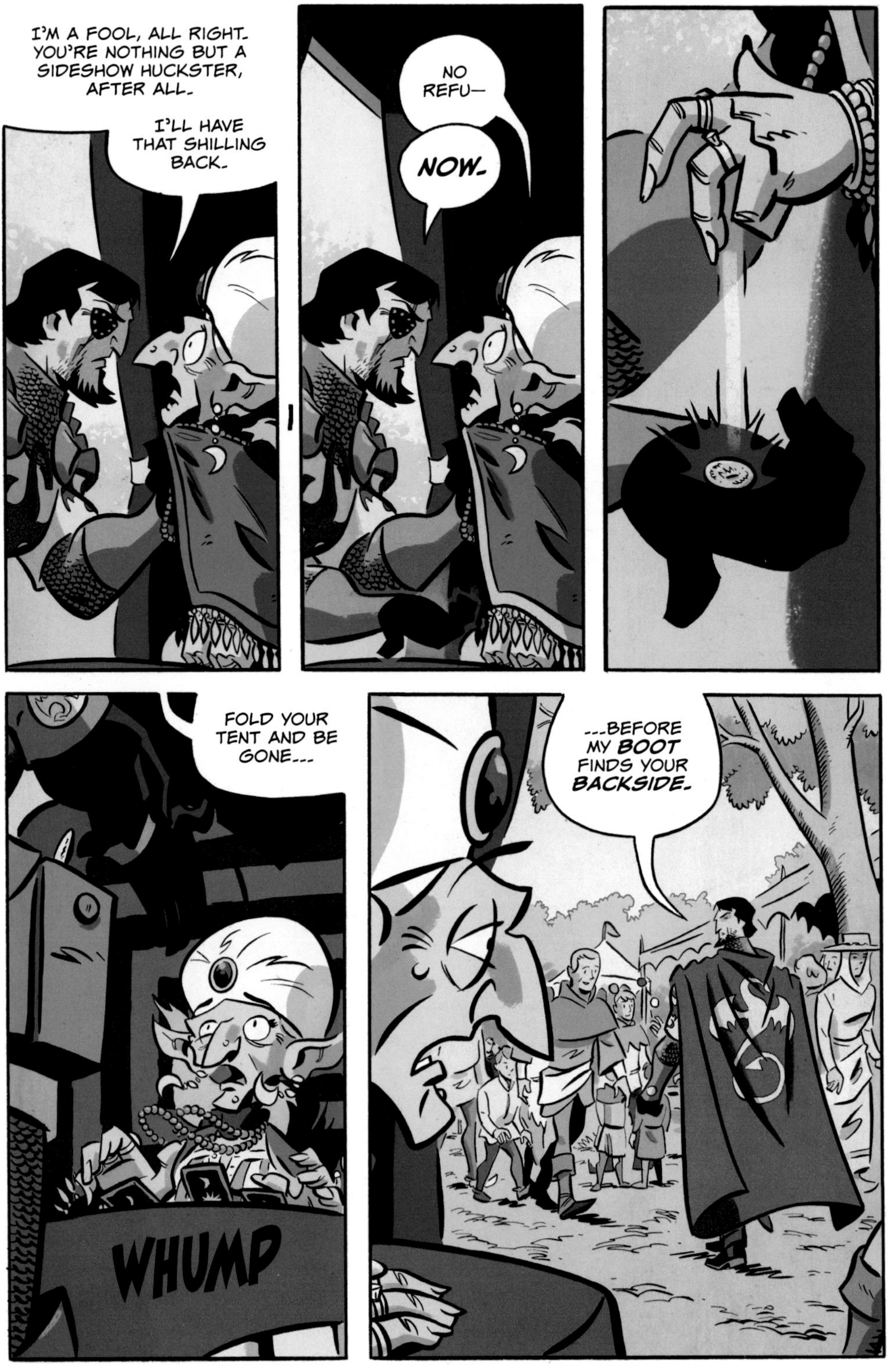
I'M A FOOL, ALL RIGHT. YOU'RE NOTHING BUT A SIDESHOW HUCKSTER, AFTER ALL.
I'LL HAVE THAT SHILLING BACK.
NO REFU—
NOW.
FOLD YOUR TENT AND BE GONE...
WHUMP
...BEFORE MY BOOT FINDS YOUR BACKSIDE.

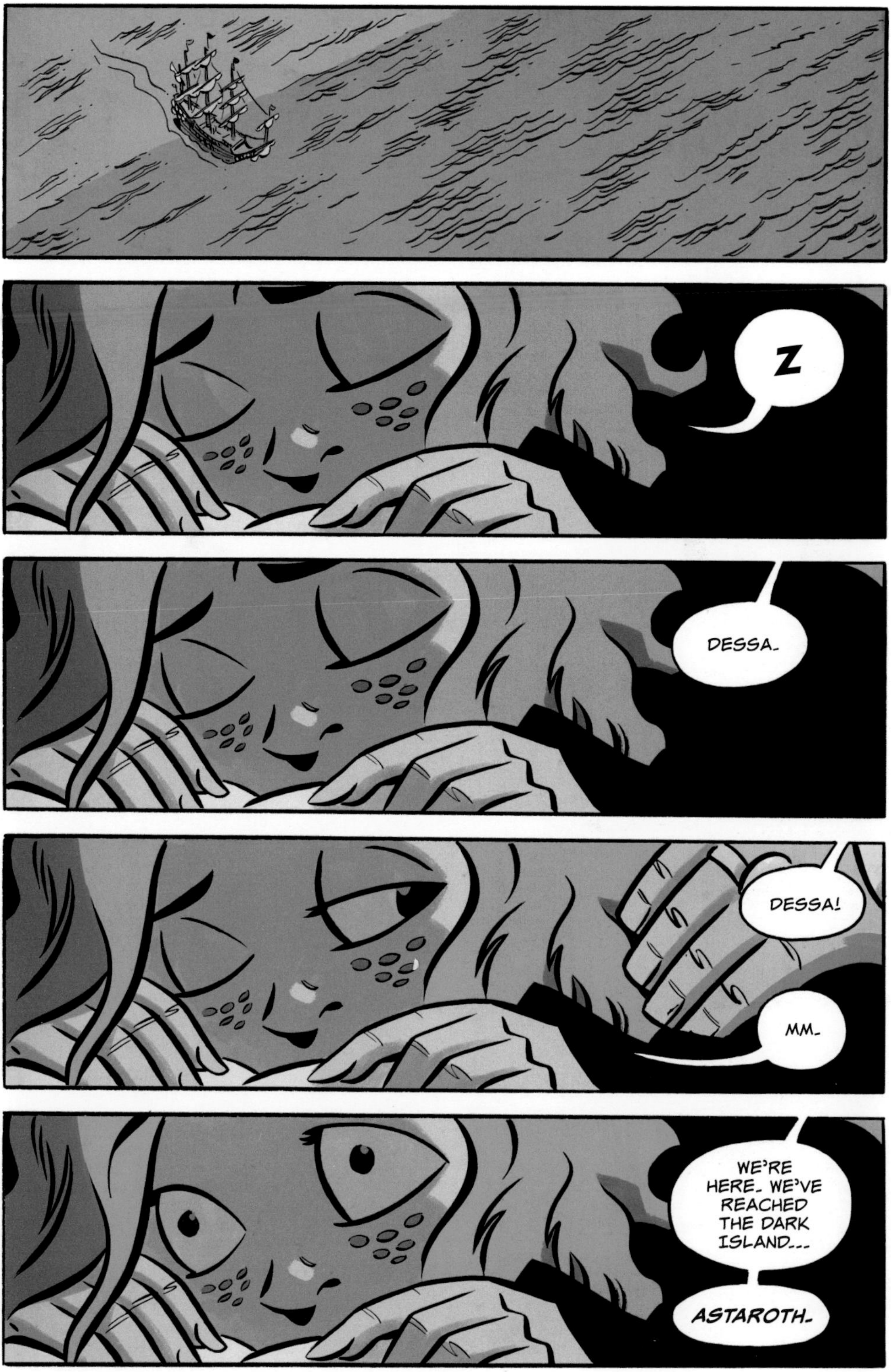
Z
DESSA.
DESSA!
MM.
WE'RE HERE. WE'VE REACHED THE DARK ISLAND...
ASTAROTH.

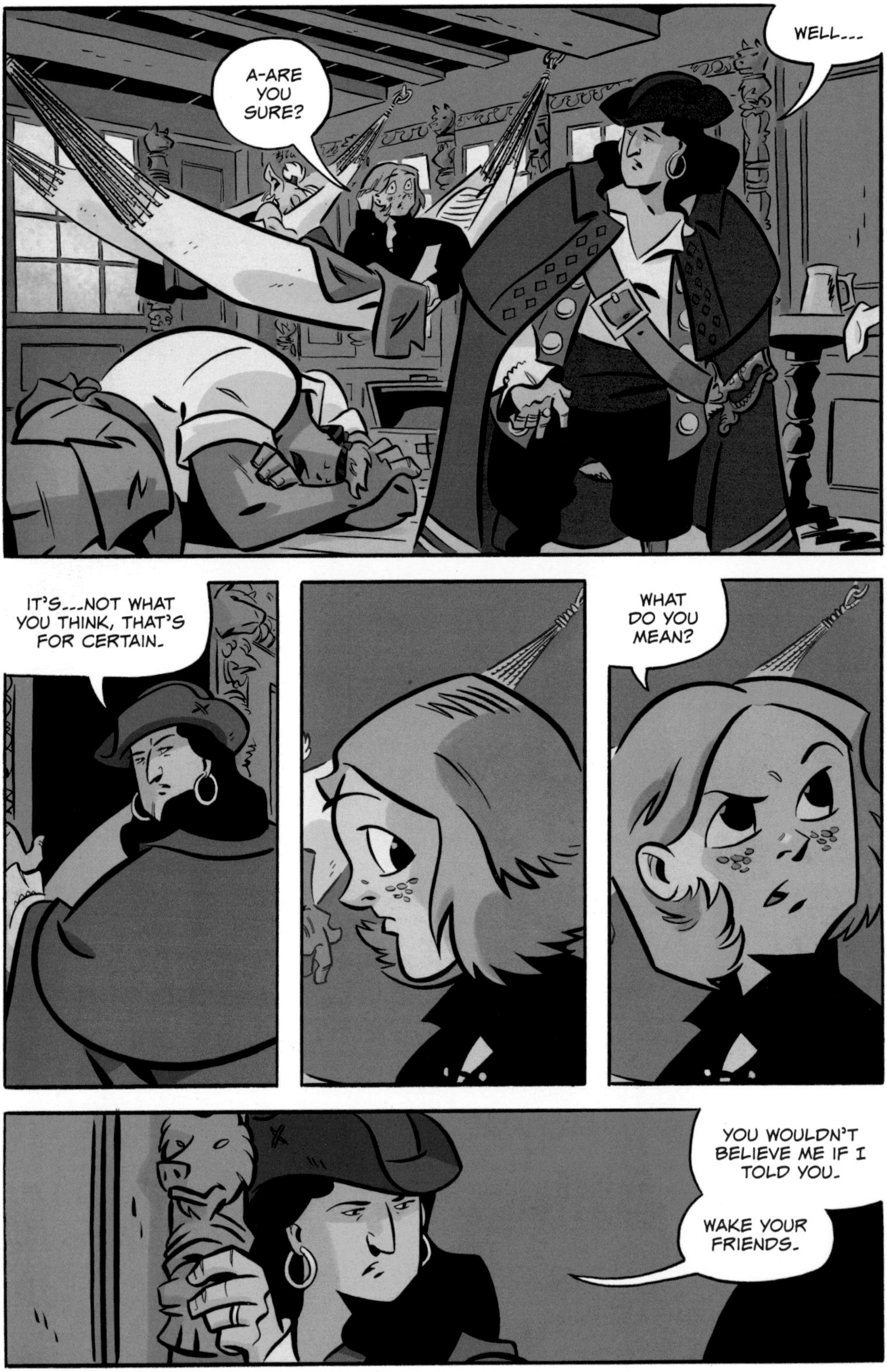
A-ARE YOU SURE?
WELL...
IT'S...NOT WHAT YOU THINK, THAT'S FOR CERTAIN.
WHAT DO YOU MEAN?
YOU WOULDN'T BELIEVE ME IF I TOLD YOU.
WAKE YOUR FRIENDS.

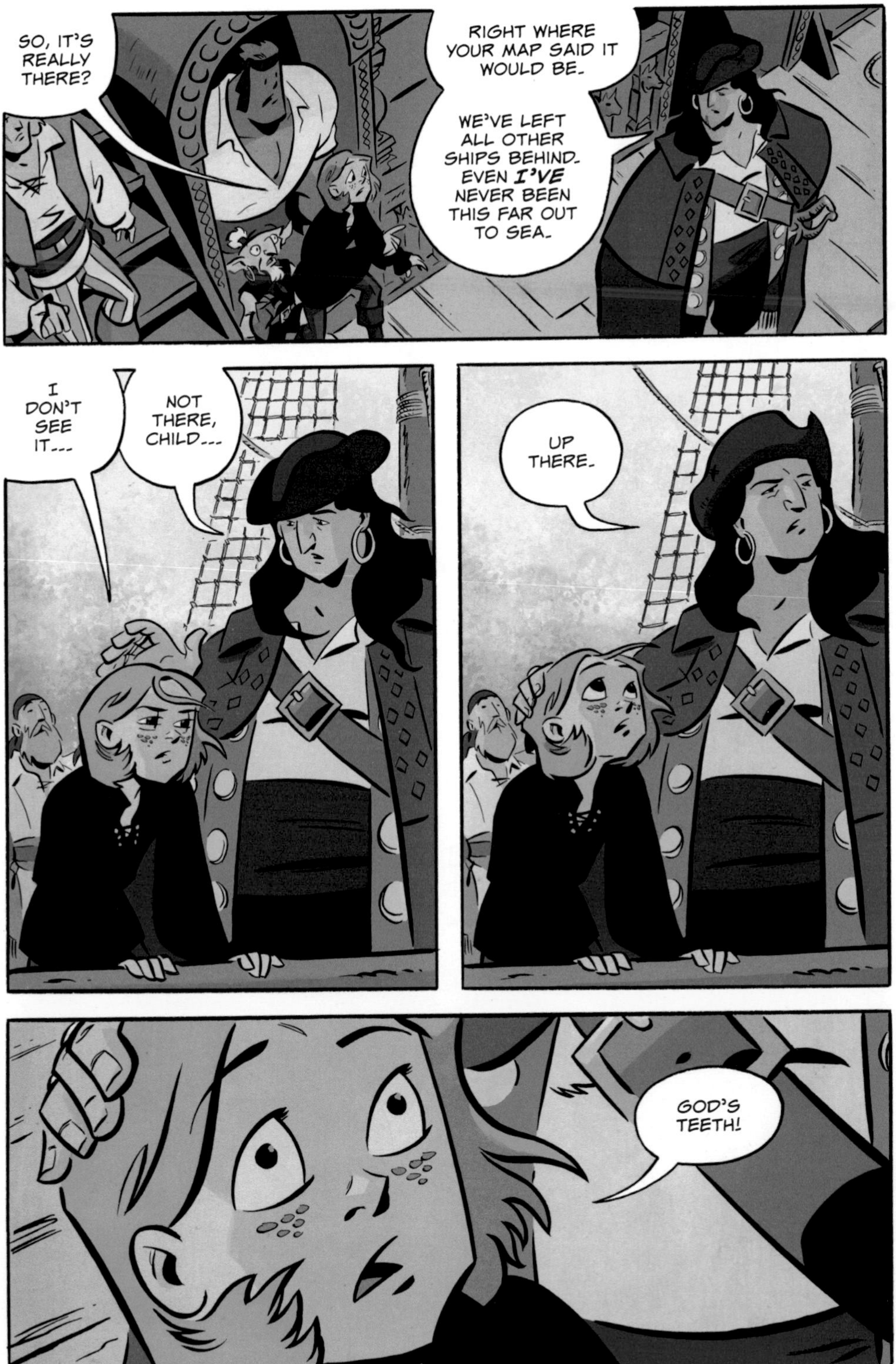
SO, IT'S REALLY THERE?
RIGHT WHERE YOUR MAP SAID IT WOULD BE.
WE'VE LEFT ALL OTHER SHIPS BEHIND. EVEN ***I'VE*** NEVER BEEN THIS FAR OUT TO SEA.
I DON'T SEE IT...
NOT THERE, CHILD...
UP THERE.
GOD'S TEETH!

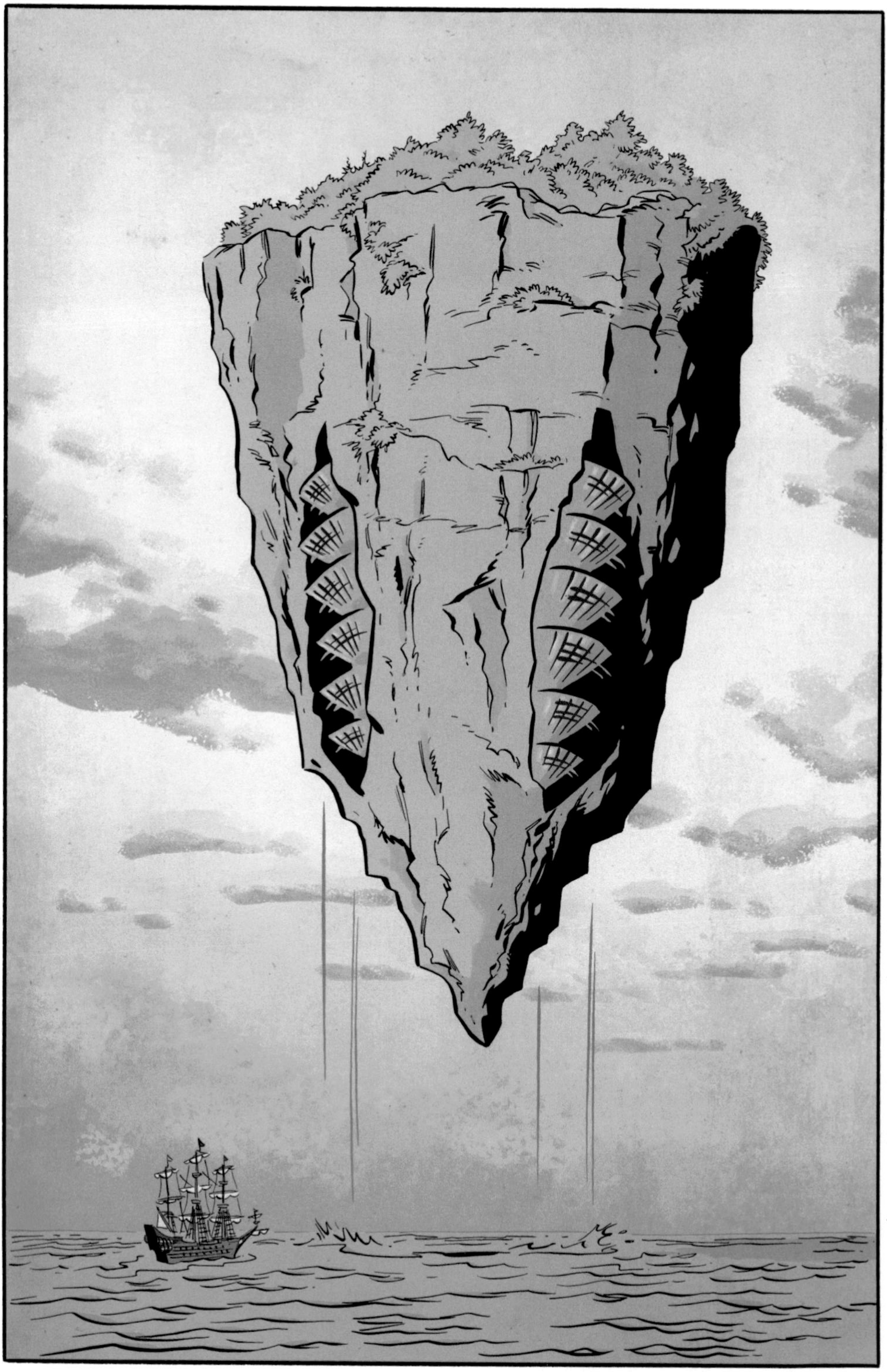

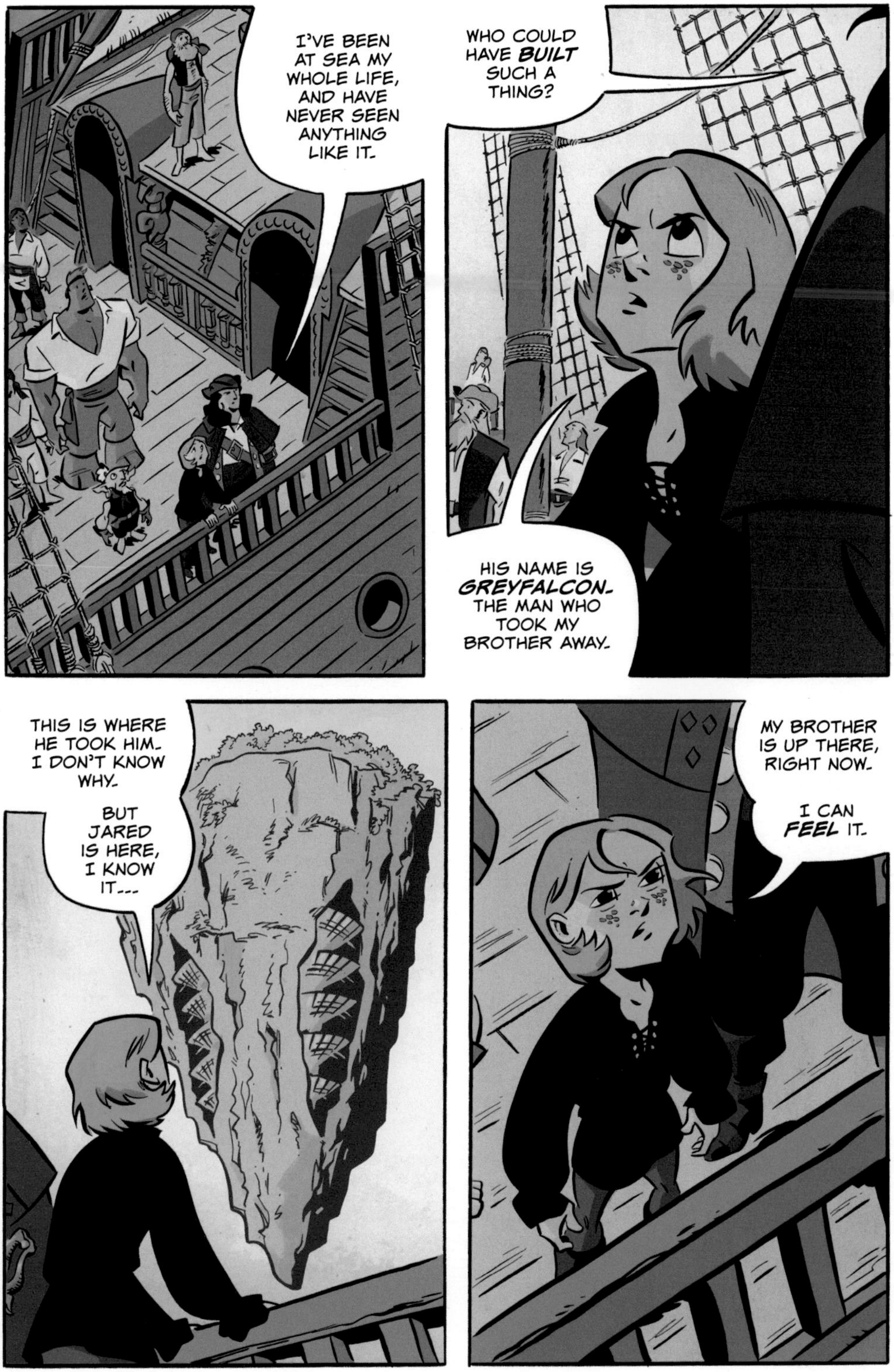
I'VE BEEN AT SEA MY WHOLE LIFE, AND HAVE NEVER SEEN ANYTHING LIKE IT.
WHO COULD HAVE **BUILT** SUCH A THING?
HIS NAME IS ***GREYFALCON***. THE MAN WHO TOOK MY BROTHER AWAY.
THIS IS WHERE HE TOOK HIM. I DON'T KNOW WHY.
BUT JARED IS HERE, I KNOW IT...
MY BROTHER IS UP THERE, RIGHT NOW.
I CAN ***FEEL*** IT.

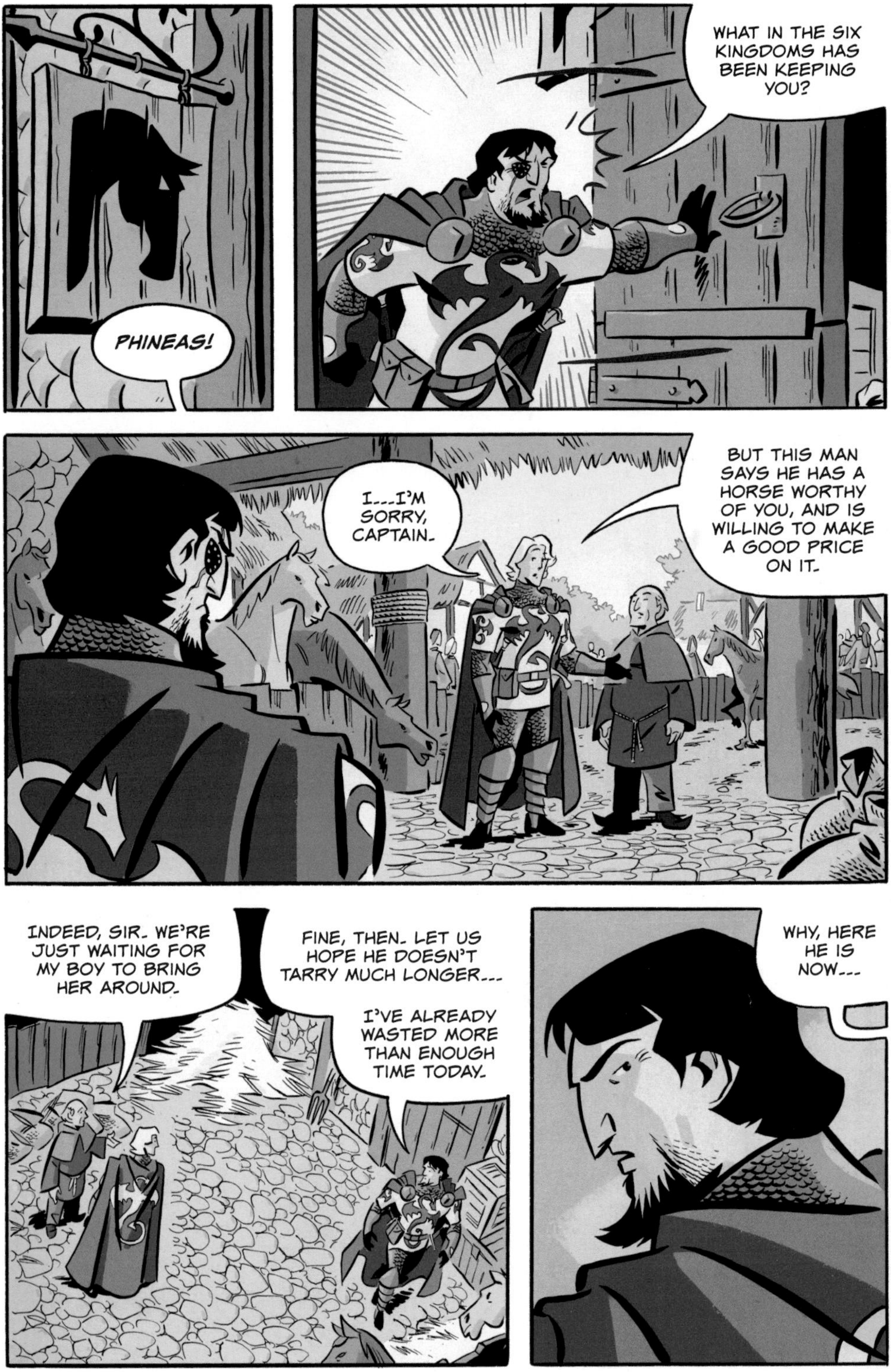
PHINEAS!
WHAT IN THE SIX KINGDOMS HAS BEEN KEEPING YOU?
I...I'M SORRY, CAPTAIN.
BUT THIS MAN SAYS HE HAS A HORSE WORTHY OF YOU, AND IS WILLING TO MAKE A GOOD PRICE ON IT.
INDEED, SIR. WE'RE JUST WAITING FOR MY BOY TO BRING HER AROUND.
FINE, THEN. LET US HOPE HE DOESN'T TARRY MUCH LONGER...
I'VE ALREADY WASTED MORE THAN ENOUGH TIME TODAY.
WHY, HERE HE IS NOW...

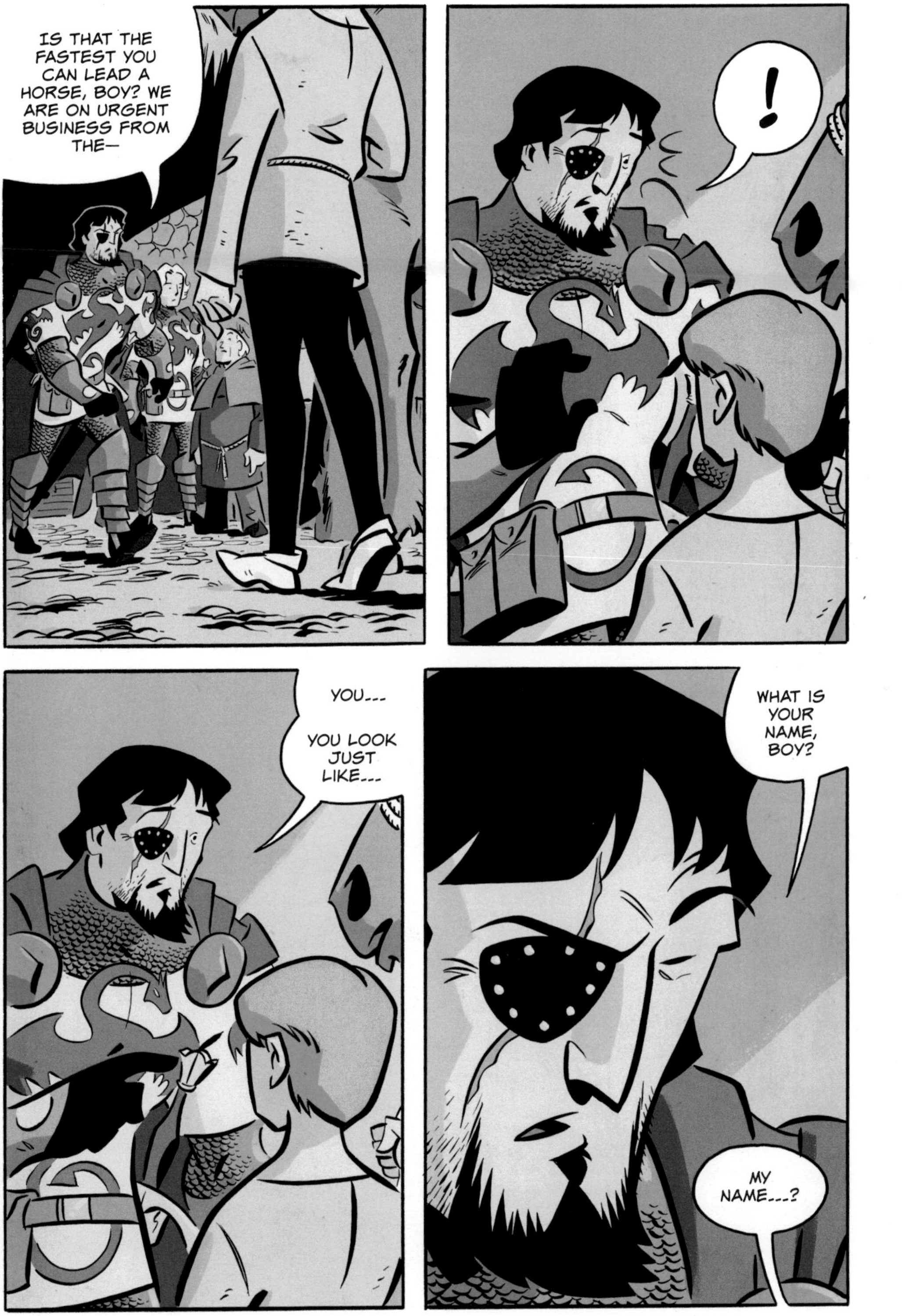
IS THAT THE FASTEST YOU CAN LEAD A HORSE, BOY? WE ARE ON URGENT BUSINESS FROM THE—
!
YOU...
YOU LOOK JUST LIKE...
WHAT IS YOUR NAME, BOY?
MY NAME...?

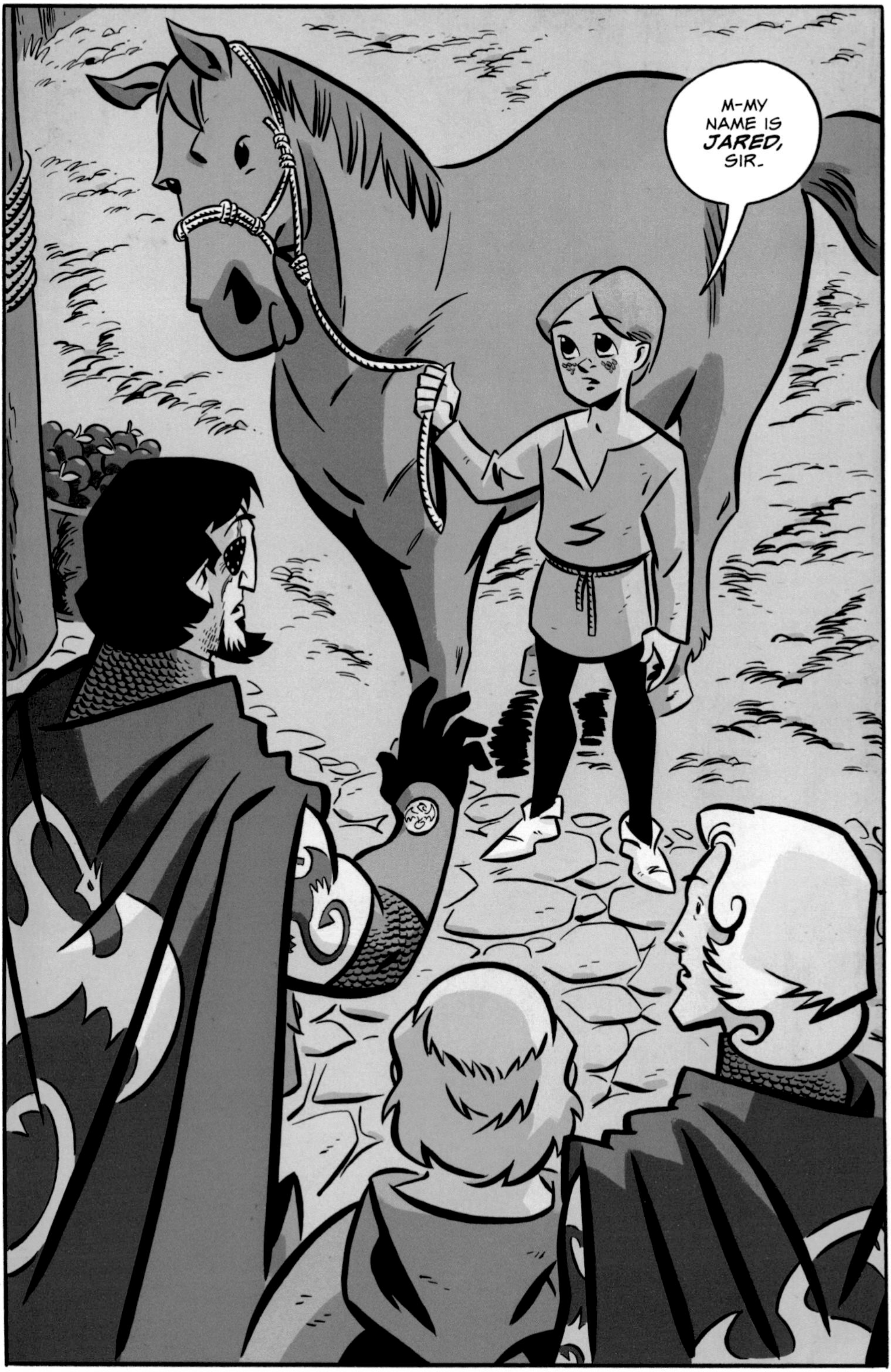
M-MY NAME IS JARED, SIR.

THREE THIEVES
BOOK SIX

Don't miss the sixth book in the Three Thieves series — coming soon!

As Dessa, Topper and Fisk begin to unravel the mysteries of Astaroth, they encounter surprises and setbacks around every corner. Captain Drake, meanwhile, hopes Jared will help lead him to Dessa, but the boy only lands him in hot water with the rest of the Queen's Dragons.

With more thrills, escapes, traps and intrigue than ever before, this penultimate chapter in the Three Thieves series has both Dessa and Captain Drake wondering if they've been headed down the wrong path since the first step of the journey.

THREE THIEVES · BOOK ONE
TOWER of TREASURE
Scott Chantler

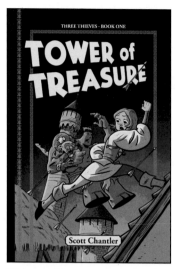

Tower of Treasure

HC 978-1-55453-414-2 • $17.95
PB 978-1-55453-415-9 • $8.95

★ Winner of the Joe Shuster Award, Comics for Kids

★ “Thrilling action sequences that don’t sacrifice sense for sizzle … the kind of fantasy tale that can be relished by children of all ages.”
— *Quill & Quire,* starred review

“An entertaining and action packed new fantasy adventure series.”
— *Publishers Weekly*

THREE THIEVES · BOOK TWO
THE SIGN of the BLACK ROCK
Scott Chantler

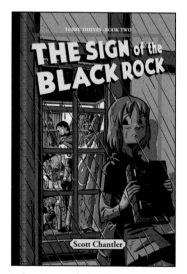

The Sign of the Black Rock

HC 978-1-55453-416-6 • $17.95
PB 978-1-55453-417-3 • $8.95

“An animated, breathlessly paced adventure that’s just hitting its stride.”
— *Kirkus Reviews*

“Touches of zany slapstick balance nicely with Dessa’s continued resolve to find her lost brother, and Chantler’s inviting cartooning captures it all with special aplomb.”
— *Booklist*

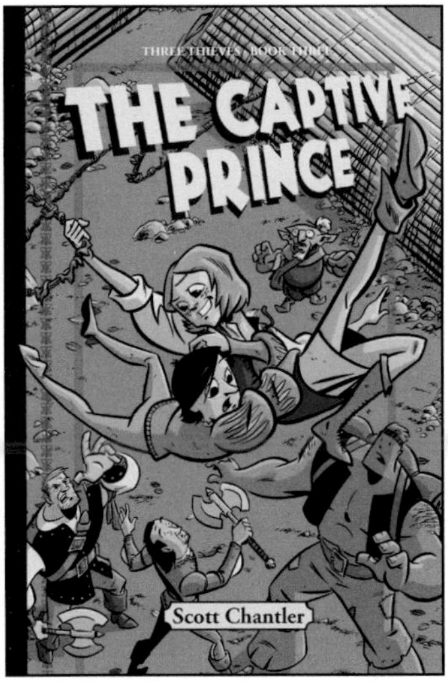
THE CAPTIVE PRINCE
Scott Chantler

The Captive Prince

HC 978-1-55453-776-1 • $17.95
PB 978-1-55453-777-8 • $8.95

"Nary a dull moment, nor even a slow one in this escapade's latest outing."
— *Kirkus Reviews*

"Heaps of charm … snappy, colorful artwork … this one can stand well on its own, though it successfully expands on the growing epic."
— *Booklist*

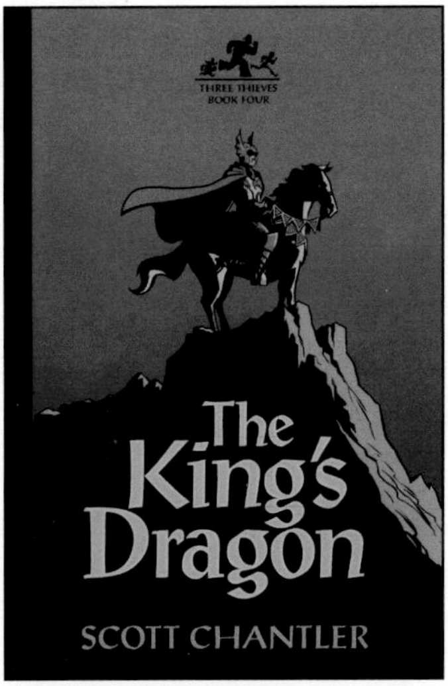
THREE THIEVES
BOOK FOUR
The King's Dragon
SCOTT CHANTLER

The King's Dragon

HC 978-1-55453-778-5 • $17.95
PB 978-1-55453-779-2 • $8.95

"Chantler's cartooning remains sharp, lively, and inviting, and his eye for rousing action sequences is top-notch. But it's his skill as a writer that shines through."
— *Booklist*

"In his cleanly drawn action sequences, Chantler ingeniously links present and past with parallel acts or dialogue … adds further depth to a particularly well-wrought tale."
— *Kirkus Reviews*